REWINDEЯ

Short Stories

"Just Another Job"—A Jonathan Quinn Story
"Off the Clock"—A Jonathan Quinn Story
"The Assignment"—An Orlando Story
"Lesson Plan"—A Jonathan Quinn Story
"Quick Study"—An Orlando Story

The Logan Harper Thrillers

LITTLE GIRL GONE
EVERY PRECIOUS THING

The Project Eden Thrillers

SICK
EXIT NINE
PALE HORSE
ASHES
EDEN RISING
DREAM SKY
DOWN

The Alexandra Poe Thrillers
(with Robert Gregory Browne)

Stand-Alones

Novels

Short Stories

For Younger Readers

The Trouble Family Chronicles

More at BrettBattles.com

REWINDER

BRETT BATTLES

Published by 47North, Seattle
www.apub.com

Amazon, the Amazon logo, and 47North are trademarks of Amazon.com, Inc., or its affiliates.

ISBN-13: 9781477830833

ISBN-10: 1477830839

Cover design by James T. Egan of Bookfly Design

Printed in the United States of America

Both thanks and a dedication
to the writers who have inspired me.
There are so many more than I can name,
but here are a few (in no particular order):
Isaac Asimov, Arthur C. Clarke,
Robert Heinlein, James White,
Graham Greene, John D. MacDonald,
Alistair MacLean, Robert Ludlum,
Stephen King, Jasper Fforde,
and Haruki Murakami.
Read them. Enjoy them

CHAPTER ONE

"Where are the others?" Lidia asks, one hand wrapped around my neck, the other pressing the tip of a knife against the skin below my ear.

"The others?" I ask.

"Bernard and everyone who was with us. Where are they?"

I shrug. "I don't know."

I start to choke as her grip tightens. "Don't lie to me!" she yells. "You said you knew when the break occurred and you fixed it. But that's not true, is it? You never fixed it."

"I . . . can't . . . breathe."

A few moments pass before her grip loosens to the point where I can breathe again.

"Where are they?" she repeats.

"They went home."

"You're lying. You obviously never changed the world back. Where are they?"

I say nothing.

Her knife presses inward, releasing a trickle of blood. "I know you know what's going on. I could see you were lying when we all met. That's why I only jumped into the woods. I wanted to see what you were going to do. When I realized that you waited to be last, I knew I was right. *What* happened to them?"

"Where's Iffy?"

"Answer my question!"

I shake my head. "I don't see her, you won't learn anything."

CHAPTER TWO

STOP.

I read somewhere that everyone is the hero of his or her own story.

Maybe that's true for most people, but not for me.

Of all the rules we were taught before we were allowed to travel in time, one stands above all: Don't screw anything up.

I didn't mean to, but, well . . .

Here I am, Denny Younger, destroyer of worlds.

You wouldn't be here if not for me.

REWIND.
MY TIMELINE.
NOT YOURS.

I was born an Eight—the level of my family's caste.

In my great-grandparents' time, Eight was referred to as the labor class, but seventy-five years ago, Parliament converted everything to a numbered system. "To avoid confusion" is a quote used in textbooks.

The most common direction in which people change caste is downward. Rarely can one rise to a higher level—something my father often reminded me. "The best you can hope for," he'd say, "is a fair boss and a decent roof over your head. If you have that, then you have nothing to complain about."

My mother, on the other hand, was not of the same mind. Though she knew we were limited by our caste, she'd tell me and my sister—when my father wasn't around—that we were different from others and that if we worked very hard, there was a chance we could be assigned a position that wouldn't include lugging tools between machines for the rest of our lives. I was eleven when my mother died after someone's vehicle got stuck in front of the tram she was on.

From my devastation grew the desire to prove her right and show my father something more was out there for me. While I always did well in school and achieved the highest marks, I began not only studying the lessons we were assigned, but reading well beyond my educational level and learning about things I would have never otherwise been taught.

History turned out to be one of my favorite subjects, becoming an obsession I couldn't feed fast enough. At the community library three tram stops away from home, I walked the roads of ancient Greece and Rome, I witnessed the sweep of Genghis Khan's army through Eurasia, and I experienced the growth of our mighty British Empire as it embraced territories around the world, including my own North America.

As much as possible, I would check out books and then stay up late reading them. Sometimes after my sister Ellie became sick, I would sit in her room and read to her. I like to think it eased her pain, and she always said she enjoyed it, but who knows.

Typically a kid from one of the lower castes such as ours enters the workforce upon reaching the age of sixteen. In my case this would have likely meant learning machine maintenance from my father at the power plant on the western edge of New Cardiff.

But my study habits paid off, and much to my father's dismay, I was granted two additional years of education beyond my sixteenth birthday. This all but guaranteed I'd be able to train for a supervisory job, something that sounded a whole lot better to me than following in my father's footsteps.

Because I knew these final two years would be the end of my formal education, I studied even harder, soaking in all I could.

Maybe that's why the two years flew by, because before I knew it, it was time for the test.

The test is officially known as the Occupational Placement Examination, and it is mandatory for all students to take at the end of their last year of formal education. The only exceptions to this are those moving on to university, but these students usually come from the middle and upper castes—Sixes and up. The students at my school are Sevens and Eights, and one girl who is a Nine. The only way one of us will ever set foot on a university campus is as a custodian or groundskeeper.

The exam is a mix of questions that we're told were designed to help determine the best place for us within the workforce. For those who take it at sixteen, it almost always results in an assignment with one of their parents, but for those who have completed the extra two years, it will determine if we are able to break our family's lot.

The exam's arrival saddens me. I'm not ready to give up learning and could easily spend years with my nose in a book. But I'm at the end of my educational options, so I reluctantly join my fellow students on the N-CAT Train to the New Cardiff Civic Testing Center overlooking the Pacific Ocean.

The facility consists of twenty identical buildings set side by side, each several times longer than they are wide. We're taken to the one with the letter *D* above the door. Inside, tables abut each other, creating five rows that run the length of the structure's single room. On both sides are chairs, many of which are already filled by students from other schools.

Over the next twenty minutes, more kids my age file in, until every seat is taken. Here and there you hear hushed conversations, but for the most part we are silent.

I can't help spending the time thinking about Ellie. My sister died before finishing her primary education, and I know she would have been granted the additional two years in school, as she was even smarter than I. In my mind, I'm taking the test for both of us.

Unsmiling exam proctors move along the aisles behind our chairs, placing testing booklets and pens in front of us. When all the materials are handed out, the head proctor, sitting on a raised platform at the front of the room, leans into a microphone and says, "You have ninety minutes. Begin."

The sound of flipping pages fills the air, but the booklet in front of me remains closed. I know it's meaningless, but I want to put off the inevitable for as long as I can. I sense confused glances from some of the nearby students, but it's the stiff hand of a proctor on my shoulder that finally ends my holdout.

"You're wasting time," she said. "Get to it."

Her accent marks her as true English, not North American. While there are plenty of people on the West Coast from the isles where our kingdom began, it's unusual to find one in such a mundane position.

"I said, get to it," she tells me again.

I open my booklet and begin.

There are questions on mathematics and language and the sciences and four whole pages on history. The last, of course, I breeze through, wishing the whole test focused on the past. There are other questions, too, ones that have nothing to do with what we've learned at school, that have us comparing ideas and ranking items and generally probing into areas society frowns on discussing. If they're designed to make us feel uncomfortable, they've done their job with me. I rush through these sections and soon find myself at the end of the test. As I close my booklet, I notice that despite my delayed start, I'm one of the first to finish.

There's no clock to tell me for certain, but it feels as if nearly a half hour passes before the head proctor announces, "Time. Close your booklets and put down your pens."

After the exams are picked up, we're dismissed with only a "You will receive your results at your school on Monday."

Relieved chatter fills the room as we file out. Even I can't help but feel a bit of elation, and I end up laughing and joking with my fellow classmates. On the tram ride home, we compare notes and realize we weren't all given the same test. Several had questions on farming techniques and others on food preparation or carpentry or gardening. None other than I had more than a handful of questions on history, which makes me wonder if each exam was tailored to test our perceived strengths.

◆　◆　◆

There are four pegs on the wall in the entryway of the home I share with my father in the western part of New Cardiff known as the Shallows. His work coat hangs from his. I place my school jacket on mine. The other two pegs, Mother's and Ellie's, have been empty for years.

I find my father in the kitchen eating some of the stew I made several days ago. More is warming on the stove, so I fill a bowl and join him. Quietly we have our meal together in the same way we've done since it's been just the two of us. What wasn't gutted out of my father when my mother died was ripped away when Ellie finally succumbed to her disease.

My sister was his favorite. The oldest child. His only daughter. I've always known it. She knew it. Even Mother knew.

Since Ellie's death my father has stewarded me into adulthood by doing only what's absolutely necessary. I tell myself it's because he fears losing me and has built up a wall so that if anything happens to me, he can go on living. But whatever his reason, I hate him for being this way. I have, however, come to accept the status quo of our emotionless coexistence.

I'm halfway through my stew when he gets up from the table and carries his bowl to the sink.

"Test day, wasn't it?" he says.

"Yes," I reply, mildly startled by the question. This is already the longest conversation we've had at mealtime in six months.

He nods to himself. "When do the results come in?"

My wishful thought that maybe the ice has finally broken vanishes as I realize the true meaning of his question. What he really wants to ask is, when am I moving out and relieving him of his parental duties? "Four days," I say, trying not to let my scorn show.

"Monday, then."

"Uh-huh."

He finishes cleaning his bowl, puts it on the rack to dry, and leaves without another word.

I wonder what conversations are like in the homes of the other test takers. I imagine nervous excitement, planning, and maybe even a little dreaming as parents hope their child might be able to achieve more than they did. Something my mother would be doing if she were still here.

I decide then and there that if I'm assigned to a position even remotely connected to the power plant where my father works, I'll run away. I don't care if it means I have to become a casteless vagabond. The drop to the bottom of society will be worth not having to ever see him again.

Suddenly having no desire to finish my stew, I toss it in the trash, wash out my bowl, and retreat to the sanctuary of my room.

◆ ◆ ◆

School is still held on Friday and Saturday, but since the test has been taken, there's little for us to do but help our professor prepare her classrooms for her next group of students.

Like on the trip home from the testing facility, everyone wants to talk about the exam. Unfortunately, the conversation I had with my father has soured me on the topic. If fate is as cruel as I've been brought up to believe, I'll be assigned to the power plant, so I spend my time thinking about where I'll escape to. A large city would probably be the best idea. New Cardiff, for example, but since we live just within the city's boundaries, it's a little too close for me. San Francisco to the north would work or even all the way up to Georgetown, but east seems like a better bet. St. Louis, perhaps, or Chicago, or even as far as the city of New York.

Once I get wherever it is I go, I'll find work that'll earn me enough to survive. That's all I need, I tell myself. Just enough so I can afford food and a place to stay.

Sunday I go to church as I always do. I'm not particularly religious, but after my mother died, my father stopped going. So it's a few hours on my only day off that I don't have to spend cleaning our home while he checks everything I do.

When Monday finally arrives, I've pretty much settled on Chicago as my initial destination. If I don't like it there, I can continue east to the Atlantic coast. What it gives me is a starting point I can hold on to for now.

There are thirty-two students in my group. My assigned spot in our classroom is in the third row, off to the side. When I walk in for my last day ever of school, the room is already half-full. This is unusual. We still have thirty minutes until the start of class. Typically, most students arrive a few minutes before the top of the hour, but of course this is not a typical day.

Professor Garner walks in right at eight o'clock and takes his place behind his desk.

After shuffling through some papers, he looks up and says, "Good morning."

"Good morning, Professor," we reply in well-practiced unison.

"A big day," he says, as if we don't already know that. "I'm sure you're all wondering about your results."

A few of the other students nod as he looks around, but most of us are too nervous to move.

"You'll be happy to know they arrived thirty minutes ago and will be brought out shortly."

A murmur of excitement runs through the room. I don't partake in this, either.

The professor raps the top of his desk with the stone he always keeps there. "This may be your last day with me, but I will not tolerate interruptions."

Once the room quiets down, he says, "Before your results are handed out, I'd like to take a few minutes to express my thoughts on your time here and how you may use it in the future."

If not for the earlier admonishment, his announcement probably would've been met by a collective groan. As it is, shoulders sag and jawlines tense, but all stay quiet.

The few minutes he promised for his lecture has so far turned out to be nearly an hour of self-indulgence. Somewhere around "discipline, such as you've learned here, will be invaluable to . . ." I

10

tune out and turn my thoughts back to plans on how best to leave town.

I'll go home right away, where I'll grab whatever I need, and leave before my father returns from work. After that, a tram to the Los Angeles district in the center of New Cardiff, where I can buy a third-class ticket on a train heading east with the money I've been saving in an envelope under my desk. Not sure how far that will get me, but it's a start.

I'm deep in these thoughts when I realize the professor has stopped talking and is walking toward the door. He pulls it open and says, "We're ready," to someone outside.

Around me, others shuffle in their chairs as they pull themselves from their own daydreams.

The professor returns to the desk and says, "Mrs. Parker is fetching your results now. When I call your name, you will come down. Once you've received your envelope, you are dismissed. Please don't open your results in the classroom, as this might interfere with others coming down to get theirs." He pauses. "Finally, I want to finish by saying it's been a privilege to instruct you. I wish you all good health and productive lives in the years ahead."

As he finishes speaking, the door opens again, and old Mrs. Parker enters, a stack of envelopes in her hands. One by one, she hands them to the professor, and he then reads the name on the front.

Nearly all the results have been handed out when I finally hear him say, "Denny Younger."

I shoot out of my seat and take the steps two at a time. I know I'm not going to like what's inside that envelope, but I want to get it over with.

After Mrs. Parker confirms I've been given the correct results, I exit the room. I'm sorely tempted to open the envelope in the hallway, but too many other students are already doing that and I'd rather express my anger privately.

I leave the school grounds and don't stop until I reach my house. A part of me is worried that my father has decided to stay home today to learn my results as soon as possible, but the house is thankfully empty.

I stand at the kitchen table, envelope in hand, hesitating before I rip open the top. I'm hovering at the demarcation point of when my childhood ends and the rest of my life begins. Given the importance of the moment, I decide to use a knife to slice a clean cut through the flap. The envelope contains a single sheet of paper.

Why would there be more? I think. It doesn't take a thick sheath of documents to tell me when to report to the plant.

The embossed symbol centered at the top and highlighted with gold ink surprises me. It's not from my father's power plant. In fact, I don't recognize it at all. Printed below this are a few lines of black type:

> Report to building J at the New Cardiff Civic Test-
> ing Center at 2:00 p.m. this afternoon. Share this
> with no one and bring your belongings with you.

I turn the paper over, but the other side is blank.

Is this a joke?

One of the associate professors carefully went over all the possible results we might receive, but he never mentioned this option.

I stuff the message back into the envelope and turn for the door. There must be someone at the school who can tell me what this is all about. But as I put my hand on the doorknob, I pause.

Share this with no one. Does that include the school administration?

I pull the letter out again and reread it. It's very clear. *No one.* I wonder for a moment if there's a problem with my test and I need to retake it. But why am I being told to bring my belongings?

What finally keeps me from returning to the school is my realization that this can't possibly have anything to do with a job at the power plant. The last thing I want to do is blow an opportunity by not honoring the letter's request.

I rush to my room, grab my bag, and shove in the things I've been planning to take with me when I run away. Worst-case scenario, the trip to the testing center delays my departure by an hour or two. Best case? Who knows?

Bag over my shoulder, I retrieve my N-CAT pass and leave the house for the last time.

At the tram stop, I run into a classmate named Nancy Cooper, who's waiting there with her mother.

"Off to your assignment already?" she asks with a glance at my bag.

I almost say yes, but the words *share with no one* flash in my mind again, so I tell her, "Uh, going to visit my aunt . . . before I start. She's been ill." I do have an aunt who lives in New Cardiff, but I haven't seen her in years and have no idea what her health status is.

"That's very kind of you," Nancy's mom says.

"So, what did you get?" Nancy asks.

I give her the answer everyone is likely expecting. "There's a management trainee opening at the power plant. I've been assigned there. What about you?"

"Accounting assistant," she says happily. "I'll be working at Lord Carlson's estate in Coventry."

"Wow, that's great. I hear it's beautiful there." Coventry is only an hour up the coast, but like with most places other than the Shallows, I have never been there.

"So I've been told."

"Is that where you're headed?" I ask, hoping so.

"Oh, no. I don't start until next week."

"We're heading downtown to find Nancy some work clothes," her mother says. "Have to look the part."

Nancy rolls her eyes so only I see, and then smiles.

I smile back, but inside I'm cringing. As I feared, we'll be traveling together, at least as far as the northwest terminal at Simi Station. I'm saved from further conversation by the arrival of our tram. I take my time getting on, pretending there's something in my bag I need to check. Once I see Nancy and her mother take seats in the forward-most carriage, I hop on in back and drop down next to an old woman who's fast asleep.

It takes twenty-five minutes to reach Simi Station. When I disembark, I check to make sure Nancy and her mother have stayed onboard and am relieved to see them still in their seats.

I wait until the train has left and then find the tunnel that takes me down to the ocean line. This is a straight shot south from Simi Station, across the San Fernando Valley, and through the mountains to the Coastal District.

I arrive at the testing center a whole hour before my appointment. Though this is now my second time here, it seems like a completely different place. Before, there were hordes of students being led to whichever building they'd been assigned. Now there isn't a soul around except me.

I walk toward building J, thinking if I show up early, maybe the person I'm supposed to meet will already be there and I'll be able to find out what the big mystery is. But when I reach the building, the door's locked, and no one answers when I knock.

The wait feels like the longest hour of my life. When 2:00 p.m. finally approaches, I push off the wall I've been leaning against so I won't look lazy or disinterested. I have no idea who I'm meeting, but it seems smart to give the best impression possible. I look back and forth along the walkway as the final minutes tick off, but see no one. It's as if the whole facility is deserted.

Maybe it *is* a joke, I think, and someone switched my real results with the letter I received. If so, I don't feel much like laughing.

But as my watch changes from 1:59 to 2:00, the door to building J opens.

I twist around and find a middle-aged, bald man wearing a dark-blue suit standing in the entryway.

"Mr. Younger?" he asks.

"Yes, sir. That's me."

"This way, please."

He gestures inside and waits for me to enter first.

CHAPTER THREE

The interior of building J looks exactly like that of the building where I took the test the previous week—only the rows of tables are missing. In their place is a single table set up in the center of the room, with one chair on one side and three on the other, two of which are already occupied.

"Follow me, please," the bald man says, leading me into the room.

He gestures to the chair sitting by itself and waits for me to take it before lowering himself into the empty one on the other side. His companions are a man and a woman, both older than the bald man by at least a decade. The second man wears a gray suit, while the woman is in an elegant but businesslike dress. They all must be Fours at the very least, but it wouldn't surprise me if they were Threes or even Twos. Four is the highest caste I've ever talked to and that was only once, so the three upper-caste people in front of me are more than enough to send a tremor through my hands.

Several seconds pass without anyone saying a word. All three faces tell me nothing, displaying the very definition of neutral. I wonder if they're waiting for me to speak. If so, they're out of luck because I have no idea what to say.

Finally, the woman sets a thin sheath on the table, unties the string holding it closed, and pulls a booklet from inside.

A *test* booklet.

For a moment I think it's the one I filled out, but I then realize the color of the printed ink on the front is different. She pulls a pen from her pocket and places it and the test booklet in front of me.

"You have sixty minutes," she says.

"I'm sorry," I say, trying to sound as contrite as possible. "I don't understand. What's going on here?"

"I would think that's obvious."

"There must be a mistake. I took my test last week." As I've been taught to do with those in castes above me, I make the tone of my voice clear that if there's a mistake, it's most likely mine.

"And you will take this one today." She leans back. "You have fifty-nine minutes. I suggest you begin."

I want to ask if there was a problem with my previous exam, but I've already pushed more than I should, so I pick up the pen and open the booklet.

At first I'm a bit unnerved, not only by the nature of the test but also by the fact that the woman and her colleagues remain in their chairs, watching me. But as I read the questions, I soon forget I'm not alone.

Nearly three quarters of the test consists of the same odd questions that were at the end of the last test. The rest is divided between practical knowledge and history. There are no mathematical questions. No language questions. And no questions even remotely connected to power-plant maintenance.

I finish with six minutes to spare.

As I close the booklet and set my pen down, the woman says, "Are you sure you don't want to use the remaining time to check your answers?"

I've already checked my answers, so I say, "Thank you, but no. I'm done."

"Very well, then. Please step outside."

I reach down to pick up my bag.

"Leave it and wait outside the door," she says. "We'll retrieve you when we're ready."

I walk out of the building, trying to make sense of what's going on. Of all the stories I've heard about the transition from school to an adult trade, none has included a second test. And yet, here I am.

A warm breeze blows between the buildings as I exit, bringing with it the smell of the ocean and a memory of sand slipping through my toes while walking on a beach. Closing my eyes I can see my sister and me holding my mother's hands as she leads us into the crowded section of the beach reserved for Sevens and below. Ellie and I used to love visiting the ocean. She'd help me dig in the sand and build forts that the waves would eventually wash away. We'd laugh and run and get wet and . . .

I know we didn't always get along, but the memories of the times we fought are hazy now, and it's the good that's clear.

I miss her. So very much. It was somehow always easier being a lowly Eight with her around.

As my eyes begin to water, the door opens, and the bald man beckons me in again. This time he doesn't accompany me all the way to the table. The only one still sitting there is the woman, and on the table in front of her sits my test booklet.

I take my seat, not sure if I should be scared or excited, then notice my bag is gone. "My things."

"Don't worry about them," she says.

"But—"

"Don't waste my time on unimportant matters." The tone of her voice is more than enough to convince me to drop the subject.

She taps my exam. "Congratulations, Mr. Younger. You did very well."

"What does that mean?"

"It means you've passed."

"Passed?" For the last two years, it's been hammered into our heads that the test is not a pass/fail exercise. It's a diagnostic tool to determine where we can best serve the empire.

"After consultation with my colleagues, it's been decided that we will offer you the choice." She shoots a quick glance past me toward where the bald man is standing, and I get the impression that whatever was decided was not unanimous. Before I can ask her what I'm choosing, she says, "Here is what you need to know. If you had not been brought to our attention and had we not then intervened, your original exam results would have placed you as an assistant librarian in the central branch of the New Cardiff library. This is one of your choices."

This revelation is stunning. I've never even allowed myself to hope for such a position. "What's the other?"

"A job considerably better than that, and one I can guarantee you'll never regret." Again she taps my exam. "One for which you're apparently well suited."

"Doing what?"

"I'm afraid that's all I can tell you for now."

"But how am I supposed to decide?"

"That's up to you. But I need your answer now."

"Now?"

"I can give you a few minutes, but that's all."

My gaze drifts to the wall far behind her. On the one hand, if I say no, I'll be assigned to work in the central library, surrounded by the books I love so much. And on the other, an unknown job I've been personally selected for. The library makes the most sense, but I can't deny the pull of this mysterious path.

"Is the job here in New Cardiff?"

Her lips curl in a faint smile. "Though I can't tell you exactly where, I can say that if you choose to join us, you will leave your old life behind and never see your family or friends again."

Words my sister said when she was sick suddenly come back to me. *There's got to be more than this. There's got to be something better. Promise me you'll try to find it.*

"Your job," I say. "I choose yours."

"Well, I can't deny that I'm surprised." She looks past me again. "You were right." When she focuses on me once more, she says, "Welcome to the institute."

CHAPTER FOUR

"Mr. Younger, if you could please come this way," the bald man says.

He leads me outside and down the pathway between the test buildings. The area is no longer unoccupied. At least a dozen men in dark suits are spread evenly along the sidewalk, each holding a powerful-looking gun.

"They're here for our protection," my escort says, no doubt noticing my wary look.

"From what?"

The only answer I get is a smile and another, "This way."

We round the corner of building L and enter a smaller structure that has no identifier above the door. Waiting inside are a man and two women.

"Lady Williams would like to depart in twenty minutes," my escort tells them.

The trio studies me for a moment. Though the women aren't identical, they look like sisters. The man is older than they are. Midthirties, maybe. From the slightly Asiatic look of his eyes, I wonder if he traces his ancestors back to the Hong Kong province.

The older of the two women turns to my escort and says, "No problem, Sir Gregory. We'll be done by then."

Sir Gregory? The man escorting me is a Three and has been knighted by the king. Not only that, he called the woman Lady Williams, which means she's at least a Three, if not higher. I'm shocked, even more so by the fact Sir Gregory doesn't exude the sense of entitlement I expect from those in his position.

"You're what? Six feet?" the male of the trio asks.

"Um, just over," I stammer.

He pulls out a sizing tape and holds it up to various parts of my body, pausing between measurements to enter his findings into a palm-size notebook.

"And, let's see . . . thirteen stones."

"Twelve and a half."

"Ah, right. Your clothes don't do you any favors," he says, then orders, "Off with them."

One of the women starts pulling my shirt over my head, while the other goes to work on my pants.

I try to push their hands away as I say, "What are you doing?"

"You can't travel in these," the woman with her hands on my pants says. "You aren't a commoner anymore." Her hands move to my belt, but then she stops and looks at me again. "May I?"

I barely get an "uh" out before she yanks my pants down to my ankles, and soon I'm standing there only in my underpants and socks. Apparently the man left the room while I was being stripped down, because he now walks back in carrying several items of clothing.

"Your undergarments will have to go, too," he says.

He tosses me an undershirt, a pair of black underwear, and matching black socks. As I catch them, I'm captivated by how soft the fabric is.

"Come on," the man says. "On with them."

"But . . ." I say, glancing at the women.

"Oh, for God's sake. Samantha, Rebecca, would you turn around so Adonis here doesn't expose you to his greatness?"

"He's just a kid, Leo," the older one says. "Ease up on him."

Both women turn away.

I stare at Leo.

"What?" he asks. "You're kidding, right? Fine."

He turns, too, and I quickly change into my new underpants. They're so comfortable it almost feels like I'm wearing nothing at all.

After I don the shirt, I say, "All right," and then pull on my socks.

The other items Leo brought are a white shirt and a black suit, similar in cut to the one worn by Sir Gregory. These, too, are made of a much higher quality material than one would ever find in the clothes markets of the Los Angeles district.

Once I'm dressed, Leo has me sit on a waist-high stool, and Rebecca and Samantha spend several minutes rearranging my hair.

"A cut is what you really need," Samantha says. "But we can do that when you arrive."

They're just finishing up when my escort returns.

"He's all set, Sir Gregory," Leo says.

"Excellent," the older man says. "Come, Mr. Younger. We have little time."

He takes me to the parking area next to the highway, where four Hayden-Norris carriages are waiting.

I've been in carriages before—beat-up things my father borrowed from coworkers, and twice in funeral carriages provided by the mortuary. But none was manufactured by Hayden-Norris, which produces some of the most elegant and expensive carriages on the planet.

Sir Gregory leads me to the second one and opens the doors. "Inside, please."

The interior is as plush as the exterior is shiny and sleek. I expect Sir Gregory to join me, but instead he closes the door, leaving me alone, and a moment later I feel the carriage's powerful motor come to life.

I spend most of the trip staring out the window, my mind spinning questions and possibilities. But I'm no closer to understanding what's going on when we finally stop nearly an hour later outside a large, busy building. Etched into the stone above a series of doors are the words HOLYHEAD STATION. I know of Holyhead and have passed through while riding the N-CAT on a few occasions, but have never disembarked here. The primary purpose of the station is not the N-CAT stop, however. Holyhead is New Cardiff's main terminal for NorAm Rail—North American Railways.

NorAm holds the royal grant giving them exclusive rights to all long-distance ground transportation in North America. It's the main way people travel around the continent. The only alternative would be if one were able to arrange a seat on a royal air transport, but only the wealthiest are able to do that. There's a rumor that in other kingdoms and a few of the independent countries, air travel is easier to use. True or not, here in the British Empire, it would never be an option for someone like me.

In fact, taking the NorAm is seldom done by those of my caste, since everyone knows there's no reason for Eights to be moving around.

The carriage door opens, and Sir Gregory peeks inside. "Hurry, please. We don't have much time."

Surrounded by the men in dark suits, Sir Gregory and I enter the packed station. Here and there I spot members of the lower castes wearing coveralls or the uniforms of servers, but most of the travelers appear to be at least Sixes. The last time I saw so many people dressed up was at Easter services, though the quality of the clothing at our local church does not compare to what I see before me.

We make our way across the main lobby and head toward the tunnel entrances that lead to the various platforms.

"My travel booklet—it's in my bag," I say, suddenly panicked.

Every citizen of the empire must have a travel book to board any vehicle going farther than a hundred miles. Even Eights are issued them.

Sir Gregory stops. "Quite right. Meant to give this to you as soon as we arrived."

He pulls a book from his pocket and hands it to me. While it *is* a travel booklet, the cover is the green of caste Five. I check the information page inside and see my own picture staring back at me.

"I can't use this," I say. "It's a forgery."

"A forgery? Why would you think that?"

"This isn't my caste level. I'm an Eight, not a Five. They'll throw me in prison if I'm found with this."

Like a patient uncle, he smiles and says in a calm voice, "Mr. Younger, when you accepted Lady Williams's offer, it came with a reassignment to caste Five. You are part of the gentry now. If you don't believe me, you're more than welcome to check with the royal registry, but I can assure you, the change is official."

I stare at him. "I don't . . . but . . ."

"I know you have a lot of questions, but better to save them for later."

As promised, there are no problems passing through the security checkpoint at the tunnel entrance. When Sir Gregory hands our tickets to a caste-Nine porter, the man's eyebrows shoot up.

"I'll be happy to help you, gentlemen," he says with more deference than I expect. "Do you have any luggage?"

"It's come ahead," Sir Gregory tells him.

"Then if you'll come this way."

Up the tunnel we go, exiting onto platform number five. There, sitting on the tracks, is a sleek, cross-country express. I've only seen these from afar as they race through the Shallows. Red, blue, and white stripes run from one end to the other, while the metal covering the rest of the carriages has been buffed to the point where I can see my own reflection in it.

What surprises me, though, is that the porter doesn't take us to the train, but instead leads us to a locked door at the end of the platform. There, he presses a button, and we wait a moment for the door to be unlocked remotely. Inside is not a room but a lift. We ride it to the very top.

When the door opens, the porter holds it in place but stays inside and says, "Go around to the other side, and you'll see it."

"Thank you for your help," Sir Gregory says as he hands the man a five-pound note.

Once we circle the elevator, our destination comes into view. Each surprise today seems to be topping the last, and this is no exception. In the center of the roof sits a Valor aircraft, its twin propellers churning the air.

Here I thought I was about to go on a long-distance train ride, and instead I'm flying for the very first time. My heart nearly stops every time the Valor tilts one way or the other in the air, and it's several minutes before I'm able to overcome enough of my fear to look out the window.

Seeing New Cardiff from this angle is breathtaking. The parklands, the sun sparkling off the Pacific, the thousands of carriages on the roads all lie below me and help me get a better idea of how nearly two million people could call my city home.

After about twenty minutes, we descend toward a more conventional airfield. Off to the side, I see several large aircraft, but don't allow myself to even think we'd be taking one of them. And yet, when we disembark, it's to the nearest of these aircraft that Sir Gregory and our bodyguards escort me.

Only this morning I was sitting in my schoolroom, waiting with my fellow students and contemplating a casteless life, and now here I am, sitting in a *royal* transport as it rises above New Cardiff, and I am no longer an Eight but a Five.

"Take this," Sir Gregory tells me, holding out a pair of white pills. "It's a long trip, and this will help you sleep."

"I'm fine," I say. I don't want to sleep. I don't want to miss any of this.

"Maybe so, but it'll be morning when we arrive, and you have a busy day ahead of you. Trust me, you'll want to take these."

"I'd rather not."

"Suit yourself. But if you change your mind . . ." He places them on the cushion between us and then folds his chair all the way back and closes his eyes.

As exciting as it is to be up in the air like this, the nighttime voyage leaves little for me to see except scattered lights below. At some point, despite not having taken the pills, I fall asleep.

The next thing I know, Sir Gregory is shaking my shoulder. "We're here, Mr. Younger. Time to get up. You wouldn't want to miss your first class."

CHAPTER FIVE

"Once you've finished training, your official title will be Personal Historian for the Upjohn Institute. But that's still three months away, so until then, you're only probationary trainees."

We are in a theater-style classroom, in six rising rows of four students each. On the stage below, our lecturer is an older man, who was introduced to us as Sir Wilfred Pell, head of institute security. He's an imposing figure. Six and a half feet tall, at least, with a chest that stretches the fabric of his shirt and arms as thick as his legs. What hair he has on his head is shaved close, but is more than compensated for by his black-dyed Vandyke beard and mustache.

"As trainees, you have restrictions on where you can and cannot go on the grounds of Upjohn Hall. You will find a map detailing these locations in your guidelines manual. I suggest you commit these to memory, because if you are found where you're not supposed to be, your participation in our program will be seriously jeopardized." He pauses, staring up at us to emphasize his point. "On occasion Upjohn Hall receives visitors from the outside. If you happen to come in contact with them and they ask what you do, you will tell them your job is to research and put together the family histories of institute contributors. If pushed, which you likely will not be, you should say you spend your days looking through dusty books and delicate parchments, and then report whoever has made this inquiry to the security bureau. We are all responsible for the secrets of the institute. Do I make myself clear?"

"Yes, sir," we reply in unison, though we're no closer to understanding what these secrets are.

"Good," he says. "Then I expect we'll have no problems."

He walks to the chairs along the back wall, where several others are sitting, so I take advantage of the break to take my first good look at the other trainees. They all appear to be the same age as me. A few meet my gaze with looks of disdain that I'm very familiar with. They come from upper castes, Fives at least. And though I'm technically a Five now, I know they see the Eight in me. The ones who don't look at me have an air about them that makes me put them in the same upper category. Am I the only one from the lower castes here?

"Good morning, everyone."

I look back and see that Sir Gregory has stepped to the lectern.

"Good morning, sir," several of us reply, though not quite as together as our previous response.

"It's a pleasure to welcome you all to our summer 2014 session. Those of you who have been here for several days, we appreciate your patience while the rest of your classmates were brought in. Now that you're all here, it's time to begin."

I realize I must've been the last one to arrive, as I barely had time to be shown my quarters before I was brought here.

"I imagine you're all wondering what profession it is you've agreed to join," Sir Gregory said.

Nods and a few murmurs of assent.

"Sir Wilfred is correct," he says. "You will indeed be personal historians, but your heads will not be buried in dusty books and delicate parchments. As rewinders you will be getting your hands dirty."

"Rewinders?" a girl in front of me asks. She wears her long hair in a style popular among the nobility and has the haughty manner to go with it. Which explains her asking the question. I'm wondering the same thing but would never have spoken up.

"It's not the official title," Sir Gregory says. "More of what we've come to call ourselves."

I see disapproval on some of the faces of those sitting behind him, making me think not everyone uses the term.

"Where was I?" Sir Gregory thinks for a moment. "Right. As personal historians, you'll be at the very heart of what we do here at the institute. Your work will take you places you never thought you could go. Never even thought possible." He pauses. "Three calendar months from today, your training will end, but to be clear, not all of you will complete the program. Those who do not become rewinders will be moved into support positions that, I can guarantee you, are also critical to the work we do."

"Like a servant?" the question comes from the same girl as before, but is whispered so only a few of us hear it. As she says it, she shoots a look in my direction.

"Those of you who do complete the program will be assigned to a senior historian, who will work with you for your first nine months, and then, as long as you've proven yourself, you'll be on your own. The job is an all-consuming one and will become your life, and you will likely only see your fellow students in passing, if at all. For that reason, attachments during training are discouraged.

"Your instruction will occur through various methods, including daily individual sessions and occasional group meetings such as this. Let's see." He looks back at his colleagues. "Have I missed anything?"

The others shake their heads.

When Sir Gregory looks back at us, he says, "I know you have many questions. The best way to get answers is in a one-on-one meeting with your personal instructor, so if you will all rise."

We stand.

"Single file, please, after me."

When we leave the classroom, Sir Gregory leads us through the building and into a hallway with twelve numbered doors on either side.

"I'll call out names followed by a number," Sir Gregory says. "Once you hear your name, proceed to the corresponding room. This will be the room you use throughout training, so don't forget your number."

As I wait for my name to be called, I try to memorize the others' names. The girl who all but called me a servant is Lidia Brewer. She's sent to room 18, and I can't help but hope I'm assigned a room nowhere near hers. When Sir Gregory says my name, though, the number he announces after it is 17.

When I enter the room, the first thing I notice is how white it is—walls, ceiling, floor—and then the three pieces of furniture that fill the space: a wooden table between two metal chairs. No one is present, so I'm unsure which seat to take. I decide I want to see who comes into the room, so I scoot around the table and claim my place.

It's several minutes before the door finally opens, and a woman in a simple gray dress with a bag over her shoulder enters. She's shorter than I am by nearly a foot, and if she weighs more than seven and a half stones, I'd be shocked. Her hair is dark, almost black, and cut so that it barely touches the tops of her ears. What I notice most, though, is the aura of confidence that moves with her. It's not something you see in the neighborhood where I grew up.

After closing the door, she takes the other seat. "Hello, Denny," she says, holding out her hand. "I'm Marie Jennings. Welcome to the Upjohn Institute."

"Thank you," I say as we shake.

"I'm to be your personal instructor during your training," she says. "And you are to be one of our potential rewinders."

"Yes, um, so what exactly is a rewinder?"

"That's the big question, isn't it? What do you think?"

I've done nothing but try to figure that out since leaving the classroom, but am no closer to an answer so I shrug and shake my head.

"The definition's very straightforward," she says. "A rewinder is a verifier of personal histories."

"Okaaay," I say, still not understanding.

"Had you heard of the Upjohn Institute before you came here?"

"Never."

She sets her bag on the table and removes a leather-bound sheath. After opening it she studies one of the papers inside and then looks up. "That's right. You were an Eight before." There's no judgment in her voice, which surprises me, as she clearly comes from a higher caste.

"I feel like I'm still an Eight."

"Give it time," she says. "Pretty soon you won't even think about what you are or where you came from. All right, let's talk about the institute for a moment. It was established with a singular purpose. People come to us to trace and verify their family histories. To have a history certified by the Upjohn Institute means that no one can dispute your lineage. No one. Our results are accepted by the very top of society."

By *very top*, she must mean the king. Just the thought of working at a job even remotely connected to the Crown is terrifying.

"So, a rewinder does these verifications?" I ask.

"Correct."

"How, exactly?"

"Quite simple. You will observe and report."

"Observe?"

She reaches into her bag and pulls out a wooden box— approximately five by seven inches and an inch thick—and holds it out to me. When I take it, I find it's not nearly as heavy as I expected, and it's not made of wood at all but some kind of metal designed to look like wood.

"Open it," she says.

On the top is a flap that's latched on the wide side. I try to open it, but it doesn't budge.

"Right here," she says, touching a smooth section next to the latch. "Touch it with your right thumb."

I do as she says, and the latch pops open.

When I look at her, she says, "It's been keyed to you."

I start to ask, "How?" but my attention's drawn to the display screen and buttons that were covered by the flap.

"What is this thing?"

She holds her hand out, and I give it back to her. "The engineers call it a temporal transmitter, but it's more commonly referred to as a chaser." She sets it on the table.

I know temporal has something to do with time, but what would a temporal transmitter be? A radio clock?

Seeing my confusion, she says, "A little history. The Upjohn Institute received its royal charter from Queen Victoria in March 1841."

I blinked. Eighteen forty-one is an extremely important year in the history of the empire.

"Yes," she says, noting my reaction. "That was only three months before she was killed. When King James III took the throne, he reconfirmed the charter, and the institute's been here ever since, serving the upper castes of the empire.

"Until thirteen years ago, the only means we had for verifying lineages were old records. This was sufficient to a point, but not always 100 percent accurate. Records can be falsified, and whole histories can be changed to suit someone's interests.

"In 1998 Lady Williams learned of a project being conducted at a small university in Virginia. She saw the potential immediately, so she made a sizable donation to the school in exchange for hiring Professor Clarke and moving his project to the institute. Under her guidance the professor turned his research in a direction more useful for our needs. It took him a little over three years, but finally he did it." She touches the chaser.

"Did what?" I ask.

"Perhaps it's time for a demonstration." She picks up the chaser. "Think of a date, sometime in the past couple years, one you know exactly where you were at a specific time."

"A date? Why?"

"Please, just think of one."

Without my even trying, a date comes to me.

"Ready?" she asks.

"Yes."

"I only need to know three things. The date, the time, and the city or district you were in."

"May 9, 2009. Three p.m. The Shallows, New Cardiff."

"All right. Now I'm going to ask you to stay in your chair no matter what happens. Can you do that?"

"Yes. Of course."

She opens the chaser's lid and works her fingers across the buttons and screen. After a moment she says, "I'll be right back."

I expect her to get up and walk out. What happens instead is that she stands up, pushes a button on the device, and disappears.

Despite my promise, my chair flies backward into the wall as I jump away from the table. I want to yell, but I can't even take a breath. She was there, standing by her chair, and then she was . . . gone.

With effort I calm myself enough so that air can flow back into my lungs.

It has to be some kind of trick. An illusion created by projections, perhaps. I'm half-convinced she was never actually in the room, but then I remember that we shook hands.

I slowly approach the table again. When I reach it, I lean forward and wave my hand through the air where she was standing. Empty.

I eye the door and consider fleeing, but my curiosity is strong enough to keep me there. If this is some kind of test, the moment I step out of the room, I'll probably fail and be removed from the program.

Without turning my back on the table, I fetch my chair and take my place again. My foot taps nervously on the floor while I wait for what happens next. Several seconds pass before I feel a slight movement of air on my fingertips. A split second later Marie reappears in the same spot she was in before.

I jerk back again, but am able to keep myself from jumping to my feet this time.

"Good," she says. "You're still here."

My hand rises, reaching to see if she's really there.

She holds out her arm. "Go ahead. You have my permission."

When my fingers touch her warm wrist, I yank my hand back.

"How did you . . . where . . ." I barely get these words out before I feel my throat tightening again.

"May 9, 2009. Three p.m.," she says. "The first anniversary of your sister's death. You visited her grave. Alone."

"You contacted my father, didn't you?" I ask. He was supposed to go with me that day but couldn't bring himself to do it.

"I've never spoken to your father."

"Okay, maybe not you, but someone here. They were probably making the call before you . . . you left."

"Would your father have seen you trace her name on the headstone? Would he have seen you take the blades of grass from above her grave and stick them in your pocket? Would he have followed you after, when you wandered through the village and stopped behind the mechanics' shop and cried?"

Brett Battles

I stare, dumbfounded. She can't know this. She can't know *any* of this.

"Someone told you," I whisper.

"We both know that's not true."

"I don't believe you. Someone must have seen me. You must have found out who."

With a patient look, she says, "All right. Why don't we try a different date, then?"

I open my mouth to give her one, but quickly shut it. What I almost chose was another date she can easily find information on. What I need is something with details only I know. I think for a moment, then say, "December 13, 2013, 4:15 p.m. The Shallows."

"Don't go away."

After a few taps on the chaser, she disappears again. This time I barely move when she vanishes. I wait a few seconds, check the air above her chair again, and confirm it's once more empty.

When Marie returns she's holding the chaser in one hand and clenching something in the other.

She says, "Quarry," and sets an old cookie tin on the table.

It's impossible.

There's no way.

And yet as I pick up the tin, I know it's the same one I kept hidden in the rocks at the edge of the old abandoned quarry. The scratches, the dents, the worn paint are all exactly as I remember them.

I'm scared to open it, but I do anyway. Inside are pictures of my mother and sister, a few odd coins, and the dried blades of grass from my sister's grave. In the excitement and mystery of the day I received my test results, the tin was the one thing I forgot to get before leaving to meet with Lady Williams and Sir Gregory.

"How did you find this?"

"You told me where to look. December 13, 2013. I just had to follow you to the quarry."

36

"Follow me? I don't—"

"Is that yours or not?"

"It's mine."

"Not a fake?"

I shake my head.

"Good. Now I need it back." She snatches it out of my hand and closes the lid.

"Wait. What are you going to do with it?"

"Is December 13 the last day you saw it?"

"No. I stopped there at least once a week."

"Then I need to put it back so it's there when you return."

"Return?"

"I guess grammatically the correct word should be *returned*, but things can get a little . . . mushy."

Before I say anything, she's nothing but empty air again, but she's gone only a few seconds before she returns without the tin.

"Will you please explain to me what's going on here?" I say.

"Let me ask you, Denny—what's the most reliable form of historic data?" she asks.

I think for a moment, remembering my history lessons at school. "Um, eyewitness accounts."

"Correct. So wouldn't eyewitness accounts be the best way to trace the lineages of the great families?"

"Sure, but it would be impossible to always find—"

"So a tool that would allow a rewinder to actually witness events would make the job easier, would it not?"

"Yeah, but—"

I stop myself. She can't possibly mean what I'm thinking she does.

"You know the answer," she says.

"You want me to believe that . . ." I can't get the words to leave my lips.

"Believe that . . ." she says, locking eyes with me.

I stare at her for several seconds before I whisper, "That you go back."

"Finish it. Go back where?"

"In . . . in . . . in time."

Marie smiles as she leans back. "So now what do you think a rewinder does?"

I remain silent, both afraid of and excited about the answer.

"When you complete your training, you, Denny Younger, will be one of those who travels back."

CHAPTER SIX

I meet up again with my fellow rewinders-in-training at dinner in the communal hall. The shocked look on their faces tells me that they, too, have seen the impossible.

Hard science has never been my specialty, but I didn't leave my meeting with Marie without asking, "How does it work?"

As expected, the answer she gave was full of words I didn't understand and concepts that tie me up and bury me under their incomprehensible weight. I came away knowing only that the chaser device is the key and it'll be my passport to everywhen.

Dinner is eaten in silence, the only noise made by our forks and knives clicking against our plates. By the time I'm lying in bed in my small, private room, I can't even recall what we were served.

I stare at the ceiling, still half-convinced Marie's demonstration was an illusion and that there's a logical answer that doesn't involve trips into the past. But I can come up with no decent alternative, so my mind begins to drift from *how could this be* to *why am I here?*

Obviously there was something on my initial test that caught the institute's eye. But what? What answers did I give that brought them all the way across the continent to test me again?

Thirty-eight hours ago, I was just another new adult from a lowly caste, waiting to be told what society thought my life should be. If given a billion chances, I would've never guessed where I am now.

◆　◆　◆

For the next seven days, we're subjected to a regimen of lectures in the morning and testing in the afternoon.

During the lectures we learn that the existence of the chaser device is known only to those working for the institute and the king himself. "This is the secret we must guard at all costs," Sir Wilfred tells us on day two. "If a chaser were obtained by the wrong person, the results could be catastrophic. For this reason you are all restricted to the institute grounds until the end of your training. After, any outside travel will need special permission. And know this—it would be an extreme understatement to say the penalty is severe for exposing our secrets to outsiders. Have I made myself clear?"

On another day he tells us this penalty is not the only threat we live under. "If at any time, you use your chaser for something other than institute business, you will face disciplinary actions that could result in your removal from the program."

"So we'd be kicked out of the institute?" Lidia asks.

The look on Sir Wilfred's face is the most serious I have ever seen. "No one ever leaves the institute. The responsibility you're being granted is so much larger than you can even imagine. If you feel you cannot handle this, you must let your supervisor know immediately."

I'm fairly certain these first lectures are designed to scare us, something I find unnecessary. I don't know about the other trainees, but there are so many inherent dangers in traveling into history—disease and war, just to name a couple—that I don't need any added threats to put the fear of God in me.

As for the afternoon tests, the best word I know to describe them would be thorough. Each exam contains hundreds of questions and is focused on a different period of history. Even with all the independent studying I've done over the years, I've never been more aware that my education has been insufficient. There are questions about things I've never heard of, points of history so precise I wonder how anyone can even know the true answer. But then I remember Marie disappearing in front of me and realize that every detail of the past is knowable. For every test, we're given four hours to finish. I'm lucky if I'm able to get halfway through in that time.

When we're not in the lecture hall or taking exams, we're encouraged to study. There's a grand library, three floors high and more than twice as large as the library near my father's house. It's located in an annex to the main building. Like several of the other trainees, I'm there as much as possible, poring through the books until my mind forces me to return to my room and drop into bed.

On the eighth day, the schedule changes, and we're told we'll be spending mornings with our private instructors and afternoons improving our physical health.

Lidia is opening the door to room 18 as I near my own. She glances at me and smirks. "Don't get too comfortable in there. They'll probably kick you out soon. I can't even understand why they chose you. You're out of place here, and you know it."

Over the past week, she's said similar things to me, often in front of others. I've been brought up not to respond to taunts from those "better" than I, so I have, to this point, kept my mouth shut.

But I can hold my tongue no longer. "They wanted me here. You probably just bought your way in."

I pull open the door to room 17 and hurry in before she can respond.

Marie is already sitting at the table, her back to the door. In front of her are a stack of books, a closed leather sheath, and a monitor and keyboard. When I take the other seat, she opens the sheath, reads the top sheet of paper, flips it over, reads the second, and then goes through the same routine with the third.

Before she even finishes the last, she says, "I'm impressed."

"I'm sorry?" I say.

"Your tests. You've done very well."

"Right," I say, sure she's trying to be funny. "I'm a genius."

She looks up. "I didn't say that. But you are far above the average for your group. In fact, you came in first."

Now I know she's lying. She's just trying to pump me up before dropping the hammer and telling me the institute has made a terrible mistake.

"Here," she says.

She pulls one of the papers out and sets it on the table so I can read it. It's a list of all those in my group, with a number next to each name. My number is highest, by a considerable margin.

"Believe me now?" she says.

I pick up the paper and stare at it. "There must be some kind of mistake. I didn't even finish any of them. I—"

"No mistake. The tests are extremely difficult. No one has ever finished them."

I lay the paper back down and allow myself to think that maybe I did do better than I thought.

"Your results will make our mornings much easier," she tells me.

"What do you mean?"

"The tests are designed to reveal the gaps in your knowledge. And our sessions are, in part, meant to fill those gaps."

Perhaps I've done well by their standards, but there's no question my gaps are considerable. "How long will that take?"

"As long as necessary." She returns the paper to her sheath and pulls the keyboard toward her. "I thought we'd start with something recent—the late twentieth century. We'll focus first on our alliance with the Russian Empire and the Mediterranean conflict of the 1960s."

◆ ◆ ◆

These morning sessions are mentally draining, but I love every minute of them. The afternoons, however, I could do without.

"Stamina is the key," we are told, so our physical training sessions always begin with a run. At first, it's "only" a mile, but within a week we're doing two and then three and then four. The rest of our time is spent building our strength. One day is chest and arms, and then abs, back, and legs before the cycle starts over again.

By the time I finish dinner each evening and drag myself to my room, all I want to do is sleep, but every day Marie gives me something I need to read before the next session, so it's always several more hours before I can finally lay my head down.

Marie and I work backward through the twentieth century as the British Empire continued its expansion, annexing the whole of Central America and much of South America after the victorious Spanish War of 1903. From there we move into the nineteenth century and the rise of the industrial world, led by Britain and fed by the vast resources of its American territories.

While much of what I learn touches on areas I've studied in the past, what Marie presents is a full version, what she calls raw history. It's not long before I realize that the past I thought I knew, the one all regular students are taught, has been sanitized and dressed up to serve the interest of the realm.

Case in point—the slave industry here in North America. I, and everyone I know, think that when King James III abolished slavery in 1841, those who had been in servitude were offered the choice of assimilation into British society here in America or a voyage back to Africa, where their ancestors were from. The truth, according to what Marie tells me, is quite different. The choice was offered only to a select few. Most were forced onto boats and shipped across the ocean, where they were dumped in a land they did not know with a language they did not speak. Localized wars broke out near many of these reintegration sites, and more than half of the former slaves were slaughtered. Of those who survived, another third died from hunger and disease.

This is not the history we were taught.

"What do you know of Queen Victoria?" Marie asks.

"She became queen upon the death of her uncle, King William . . ." I pause, closing my eyes to remember ". . . the Fourth, in the late 1830s."

"Eighteen thirty-seven," she says.

"She was queen for three years until her assassination by Edward Oxford."

"The date?"

Every student knows this one. "June 4, 1840."

Oxford lay in wait for the queen and her husband, Prince Albert, to ride by in their open carriage. The first bullet took her life, while the second ripped through the prince's shoulder, puncturing his lung. He lived, but only for a few more months. Officially his death was caused by infection from the wound, but the popular story was that he died from a broken heart.

"And the succession?" she asks.

"James the Third took the throne."

She cocks her head. "Surely you were taught more than that."

From a young age we're expected to memorize the order of royalty. Any kid older than eight can recite it up to at least the early eighteenth century: The four Georges (I, II, III, IV), William IV,

Victoria, James III, James IV, John II, Catherine, James V, and the current king, Phillip II. But she's right. I do know more.

"There was something about one of her uncles," I say as I dig into my memory. "The king of. . . Hanover. Right?"

"Correct. Ernest Augustus. The queen had produced an heir the year before she died, a daughter. But since she was still a baby, he claimed the throne should be his."

"But that didn't happen," I say. "He died before he could be crowned. So did the child."

"Correct again. And how did they die?"

"Some kind of disease."

"Pneumonia? Is that what you're looking for?"

"Yes. Right. Pneumonia."

"Then you'll be surprised to learn the king of Hanover was poisoned."

"Is that true?"

"It is."

"What about the girl?" I ask.

"Suffocated."

Though the revelations are unexpected, they occurred nearly 175 years ago, so I don't feel the need to get too worked up over them. Still, I'm curious enough to ask, "Why?"

"Why would you think?"

I shrug. "I guess someone didn't want either to take the throne. Would it have been that bad if one of them had?"

"It wasn't a matter of good or bad," she says. "Let's say you're a member of a group that's not happy with the direction the empire is heading in, and you want to do something about it. Say, in the wake of the queen's death, confidence in Parliament plummets, and a special election is quickly held."

I know this isn't conjecture. It's what happened in the aftermath of Queen Victoria's assassination.

"Now," she continues, "say that your group is able to secure a majority of seats in the lower house, and at the same time gain influence over a large number of those in the House of Lords."

She looks at me, waiting.

"You would control the government," I reply.

"Completely?"

"Not completely." By that point in history, much of the power of the British Empire was held by Parliament, but it didn't control everything.

"If you wanted it all, what would you need?" she asks.

"You'd need to control both Parliament *and* the Crown."

"Exactly."

It takes me a second, but then I get it. "The Home Party," I say.

The Home Party has controlled the empire without a break since right after Queen Victoria's death. While other political parties do exist, none ever gain enough seats to make a dent in the Home Party's rule.

Marie smiles again. "Then you have your answer."

CHAPTER SEVEN

"Don't sit down," Marie tells me as I enter my study room.

We have just started the fifth week of my individual training, but this is the first time I've arrived to find no books on the table. Instead, there are two leather, over-the-shoulder satchels.

When I reach the table, Marie pulls one of the bags forward and says, "This is a standard mission kit."

My skin tingles with excitement. We've discussed the kits before, but this is the first time I've seen one in person.

"Open it," she tells me.

Like a child on his birthday, I throw open the flap.

"Now carefully remove the contents and lay them on the table," she instructs.

A sweater is on top, brown and nothing fancy. It's designed, I know, to blend in with whatever time period this kit has been prepared to visit. There are other clothes, too—a shirt, a pair of pants, and one pair each of underwear and socks. Marie has told me that at most a kit will contain two sets of clothes. If in the very unlikely event a trip would last long enough to need more, items could be locally obtained. Next comes a plastic food box.

"What does that tell you?" she asks as I open the box.

Inside is enough room for several prepackaged meals, but it contains only one and a couple energy squares. "This isn't for a long trip," I say.

"And?"

Her question trips me up for a moment, until I realize the answer is the box itself. "And the trip can't be going very far back, thirty years at most, I would think." Any earlier, and the box might draw unwanted attention.

She nods. "Keep going."

I set the box down and pull out a notebook with attached pen, a cloth pouch that holds the medical kit, and a second pouch that contains several tools—knife, wrench, small screwdrivers, and a measuring tape.

The final item is inside a padded sleeve. I remove it from the box and pull off the sleeve.

A chaser device.

When Marie showed me one at the beginning of training, I had no idea how to even turn it on. But in the weeks since, she's taught me the meaning of every button and dial, gone over the steps for various operations, and tested me repeatedly until I know it all by heart. I look at it now with educated eyes, but it still holds so much wonder.

"This is yours," she says.

"Mine?" I say, still looking at it.

"It's the same one as before, but is keyed to you. Can you open it, please?"

After I unlock the latch, she takes it back and turns the power on. Once the screen comes to life, she navigates through several displays until she comes to one with the heading TRAINEE SETTINGS. There she touches a button labeled SLAVE. Immediately a box pops up, with the word AUTHORIZATION at the top, an empty entry line in the middle, and a row of numbers, 0 to 9, at the bottom. She quickly taps in seven numbers, and as the last is entered, the authorization box is replaced by another, with the word LINKING glowing in the middle.

"Right now it's trying to link with my chaser."

She sets it on the table and removes her device from the other satchel. When she turns it on, the word LINKING on mine begins to pulse. After about five seconds, the word is replaced by READY.

"Repack the bag," she tells me. "All but this." She touches the chaser.

I carefully put the items back inside.

When I'm done she says, "Strap it on. You may need some of it on the trip."

My hands begin to shake. *Trip? Now?*

She pulls the strap of her satchel over her shoulder, and after I do the same, she hands me my chaser. "Technically the two of us could jump with just mine if you held on to me tight, but you need to get used to what it feels like to be alone. After training is done, you'll always leave from the departure hall. But we don't have to worry about that at the moment. All set?"

I nod, though how can one ever be ready for this moment?

"We won't be going far. Five years only. So the most you may feel is a mild headache, and likely not even that." She pauses. "What is the mission?"

"To observe and record," I say automatically. It's a phrase that has been drilled into us during both mental and physical training. It's also printed on a banner in the dining hall and a plaque above my bed. As Sir Gregory has stressed countless times, "It's not just what we do. It's *all* we do."

"All right. Then I guess we should go."

She pushes the "Go" button on her chaser, and—

◆ ◆ ◆

A dark gray mist surrounds me, but it's there only long enough for me to register it before a different kind of darkness replaces it. A starry, moonless night.

I gasp. I don't know if we've really gone back in time, but we have gone someplace other than my training room.

"Steady," Marie says from beside me. "On first arrival, what do you do?"

On first what? My head aches with dull pain.

"Denny, take a breath and tell me what you're supposed to do."

I take three, not one, each slower and deeper than the last. Finally the pain fades enough for me to answer. "Check your surroundings."

"Then do it."

I scan the area and see we're in what appears to be a deserted alley.

Our location and time of day fit standard rewinder procedures. *First arrivals should occur at an out-of-the-way spot in the dead of night, suggested time between 3:00 and 4:00 a.m.* This rule allows a rewinder to get the lay of the land before daylight hours.

My chaser displays a local time of 3:21 a.m. on May 16, 2009. The actual location is given as a string of numbers that can only be deciphered using the device's calculator program, so I ask, "Where are we?"

"Chicago," she says.

The Midlands, I think. Though I flew over this part of the continent on the way to New York, I have never set foot in it before. But the same could be said for anywhere that's not New Cardiff.

"Come on," she says, and then leads me to where the alley dumps onto a road lined with parked carriages.

I'm not an expert on vehicles, but none looks like any of the newer models I've seen advertisements for. The buildings on either side of the street are apartments, some with businesses on the ground floor. It could be 2009, and it could be 2014. Nothing stands out. There is one fact, though, I can't ignore. When we left my training room it was morning, and here it's the middle of the night. Given that there's only an hour's time difference between New York and Chicago—if this is indeed Chicago—then I've either been unconscious for several hours or we've really traveled through time.

Marie turns down the sidewalk, and I quickly step after her to catch up.

"I assume you saw the date?" she asks after a few minutes.

"Uh-huh."

"And does it mean anything to you?"

The date? I look back at my chaser to confirm. May 16, 2009.

May 16, 2—

I stop walking. Marie looks back at me.

"Oh, my God," I say.

"Hold that thought." She pushes the "Go" button again.

The change from darkness to a blink of the gray mist to sunlight is so abrupt that I have to slam my eyes shut.

"We don't have much time," Marie says. "Come on."

She grabs my arm, pulls me to the left. Through narrowed eyelids I see we're in a field. Weeds and wild grass brush against my legs, and I almost trip on what I at first think is a rock, but realize it's the edge of the old foundation for a long-destroyed building.

As my vision continues to adjust, I see we're headed toward a group of brick buildings that look to me like old, abandoned warehouses.

"Still Chicago?" I ask.

Marie nods. "Southern industrial zone."

When we reach the end of the field, she crosses the street and races over to one of the warehouses. As I follow I once again have the feeling this is a place she knows. The feeling is reinforced when she jogs up to a set of metal doors and pulls them open like she already knew they'd be unlocked.

On the other side of the doorway is a staircase, but I don't catch up to Marie until I reach the top landing, and this is only because she's stopped to wait for me.

"We're here for one purpose only," she says. "This place gives us a good vantage point. Whatever else you see here is not important. Okay?"

"Sure," I say. "Got it."

She opens the door, and we walk onto the sunlit roof of the warehouse. The weather-protection material that once covered the roof is torn in several places and missing altogether in others. There are at least half a dozen spots where the wood beneath has rotted away, leaving holes that offer a swift trip down to the concrete slab four floors below.

I'm so focused on avoiding these traps that I don't realize we aren't alone until we almost reach the raised lip at the edge. Looking around I spot four other pairs of people scattered along the roof and immediately note a disturbing similarity. In each group there is one person who looks to be around my age. That's not the crazy part, though. The second one of each pair is Marie.

The same woman who brought me here.

Counting the one I'm with, there are five of her.

"Focus," my Marie hisses at me.

I turn to her, and though I'm sure she can see the shock and confusion in my eyes, she ignores my unspoken questions and points toward the city.

"You see it? The tallest one?"

I have to force myself to look toward downtown.

"Yes," I say, picking out the infamous Dawson Tower. From here it looks like a sparkling finger pointed at the sky.

"Just a few seconds now," she says.

So much is running through my mind that I almost miss the very thing she's brought me here to watch. From this distance we're unable to see the exact moment the twenty-third floor begins its collapse, but we can't miss the hundred-plus floors above it beginning to tilt. One of the others with us on the roof shouts in horror as the giant structure breaks into pieces, and a part of me is surprised I haven't yelled, too.

It was supposed to be the tallest building in North America when it was finished, but on May 16, 2009, less than a month from completion, the tower collapsed onto the city, taking several other structures with it and killing thousands. That bit of history from five years ago is happening now right in front of my eyes.

"We could have saved some of them," I say as a great cloud of dust rises. "We could have saved all of them if we wanted to."

"And if we did?" Marie asks.

I know what answer she wants me to say, but I find it impossible to voice. Who cares what happens after? Who cares what changes would occur to our present? We could have *saved* them!

"Suppose we did," she says when I don't answer. "Perhaps we convince a worker who would have been on the seventy-sixth floor to stay home. What if, in his relief for not having been in the accident, he gets drunk and causes the death of someone who wasn't in the tower, someone who, in our home time, was still alive when we left? Now that person is not. Babies will be born who shouldn't have been, and others who *were* born will cease to exist. Relationships with husbands and wives and lovers and friends and enemies and business partners will all play out differently. There's no way to predict what will happen, except to say that our time will be forever altered. All this because we save the lives of those who were already dead. As much as we all wish it were different, a rewinder is not a god. A rewinder is an observer, who keeps his contact with those in the time he's visiting to a bare minimum."

"I get it," I say. "I just . . ."

"It's human nature to want to help," she says.

I nod. That's it exactly.

"I feel the same way every time I watch this happen," she says.

"How do you keep from acting?"

She's silent for several seconds, then says something that sounds more like she's reading it from one of the institute's manuals than feeling it in her heart. "By doing nothing you are serving the greater good of humanity."

I have a hard time believing that but don't know how to respond, so I quietly watch the dust cloud grow. When I can take the tragedy no longer, I look over at the others along the lip.

"More of your students?" I ask.

"Three of them are. One is someone I haven't met yet, but I see him here every time."

I look at her. "You've seen me here, too?"

"I have."

My brain is starting to hurt. "Everyone's in the same position?"

She nods.

"Doing the same things?"

Another nod.

"Did you notice us having this conversation before?"

"I'm watching us right now."

She nods past me, and I look back to see the second Marie over looking in our direction.

"What if you do something you haven't seen before?" I ask.

She looks uncomfortable. "Like what?"

"I don't know. What if you wave? Have you waved at the others before?"

"No, but I'm not so sure that's a good idea."

"You mean it's kind of like if we tried to save those people?"

After a silent moment, she suddenly raises her hand above her head and waves at the other groups. A few respond in kind.

"Whoa," I say, surprised. "Do you now remember seeing you do that?"

"It doesn't work like that. My memory doesn't change."

"So what does that mean?"

She looks back toward the city. "What's your understanding of what caused the Dawson Tower disaster?"

I'm actually glad she's changing the subject, because any answer she might give would undoubtedly lead to more questions, and my head is already overfilled. "Disgruntled workers sabotaged the project," I say, following her gaze. "They were led by a guy named, uh, Wendell something, I think."

"Wendell Barber," she says.

"Right."

"They were scapegoats," she says. "He and the people who were executed with him knew nothing about what caused the disaster."

I get the sense this conversation is turning political, and as an Eight who was taught long ago what should and shouldn't be discussed, it's not a comfortable direction for me.

"There was sabotage, all right, but not by disgruntled workers," she goes on. "The building was brought down by budget skimming through the use of inferior materials and bribed inspectors. The true causes are the same ones that invade most aspects of our society—greed and corruption."

It's impossible to keep the discomfort from my face.

She says, "I'm telling you this because you need to know. When you go on a mission, you will come face-to-face with this same greed and corruption time and again."

I say nothing.

55

"I know you were taught to ignore it and pretend it's not there. But this is reality, Denny, and you're going to be waist-deep in it. It's a part of the empire and has been since . . ." She pauses. "Well, you tell me."

For a moment I'm at a loss, but then it comes to me. I have to fight through my fear to give her the answer. "The Home Party."

"I knew you'd get it. After they took power, everything changed. There'll be a lot of times you'll need to navigate through layers of corruption to find the truths you're assigned to uncover." She's quiet for a moment before adding, "One other thing. It's something the other trainees probably won't be told, but everyone figures it out eventually. The true histories you uncover may not be the ones we initially present to the clients."

"Wait. Are you saying our job *isn't* to report the truth?"

"No, that's not what I'm saying. The institute expects you to always report the facts exactly as you've observed them. Records of those truths will be kept in the archives, but there will be times when the directors decide it's better to tell a sanitized version to the family who engaged us."

"But why?" I ask.

A flash of disapproval appears in her eyes but quickly vanishes. At first I think it's meant for me, but when she speaks, I'm not so sure. "The truth isn't necessarily good for all to have." Like earlier when she spoke about the "greater good of humanity," the words come out as if she's said them a million times before and they've lost all meaning to her.

I look back along the edge of the roof and see that two of the other Maries and their students are gone.

"Time we go home," my Marie says.

A second later, 2009 is history again.

CHAPTER EIGHT

For the first time in several weeks, the other trainees and I are gathered together in the lecture hall. Or, I should say, some of us. Twelve—exactly half of our class—are missing.

We whisper among ourselves, asking each other if we know what's going on. But no one seems to know anything.

At precisely 8:00 a.m., the door at the front of the classroom opens, and Lady Williams enters, followed first by Sir Gregory and Sir Wilfred, and then by Marie and the personal instructors of the other trainees present.

After greeting us Lady Williams says, "Congratulations are in order. You are the chosen."

We look around at each other, confused. Well, most of us. There's a satisfied sneer on Lidia's face, like she already knows what's going on.

"I'm sure you are wondering why several members of your group are missing," Lady Williams says. "That's because the twelve of you have excelled at your studies and have shown us that you will make the best personal historians. The other twelve have not left the institute. In fact, they will play a very pivotal role in your coming career. They will become your chaser companions, and each of your devices will be permanently linked to one of theirs."

I have no idea what a chaser companion is. I was under the impression that, with the exception of the first nine months when we'd be working with supervisors, we would each be traveling alone. Having someone accompany us would double the chances of something going wrong.

"Starting tomorrow," Lady Williams goes on, "and every day from now until your training ends, you'll be traveling with your trainer, putting to practical use the lessons they have taught you by rewinding family histories that are already known to us. This will allow us to better judge and focus your efforts when need be."

She continues, rehashing some of the things Marie has already taught me, and then wraps up with the warning that if our performance fails to meet expectations, we can still be removed from the program. "But I'm certain you will all do just fine. You are on the cusp of a great adventure, and for that I envy you. You'll be seeing what no others can. You'll be witnessing *history*. It's an honor so very few will ever have. Never forget that."

With that she turns and walks out the door, followed by Sir Wilfred.

We sit silently for a moment before Sir Gregory moves up to the lectern. "As I call your name, please join your instructor. Hayden Adams."

Hayden, sitting in the row in front of me, gets up and heads down the stairs to the front of the room. When he reaches his trainer, they exit through the same door Lady Williams and Sir Wilfred used.

One by one the process repeats until I'm the only one left.

"Denny Younger," Sir Gregory says. As I walk by him to where Marie waits, he smiles and pats me on the shoulder. "I'm very impressed with your work, Denny. I knew you would do well."

"T-t-thank you, sir." I'm caught off guard by the compliment.

As soon as Marie guides me out of the room, I ask, "What are we doing?"

"You'll see," is all she tells me.

We turn down several halls and descend a flight of stairs to a level I have never visited before. We soon come to a set of double doors that cuts off the hallway.

As Marie opens one side, I can see that the room beyond is small and unlit. "Step in but don't go any farther," she says.

I do as told. When she joins me and shuts the door, we're plunged into complete darkness.

Marie moves past me, and I hear a handle turn. Dim light streams in from another room.

"This way," she says.

Worried that I might trip on something, I carefully follow her shadowy form through the doorway and into what turns out to be a large, rectangular room. Doors line all the walls but the one at our end. Their close proximity to each other reminds me of our trainee instruction rooms, only these doors are constructed mostly of glass.

Down the center of the room are two long, parallel counters divided into dozens of data stations, all but a few occupied by individuals wearing headphones and staring at their screens. I also spot a couple of fellow trainees and their instructors standing behind the data operators.

"This is the companion center," Marie says. "One of four at the institute."

My brow furrows.

"Come."

She leads me behind one of the manned data stations. I can now see that the user has two monitors in front of him. One is displaying moving digital graphs, while the other is showing an alternate spectrum shot of someone lying on a bed.

Marie whispers, "This man's job is to monitor one of the companions."

"What—" The word comes out louder than I intended, and a few people sitting nearby glare at me. "Sorry," I whisper, then look back at Marie. "What exactly are companions?"

She motions for me to follow her again, and we head over to one of the glass doors. Though it's dark on the other side, there's enough light bleeding in that I can make out a narrow, occupied bed.

Marie moves to the next door. After checking through the window, she opens it and ushers me inside. The room is exactly like the one before, only the bed is empty.

"Was that a companion?" I ask, more confused than ever.

"Yes."

"What was he doing? Sleeping?"

"Basically."

"Why?"

"Because that's what his job requires." She sits on the bed and urges me to do the same. Once I'm beside her, she says, "We've talked about the pain of time travel."

I nod. She's told me the longer the trip through time, the more pain a rewinder will experience.

"The effect is considerably worse without a companion. When it's paired with another chaser, the device deflects onto the companion a considerable amount of the pain its rewinder would otherwise experience." She sees I'm having a hard time following her and says, "Let's say you travel back five years, like we did the other day. You experience, at most, a minor headache. Your companion, resting here in one of these rooms, will have a headache, too, only a much stronger one."

"But I didn't have a companion when we went back." I pause. "Did I?"

"You were slaved to my device, so my companion served both of us. Since we weren't going back too far, it wasn't difficult for her. All right, so now let's say you go two hundred years into the past, taking it in a single jump. Your head would pound, you'd likely be sick to your stomach, and it'd be an hour or so before you felt normal again. Your companion, however, would be consumed by a migraine and muscle spasms that could last all day, if not longer. If you didn't have him, all that pain would be on you, and you'd arrive unable to function at all, meaning the chances of you being discovered skyrocket."

"So we don't make trips without companions," I say.

"Technically it's possible, but I wouldn't try it if I were you. Especially since your companion serves the second and perhaps even more important role of being your beacon home. The farther you have to travel to get back here, the less accurate you become. Not in time. You'll always get the time right. What I mean is physical location. A jump of a few hours or even a couple of days, and you can land precisely where you want without any help. Even a week or two will get you within a few feet of your desired location. But when you stretch that to years—again, like two hundred—no matter what location you've entered into your device, you could end up hundreds of miles away without your companion. Which, on a bad day, might put you in the middle of the ocean. The chaser is able to use the companion's gene signature—which is what the devices use to bind together—to deliver you directly into the arrival hall here at Upjohn Hall."

I feel as if I've fallen through a magic hole into a dreamland where nothing is real. And yet I've traveled through time myself, so is this really that much more to accept?

Someone taps on the door and then opens it. It's one of the data monitors.

"We have a departure in a couple minutes," he says.

"Ah, good. Thank you," Marie tells him. She turns back to me. "This is what we came to see."

◆　◆　◆

I peek over the shoulder of the attendant, careful not to get in the way of Lidia or the other two trainees who have joined us. On the video screen is an alternate spectrum shot of a female companion lying on her bed. The colors of the image range from bluish white to dark blue to black. After a few seconds go by, another person enters the room and connects some wires to the reclining woman's head and upper chest, then straps her arms and legs into padded restraints.

"Those are for monitoring her vital signs," the data attendant says, then points at the other monitor. The graph on it was flat when we arrived but now has sprung to life.

I look at it for a moment but can't even pretend to understand what the lines mean, so I focus back on the other monitor.

"And the restraints?" David, one of the other trainees, asks.

"Just watch," his instructor tells him.

A small square opens on the lower left portion of the main monitor, displaying another camera feed, this one originating from what I recognize as the departure hall. It's focused on a man probably twice my age standing on one of the platforms.

After the man gives a hand signal, the data attendant leans forward and says into a microphone, "Stand by."

The person in the companion's room checks the restraints. When he waves at the camera, the data operator touches a button and says into his mic, "Taylor, clear."

On the departure-hall feed, the rewinder nods and lifts a chaser.

The very instant he disappears, the companion arches on her bed as if shot through by a jolt of electricity. She then drops back down and writhes on the mattress, her hands clenching and unclenching as her arms jerk against the restraints. This only lasts a few seconds before she arches again.

The process plays out four times before she lands back on the bed and stays there. With skill and speed, the room attendant plunges a syringe into her arm. After a moment her tremors begin to subside, and she falls back, either asleep or unconscious.

Marie steps forward. "Can you play back the event, please?"

The data attendant does so, and it's no less disturbing the second time around.

"There are two stages to each jump," Marie tells us. "Pre-arrival and post-arrival."

The attendant runs the video once more, this time pausing on a frame in which the companion is arching her back.

"Pre-arrival," Marie says. "The 'Go' button has been pushed, and the rewinder is in transit. We call this the journey arc."

She nods at the attendant, and the video moves forward, pausing again when the woman is twisting on the bed.

"Post-arrival. The shot she was given helps mitigate the pain and allows her to rest."

"Why wasn't it given to her before the jump?" I ask.

"Because that would reduce her ability to deflect the pain," the attendant says.

"Idiot," Lidia whispers in my ear.

"You saw four journey arches," Marie says. "This is because the rewinder is going quite a distance back and has used the automated controls to make the journey in smaller hops. This helps alleviate much of the pain he would feel upon arriving at this destination if he did it all in one jump."

"How far did he go back?" I ask the attendant.

"One hundred fifty-three years."

Incredible—1861.

"So a short trip wouldn't be so bad on a companion, right?" Kimberly, one of the other trainees, asks.

"The post-arrival phase would be less painful," Marie says. "But for the journey arc, the pain is consistent no matter the span of time traveled."

"Even just five years?" I ask, thinking about our trip to Chicago.

"Even just five years."

Marie and I witness two more departures before we leave the companion-monitoring center.

Once we're alone, I ask, "Do the companions have to stay in those rooms all the time?"

She shakes her head. "If their rewinder isn't traveling, their time is their own."

I'm relieved to hear this.

"Who will my companion be?" I ask.

"One will be assigned at the end of training. You'll find out then."

I was kind of hoping she'd say I would never find out. I'm not looking forward to knowing who it is I'll be putting through agony every time I jump.

CHAPTER NINE

From the beginning we were told training would last three months. What wasn't made clear to us was that this only meant three months in 2014. The reality is that the final three weeks of practical experience last as long as one's instructor feels is necessary. When you go back in time, you can stay there as long as you want and still return minutes after you left. So for those who are still plodding away in my home time, three and a half weeks for them could be four months for me.

I'm not complaining. The time I spend with Marie traveling into the past is nothing short of amazing. Our first "case" is to trace the family lineage of an institute patron named Sir Lionel Mason. We move slowly, rewinding first Sir Mason's own life, witnessing snippets of his successes and failures, making sure to note everything. We then move on to his parents, and then his parents' parents, and so on, each step back expanding the number of people we must track. We're on the job for nearly three weeks of real time—living and breathing time—before Marie is satisfied with my work and allows us to return to the very day we left.

I will grow old very quickly this way, and I say as much to Marie.

"It'll be different after your training is done," she tells me. "Once you're officially a personal historian, when you push the 'Home' button, your real time in the past will equal the amount of time you've been gone. No unnecessary aging." She thinks for a moment. "I should say that's how it *usually* works. You may, on occasion, be asked to make an expedited trip, and you'll return right after you leave."

"Is there a reason why that happens?"

She shrugs. "Whatever the reason, you're not likely to be told."

"A rush for a client?"

She hesitates. "That could be it." Like on a few previous occasions, she seems to be holding something back. Whatever that might be, she continues to keep it to herself.

By the time my training nears its end, I have visited nearly every year going back to 1900, and dozens of years earlier than that. On most trips going more than eighty years back, we use the automated function and do them in hops to reduce the side effects. Marie made me take one long trip all the way back to 1645 so I'd understand why the hops were necessary. The pain was so intense I passed out moments after we arrived. When I came to, I made it clear to her it was a lesson that did not need repeating.

When I arrive for my very last day of training, I ask Marie, "So, who are we tracing today?

"No one."

"No one? We're not going anywhere?"

"Did I say that? Pull out your chaser, please."

As soon as I do, she pushes the "Go" button on her device, and we wink out of 2014. In the now-familiar gray mist of the journey, I can sense Marie's companion. This is something that's been building from trip to trip. It's like that feeling that someone's watching you, but you're never quite able to figure out who. Marie tells me the link will be even stronger with my own companion after I've worked with that person for a while. There are pairs of rewinders and companions who are so compatible that they're able to communicate through the link. I'm not sure if I want that or not.

Our journey is apparently a long one, as we end up making five different stops before we settle on the bank of a river. Having unexpectedly—at least in my mind—arrived during daylight, my training immediately kicks in, and I drop to the ground, my head moving back and forth as I scan the area to make sure we haven't been spotted. But we're completely alone.

"Good response, though you could have probably dropped a second sooner," Marie says.

A half second at most, I think, but I'm not going to argue. I rub away my headache as I look out at the wide river. "Where are we?"

"Spain. The Guadalquivir River."

That would explain the sweat on my brow. "What are we doing here?"

"Is that the right question?"

Of course it isn't. "*When* are we?"

"The tenth of August, 1519."

The date is a familiar one. But with all the practical training we've been doing, I'm a bit rusty with my studying.

"There," she says, pointing upriver.

The bow of a ship is just coming into view, and that's when I remember. It was even a question on the very test that brought me to the institute's attention.

There are five ships total. I don't remember the names of all of them. One, I believe, is the *Victoria*, another the *Santiago*. There is one whose name I do know for sure. The *Trinidad*, flagship of Ferdinand Magellan's fleet. This is the day he sails to the coast, where his journey around the world will begin, a trip Magellan will not finish. But both he and I are here at the start, separated only by the flowing river.

When the ships finally sail out of sight, all I can say is, "They're smaller than I pictured in my mind."

I look over at Marie to see if she's heard me, but she seems lost in thought.

When I open my mouth to ask if she's all right, she says quietly, "And look what we've become."

"I'm sorry?"

She glances over as if she momentarily forgot I'm here. "Don't get used to this," she says, ignoring my question. "Historical moments will seldom be on your agenda. Consider this a present from me, for doing a good job." She looks back at the now-empty river. "Remain true and keep your eyes open, and you'll be one hell of a rewinder."

She short-hops us back to 2014.

Before dismissing me for the last time, she takes my chaser and disables the slave mode. It may not be official yet, but I feel like I'm already a rewinder.

◆　◆　◆

Graduation is a formal affair in the gardens behind Upjohn Hall. There must be two hundred people in attendance. The first group to be honored consists of the twelve people who started out as rewinder trainees but have been reassigned as companions. None of them appear particularly happy, and a few even shoot scornful looks in our direction. And why not? I wouldn't be happy, either.

After the new companions have been acknowledged, Lady Williams gives a speech about the obligations that come with being a personal historian, and the absolute dedication each of us needs to bring to our role every single day. She then focuses on the importance of the Upjohn Institute to the empire and talks wistfully about the beginnings of the organization and all the families it has helped. Her words are met with polite applause, making me think this isn't the first time she's given this speech.

Finally, she calls the new rewinders one by one to the stage, where each personal instructor gives his or her student a certification of completion. When my turn comes, Marie whispers as she shakes my hand, "Do good."

The student in me wants to ask her if she meant to say, "Do well," but something in her eyes tells me she meant exactly what she said.

When we leave the stage, we are guided over to where the new companions stand.

Sir Gregory then takes the microphone and says, "It's now time for the pairing. The selections are not arbitrary, but the result of considerable analysis and consideration. As each pair is called out, you will stand together." He reads the pairs but foregoes the usual alphabetical order. Instead of being last, I'm third.

"Denny Younger and Palmer Benson."

What I remember most about Palmer is that he'd often hang out with Lidia during off-hours, which is probably why we've never shared more than a few words.

And probably why we share only two now.

"Hi," I say as I move next to him.

"Yeah," he replies.

Sir Gregory encourages us to spend the afternoon with our companions, but as soon as we're dismissed, Palmer takes off. I'm actually glad he's uninterested in forming a friendship. It'll be easier for me to forget the pain I'll be causing him later.

As Palmer walks away, I notice Lidia watching him, too. Suddenly she turns and looks in my direction, hate oozing out of every pore, and I instantly know what she's thinking. Palmer should be standing in my spot, ready for his life as a rewinder, while I should be the companion.

◆ ◆ ◆

The supervisor I'm assigned to work with for my first nine months is a veteran rewinder named Merrick Johnston. He makes it clear from the beginning that ours is strictly a working relationship, and as long as I do exactly what he tells me, we won't have any problems. I have no doubt the types of question I often asked Marie would not be welcome.

Johnston turns out to be a master at blending into whatever era we visit. Vowing to myself to be as good as he is, I watch his every move and study each choice he makes. Through the last months of 2014 and the first few of 2015, we trace the histories of dukes, lords, and barons and leaders of industry and business. We delve into the past and uncover the expected ancestral triumphs that lifted families to prominence, and the ugly, buried secrets those in bygone generations assumed would never be known.

I immerse myself in my work, and even when we're not traveling, I continue my studies into the past so no decade I visit will be unknown to me. It's purely by accident that I see the story in the newspaper.

The world of my home time has become all but invisible to me. The institute is my life. The only time I leave the grounds is when I go into the past. The world of today is something I never think about.

I'm in the library, where I spend most evenings researching, when I see it. Johnston has told me that tomorrow we'll be traveling back to 1943, so I'm in the mid-twentieth-century section for a quick refresher.

It's a tense era. The Russian Empire is dealing with internal revolts that will last until the czar's army is finally able to squash them in 1948. Closer to home is the growing tension between the British Kingdom and China. The war neither empire really wants is still another decade away, but the people of '43 don't know that. For them, the Chinese desire to reclaim the coast from north of Shanghai all the way to southeast Asia could turn hostile at any moment.

I roll my head from side to side, trying to work out the ache in my neck and shoulders, but I know the only thing that will make it go away is rest. I could continue reading but I'm more than prepared for the trip, so I shelve the book I've been reading and turn to leave.

The newspaper sits on one of the stuffed chairs along the wall. It catches my attention because it's the first one I've seen since coming to the institute. The paper is folded so that an article on one of the inside pages is showing. The headline is why I pick it up.

PROMINENT BUSINESSMAN HARLAN WALKER DEAD

It's a name I know very well. Less than two months ago, Johnston and I rewound the man's history. Though we've traced two other families since then, Walker's has stuck in my mind because of the irregularity we uncovered.

I read the article and learn that Walker—owner of the largest construction company on the East Coast of North America, and the fourth Harlan of his family—was found in his office, dead of natural causes. Unnamed medical sources report he had a hereditary heart condition that resulted in a massive coronary the previous afternoon.

I frown. Someone doesn't know what he or she is talking about. Here's what *I* know.

Harlan Walker was thirty-seven years old. I've seen Walker's medical records. I have seen his father's and mother's medical records. I have seen the medical records belonging to his grandfathers and grandmothers and great-grandfathers and great-grandmothers. Not a single one of them had a heart condition.

71

I flip the paper over so I can read the rest, and have to go over the second-to-last paragraph twice to make sure I didn't read it wrong.

Again, what I know. Harlan Walker was unmarried but on the cusp of becoming engaged. This was the reason he hired the institute. He needed to verify his lineage before he could marry the daughter of a duke. What we found was that his grandmother on his father's side had an affair. His father, Harlan III, was the result, making Harlan IV the son of an illegitimate heir.

We collected hair samples that the institute's lab tested to confirm this discovery, and we included the evidence in our report. Though it was never said outright, Johnston all but told me this information would not be given to the client, meaning the official report Harlan IV received would be clean.

The next-to-last paragraph in the news article makes me wonder if what we learned was truly buried.

> Walker Construction's board of directors confirms that ownership of the company will pass to Walker's cousin Teresa Evans and her husband, Mathew Evans. In addition, a family source reports the estate will be making sizable donations to several organizations, including the Health Fund of the Atlantic, Catherine University, and the Upjohn Institute.

As a personal historian, albeit one who's still very new to the job, I've been trained to look for connections that will help unearth real stories. So I can't help but make the connection that's staring me in the face. Walker hires the Upjohn Institute. The Upjohn

Institute—via Johnston and me—uncovers a shattering truth about Walker's past. And now Walker is dead, and the institute has come into a "sizable donation."

This is one of those things I desperately want to talk to someone about, someone who can tell me I'm just overthinking. I decide I'll risk bringing it up with Johnston—very cautiously. After I go back to my room, I lie awake until well after midnight before I come up with an approach I hope will work.

◆ ◆ ◆

I arrive in our prep room early the next morning and place the newspaper on the counter along the back wall.

Twice I go back and adjust its position. I'm not satisfied that it doesn't look planted, but I finally force myself to leave it alone.

At my closet I begin changing into the era-appropriate clothing that's been left for me. I'm buttoning up my shirt when Johnston enters.

"Morning," I say.

When he glances over and grunts, I think he knows I'm up to something. I turn away so he can't see my face, and I take a deep, silent breath. I listen as my supervisor dons his wardrobe, and when I hear him start tying his shoes, I wander toward the back of the room.

"What's this?" I say. *God, could that have sounded more fake?*

I pick up the paper and pretend to read. I'm not so stupid as to have left the article about Walker front and center, so I scan the front page and then open it to take a look inside.

"Where did you get that?" Johnston asks, his tone accusatory.

I glance over and see him walking angrily toward me.

"It was, uh, sitting here." I point at the counter.

The thumb of my other hand rests right below the headline proclaiming Harlan Walker's death. As I start to look down so that

I can "notice" the article, Johnston snatches the paper out of my hands.

"This shouldn't be here," he says and crumples it up.

"It's just a newspaper."

Using the paper to emphasize his words, he says, "Our concern is the then, not the now. The only thing about 2015 that's important is that it's where you learn your next assignment. Got it?"

"Of course," I say, trying hard not to glance at the paper.

I'm hoping he'll toss it on the floor and I can lag behind, hide it somewhere, and retrieve it later, but it's still in his hand as we walk out. When we pass one of the institute's security men, Johnston shoves the paper into the guy's hand and says, "Dispose of this."

The pit of my stomach plummets toward the center of the earth. That did not go anywhere near how I was hoping it would. Not only is the article gone, but I can't bring up the subject of Walker now without risking Johnston finding out I brought the paper into the prep room in the first place.

I tell myself I need to forget the whole thing, but throughout our assignment, I keep thinking about Walker and the money the institute is receiving.

When we return the next evening, it's bothering me so much that I go in search of Marie. Though I haven't seen her since graduation, I know she'll at least listen to my questions. But she's not around. Over the next several days, I continue trying to see her, but either my timing's bad or she's avoiding me; I'm always told she's busy elsewhere.

I decide that if I can't find her, maybe I can at least find another newspaper. Everywhere I go in the institute, I keep my eye out, but I never see one. This is when it dawns on me that, with the exception of the paper I found in the library, the last one I saw was back in New Cardiff.

Several weeks after my failed attempt to talk to Johnston, we return early from an assignment, and I find myself with my first open afternoon. I decide to take advantage of the opportunity and head for the gate leading into the city, where I can find a newspaper. But as I approach the main gate—a thick wooden door in the stone wall surrounding the institute—a security man steps from a nearby hut and says, "May I help you?"

"I can get the gate myself, thanks."

When I step toward it, he moves in front of me. "Do you have authorization?"

"I'm only going to be gone a half hour at most," I tell him. "Just taking a walk."

"May I have your name?"

"Why do you need my name?"

"If you don't want to tell me, I can easily look you up."

He's right about that. There's a directory with everyone's name and picture in it. "Denny Younger," I say.

"And your position?"

This makes me feel even more uncomfortable. "Junior personal historian."

He pulls a notebook from his back pocket and writes down the information. When he finishes he says, "Mr. Younger, I'm sorry. Without authorization from your supervisor, I can't let you leave. If it's walking you're interested in, the institute grounds provide plenty of options."

His smile tells me our conversation is over and that he doubts I'll be back. He's right. Johnston would never give me authorization without asking questions I don't want to answer.

I head straight back to my room only to find another security man waiting by my door.

"Mr. Younger?" he says.

"Yes?"

"Please come with me."

CHAPTER TEN

A chill passes through me. "What's this about?"

The guard turns and walks down the hallway without answering. Seeing no other choice, I follow. He leads me into the administration section, and then to a room about three times the size of mine. Behind a desk sits a woman with graying brown hair.

"Mr. Younger," the security man announces.

After a nod of acknowledgment, the woman points to a chair along the wall and says to me, "Wait there."

When I sit she picks up her com-phone and says, "He's here," then listens for a moment before cradling it again.

I glance nervously at her while she busies herself with some papers as if I'm not even here. After a few minutes, a door behind her swings open a few inches. "You can go in now," she tells me.

The new room is twice as large as the woman's, with walls covered in dark wood paneling and bookcases stuffed end to end with leather-bound volumes. A beautiful carpet covers the floor, but the desk is the focal point of the room. Massive and old, it looks as if it were carved from a single piece of wood. What's missing is the room's occupant.

Hesitantly I walk over to the guest chair in front of the desk, but I know sitting first would be disrespectful so I remain on my feet. About thirty seconds later, I hear the faint squeak of a hinge. I look over just in time to see a small section of a bookcase open outward, revealing Sir Gregory.

"Mr. Younger." With a smile he walks over and shakes my hand, then gestures to the chair. "Please. Sit down, sit down."

I wait until he's lowered himself into his before I do as he asked.

"Something to drink?" he offers. "Tea? Coffee? Water?"

"I'm fine, thank you," I say, though I'm far from it.

"Very well, then." He picks up several sheets of paper off his desk and looks them over. "Let's see . . . ah, yes." He glances up and smiles again. "We first met in New Cardiff last spring."

"Yes, sir."

"And now you're a full-fledged personal historian."

"Junior, sir. But yes, since September."

"I never doubted you'd pass." He gestures to the file. "When I first learned of your Occupational Placement Examination scores, I knew you would be perfect for the program."

"Um, thank you," I say, not knowing how else to respond.

"And how do you like it?"

"Sir?"

"Being a rewinder."

"Oh, it's, uh, it's more than I could've ever imagined. I still have a hard time believing it."

"Of course you do. That sense of wonder will likely stay with you throughout your career. It does with most rewinders. God knows, I still can't believe it sometimes."

He's quiet for a moment as he reads through another one of the sheets. When he looks back at me, he says, "I see here that you wanted to go for a walk today."

"I'm sorry, Sir Gregory. I forgot I needed authorization. I haven't been out since I arrived here, and I ended up with some extra time this afternoon so I thought . . ."

"But you get out all the time on your assignments."

"You're right, sir. I do. It's just . . ." I pause, thinking quickly "I'm always working then."

"Of course. I understand. Truth is, there are times when I wish I could take a walk outside."

"You don't go out, either?" I ask.

He studies me for several seconds and then sets the papers down. "This was going to happen eventually. It always does. You should feel honored. You're the first from your class I've had to talk to about it."

"About what exactly, sir?"

He leans back in his chair. "There was a time when members of the institute freely moved in and out of our gates. In fact, when I started as a personal historian, it was a necessity. Our work at the time meant tedious hours spent combing historical archives and records that were often not accessible via data monitors, so we traveled throughout the empire to consult and decipher the original texts. For over 160 years, this is how the institute did its work. But then everything changed." He pauses as if he's given me the answer I'm looking for, but he hasn't, and my expression tells him as much. "Mr. Younger, what is the most powerful thing on earth?"

I say without hesitation, "The king."

"Yes, yes, naturally," he says. "But I'm not talking about a person. I'm talking about a *thing*."

I shrug and say the next thing that comes to mind. "The nuclear bomb." I'm not sure how it works—something about atoms smashing together—but everyone's seen the destructive results in photos of the cities in China and Africa where the bombs have been dropped. One bomb can destroy miles of land, its radiation continuing to kill weeks and months and often years later.

"An understandable choice," he says. "But not even close."

I consider the question again. "Volcanoes?"

"That's a much better guess, but still not correct." He opens one of the desk's drawers and pulls out a chaser device.

It's different from the one I've been using. It's dinged and scuffed and has several more buttons and switches than mine.

He admires it for a moment before setting it on the desk between us. "Beautiful, isn't it?"

That's not exactly the word I'd use, but I nod.

"This is one of the early devices. Second generation. Mine, actually."

He flips one of the switches and I pull back, half expecting him to disappear.

With a chuckle he says, "The battery cell was removed long ago. I like to keep it here, though. A reminder of the whens I've visited and the things I've seen."

He picks it up, and without warning tosses it to me. It bounces off my hands as I'm reaching out, but I manage to snag it before it falls to the ground.

"That, Mr. Younger, is the most powerful thing on earth," he says. "In the wrong hands, can you imagine the devastation one of these could cause? Someone could go back and ensure someone else is never born. Or worse."

Having traveled as much as I have, it's easy to imagine the things someone could do—assassinating world leaders before they gain power, introducing technologies decades or centuries prior to their development, using knowledge of the past to increase one's wealth in the present. I could spend hours writing a list and still not cover everything.

"That's why the only person living outside our walls who knows of the chasers and what they do is the king, and even his knowledge is limited to believing that we can only witness the past, not interact with it. If he knew the full extent of its abilities, well . . ."

With the experience and education I've gained at the institute, I can see the necessity of limiting the Crown's knowledge, but I can't stop the feeling of dread that grips my chest for holding knowledge back from the king. It's a reaction rooted in how I was brought up, how all in the empire are brought up.

"You can see now that it's imperative we guard against those who might attempt to obtain our secret," Sir Gregory continues. "Abducting one of our members while he's out for a walk would be a simple thing. We can't expose institute personnel to that kind of danger. The chaser and what it allows us to do must be protected at all costs."

"So we're imprisoned here."

"The institute would never phrase it that way. The grounds are expansive, and you are one of the lucky ones. As a rewinder, you get out all the time. Think of the others here—the companions, the administrative staff, the security officers. If anyone is imprisoned here, *they* are."

Up until this afternoon, despite some of the lingering questions, I've never felt any doubts about joining the program. Now I can feel them starting to creep in.

"You do understand, don't you?" Sir Gregory asks.

"Yes, sir. I do."

"And you'll be able to live with these conditions?"

Do I have a choice? "Absolutely."

◆　◆　◆

I focus all my energy on work so that I won't think too much about what Sir Gregory has told me.

I'm aided in this by the project Johnston and I are assigned. It's a comprehensive rewind of an old and influential Midlands family. Their ancestral lore speaks of deep roots in England, and while those are indeed there, lines also lead to German, Dutch, and—the family will not be pleased about this—French relatives.

It's usually at night, as I'm waiting for sleep to take me, that my mind drifts in directions I don't want it to go. Some nights I see myself running along the institute's outer walls, screaming, "Let me out! Let me out!" Other nights I see a dead Harlan Walker IV in his open casket, surrounded by bags of cash labeled Upjohn Institute, or Johnston balling up dozens of newspapers that he buries me in, or Palmer arching in pain over and over and over as he screams, "Denny!"

It's a beautiful spring evening, and I'm taking advantage of it by reading a book in the back gardens. The topic is the Protestant Reformation, a period I'll be visiting on an upcoming assignment. It's a dry subject not holding my interest, so the moment I hear loud footsteps, I look up and see Lidia racing out of the main building. I've seen her in foul moods before, but I'm not sure I've ever seen her this angry.

When she nears the reflecting pool, she begins turning around as if she's decided to go back inside, but then she spots me and makes a beeline in my direction.

"Did you know about this?" she asks as she nears me.

"About what?"

"You know very well what I'm talking about."

"Go bother someone else, Lidia." I look back at my book.

She points past me. "I'm talking about *that*!"

When I twist around, all I can see is the wide grass field and the distant institute wall.

As I turn back, she says, "How long have you known that we're locked in here?"

So that's it. She's just had the talk with Sir Gregory. Despite the tension between us, I can't help but feel some sympathy. "I was told only a few weeks ago. Before that I didn't know, either."

She gapes at me. "A few weeks ago? It didn't cross your mind to *share* that information?"

"Before I left Sir Gregory made me promise not——"

"I don't care what he told you to do. You had an obligation to your fellow trainees. You should have told us as soon as you left his office!"

I consider letting her know she's the first from the group I've seen since then, but it'd probably fall on deaf ears so I only say, "Sorry."

"Sorry?" Her face twists so tight that I'm sure she's about to unleash a torrent of rage on me, but then she takes a breath and looks toward the wall again. "My father won't stand for this."

Without another word she whirls around and races back toward the main building.

I see her the next evening in the dining hall, sitting alone. The anger from the night before has been replaced by a distant stare. I know I should let her be, but her words about my obligation to my group have stuck with me. It's the Eight in me, always feeling the need to do more for others than they do for me. So I stop at her table before collecting my meal.

"How are you doing?"

I'm not sure she's heard me until she slowly tilts her head up. Her gaze is on me, but I feel like she's looking through me. "He already knew," she whispers. "He arranged for me to be here, and he already knew."

Her eyes remain on me for a few more seconds before she looks away and stares off at nothing again.

I ask if she's all right, but she doesn't respond this time. I decide to let it be and retrieve my meal.

Lidia must have been talking about her father. But how would he have gotten her into the institute? I've been under the impression we're all here because of our test scores. It's clear, though, that she thinks he had a hand in it and that he already knew she'd never leave once she was inside. If that's even partially true, I actually feel sorry for her.

As I eat my meal, I think things have gotten as strange as they could get.

But I'm wrong.

Two days later in the prep room as I dress for a trip back to 1924, I find a note.

CHAPTER ELEVEN

The note is in the pocket of the trousers I'll be wearing on my mission. I initially think it's a piece of rubbish that somehow was missed by the support staff, but when I pull it out, I find it's not all stuck together as if it's been through the wash. It's folded into a small square. Curious, I open it.

There are four lines of machine-printed type: my name on the first, a chaser location number on the second, a date and time—MARCH 16, 1982, 4:30 P.M.—on the third, and the words COME DISCONNECTED ONLY on the last.

I've no idea what the final line means, but it's obvious someone wants me to travel to the coordinates.

As to who might have left it for me, the first person that comes to mind is Lidia. Perhaps she's still furious with me for not telling her about our confinement and wants to take it out on me somewhere outside the institute's grounds. But the last time I saw her, she was more in a state of resignation than fury.

Perhaps the note is some sort of institute test to see if I'm willing to make an unauthorized jump. We've been told that doing so without the knowledge of the mission staff is grounds for immediate reassignment.

I hear the door start to open, so I slip the note back into my pocket just as Johnston enters the room. Ten minutes later we leave 2015 behind.

As we work, my mind drifts now and then back to the note in my pocket, but at least I'm smart enough not to pull it out. When we come back to our home time, I slip the note from one pair of trousers to the other as I change.

◆ ◆ ◆

Back in my room, I sit at my desk, staring intently at the note. I can't deny I'm more than a little tempted to make the jump. But even after putting aside the questions of who gave me the coordinates and why the person wants me there, I'm confronted with a third unknown: If I were to make the trip, how would I do it without anyone at the institute knowing?

```
Anytime I use my chaser, my com-
panion Palmer feels it, and those
who monitor him know I've gone
somewhere. If I travel at an un-
scheduled time, Sir Wilfred will
be informed, and security will be
waiting for me when I get back.
Or quite possibly, based on the
fact we've been told our destina-
tion can be tracked, the guards
may even come after me.
```

So, as tempted as I am to go, I see no way to make it work without putting my position in danger. I tuck the note away and try to forget about it.

Exactly one week later, I receive a second message.

◆ ◆ ◆

Like the one before, the new message is machine-printed.

        If you want answers, go. Discon-
        nect. It's safe.

This is followed by a short list of instructions.

Disconnect. There's that word again. I try to recall if I've ever heard anyone at the institute use it, but nothing comes to mind. When I read the instructions, however, I finally understand what it means. The instructions concern making adjustments to my chaser, but it's the last line that explains it:

        5. Once done, enter the coordi-
        nates and go. You are disconnected
        from your companion and cannot be
        traced.

My skin tingles from both fear and excitement. Thoughts of *do it* and *go* are matched in strength by ones like *the note is a lie* and *it can't be safe.*

Even if I want to go now—which I'm not sure I do—I can't. My next mission is about to start, and Johnston's already waiting by the door.

Today our work takes us to Pittsburgh, 1971, in the business district near where the rivers meet. Johnston, as he often does, has told me to stay where I am while he checks ahead, so I'm blending in by leaning against the side of a building and reading a local newspaper I found on the ground.

It's a nice day, and a lot of people are out, walking along the sidewalk. None pay me the slightest bit of attention. That is, not until someone tugs at my arm.

I keep my eyes on the paper and pretend I haven't noticed, hoping whoever it is will go away. But there's a second pull, followed by a young boy's voice saying, "Excuse me."

Thinking he's looking for a handout, I say, "I don't have any change."

This isn't the first time I've talked to someone in the past, but the encounters are always unnerving, and, per training, I do everything I can to end them quickly.

"Who's asking for money?" he says.

I move the paper to the side and take my first look at him. Though his clothes are not new, they're relatively clean, and there's no dirt on his face or hands. Not a street kid.

"I'm busy," I say, and start to open the paper again.

"I have a message for you. You want it or not?"

A message? "You must have the wrong guy."

"You're Denny, right?"

I lower the paper all the way to my side. "Yeah."

"So, do you want it?"

Johnston must be in trouble, I realize, and this is the only way he could reach me. "What is it?"

"They can't track you if you go farther than ten years."

I stare at him, dumbfounded. "What?"

"They can't track you if you go farther than ten years."

"Who told you to tell me that?" When he doesn't answer, I say, "Who?"

I reach out to grab him by the shoulder, but he jumps back.

"Hey, leave me alone."

I step toward him. "I just want to know who it was."

As he turns to run away, I notice we're beginning to attract attention. My need to know who gave him the message struggles with my training to blend, and it takes all my will to move only a single step after him.

That's when the boy stops and looks back. "Oh, yeah. One more thing. Disconnect and go!"

My feet sink into the cement sidewalk as he disappears down the street.

Perhaps if I really want to play the fool, I could dismiss the first part of the boy's message as coincidence. But there's no way the last is.

Whether it's true or not, I don't know.

What I do know now is that I'm going to make the trip.

I can hardly wait to get to my room when we return.

After I finally close and lock my door behind me, I dig out the note containing the instructions and set to work disconnecting my chaser from my companion. It's not difficult. Only two wires need to be decoupled and a third rerouted.

I check my work several times to make sure I did it right. The only way to know for sure, though, is to make the trip.

I enter the date and location information from the first note, key in the time, then stare at the device, my confidence wavering.

Should I really do this? Is it worth the risk?

My answer vacillates with every second, until, with *yes* still in my head, I press the "Go" button.

As always the world around me winks out, and I'm shrouded in gray mist. What's missing this time is the faint but ever-present sense that Palmer is there, too. As quickly as I register this, the mist is gone, and the world of March 16, 1982, appears. The note told me to arrive at 4:30 in the afternoon, but per my training, I've arrived thirteen and a half hours early at 3:00 a.m.

A trip of thirty-three years would typically result in nothing more than a headache that might last a few minutes. What I experience is a spike of pain more reminiscent of a hundred-year jump. It forces me to a knee as I ride out the sensation.

Once the pain has abated, I look around and see that I'm not, as is usually the case, behind a building or in an alleyway or some other hidden spot in a city. In fact, there are no buildings in sight. I'm at the edge of a forest in a grassy meadow, where boulders stick out of the ground here and there like skullcaps of buried giants. The only sound I hear is a gently flowing river somewhere to the right.

It's a perfect place for an out-of-the-way meeting.

Or ambush, the cautious part of my brain thinks.

I choose a spot just inside the woods, use the chaser's calculator to refigure my arrival location, and pop to 4:30 p.m.

As soon as my eyes adjust to the tree-filtered daylight, I creep up to the edge of the meadow and look around. At first I think something must be wrong. No one's waiting for me near the spot where I'm supposed to appear. I scan the meadow, wondering if this is someone's idea of a joke, perhaps Lidia trying to get me into trouble. But then I spot someone sitting on one of the rocks about fifty yards away, back to me.

By the time I'm halfway there, I'm pretty sure I know who the person is, and when I'm near, I know I'm right.

"Gorgeous here, isn't it?" Marie says.

I take a look around. "It is."

She motions to a spot beside her. "Join me."

The rock is easy to ascend, and within seconds I'm sitting next to my old instructor.

"If you're hungry, I have some snacks," she offers. "Water, too."

"I'm fine, thanks."

After a quiet moment, she asks, "When did you come from?"

I give her the date of my home time.

"Took you a whole week, huh?"

"When did *you* come from?" I ask.

"I put the note in your pants ten minutes before I got here."

"Which note?"

She raises an eyebrow. "Well, I guess it would be the first one. I take it I needed to give you another."

I nod and reach into my pocket to get the second note, but she lays a hand on my wrist.

"No. I still have to give it to you, so let me surprise myself."

I pull my hand back out, empty.

"Since we're not surrounded by security officers, I'm guessing you figured out how to disconnect."

"Not on my own."

She raises an eyebrow but says nothing.

"Are you sure we can't be traced here?" I ask.

She nods. "It's a hole in the system the institute's science department hasn't been able to plug. Any jump more than ten years, with or without a companion, doesn't even show up on their scanners." Her eyes narrow, assessing me. "You already knew that, too, didn't you?"

I shrug.

"I tell you that in the second note?"

"No. You had a boy tell me on one of my missions."

She chuckles. "Still more work you're making me do, I see."

I hear the cry of a bird. I look up and spot it soaring above the far end of the meadow. When it disappears in the trees, I ask, "What did you want to see me for?"

"You've got it backward. You wanted to see me."

"So you knew I was looking for you."

"Of course I did."

"Then why wouldn't you see me back at the institute?"

"Because I have a feeling what you want to talk about would be best discussed elsewhere." She gives me a sideways glance. "Was I wrong?"

"No." She's given me an opening, but I hesitate. "You won't report what I ask you about?"

"Would I have brought you here if I was going to do that?"

I shake my head.

The original questions I wanted to ask her were about Harlan Walker, but in the time since I first started looking for her, more important ones have surfaced. "Are we really not permitted to leave the institute in home time?"

"You've had the talk, huh?"

I nod.

"I've been with the institute for fifteen years and can tell you that since we started using the chaser, I've only set foot outside in our home time twice. Both were as part of recruiting missions, such as the one that brought you to us."

"They really should have told us that ahead of time."

"If you'd known, would you have refused the offer?"

"I didn't even know what I was coming to."

"But you did know it was going to be a hell of a lot more interesting than the life you would have had otherwise."

"You're right," I say after a moment. "I would've still come. But I don't think Lidia would have."

"Lidia?"

"She was in my group. Trained in the room next to ours."

"Ah, right. Lidia Hampstead. She was a . . . placement."

"What's a placement?"

"Rewinders typically come from families who are Threes, Fours, and Fives. Now and then we'll get the occasional Six."

"I'm an Eight," I say.

"You *were* an Eight. Yours was a . . . rare case. The institute's only taken two others from that far down, but they couldn't ignore your test scores. Still, Lady Williams had serious doubts. That's why you were tested again and why she was personally there. And it took Sir Gregory to convince her to take you. It's good to see his belief in you has paid off."

I never even considered that I was the lowest caste member in my training class. That's probably why most of the others ignored me, and a few—Lidia at the lead—did nothing to hide their contempt.

"Why would Sir Gregory do that for me?"

She looks at me as if I should already know the answer. "Why would you think?"

A potential answer comes to me, but I find it hard to believe so I say nothing.

Before the silence stretches too long, Marie continues. "There's a certain prestige among the elite for having an offspring at the institute. Those with eighteen-year-olds who achieve a certain score level on the tests can request placement within the program. Usually these candidates come from large families who have children to spare. Per the institute's royal charter, names of new institute members are sent to the king. By offering one of their own, a family can gain favor with the Crown and receive advantages such as tax breaks, knighthoods, and even the possibility of moving into the nobility if they aren't there already."

"I'm on the list?" I asked, surprised.

"Of course."

I can barely get my head around the thought that the king has seen my name.

Marie looks at me. "Is this what you wanted to discuss?"

I push away my thoughts of the king and shake my head. "Not just that." I tell her about Harlan Walker, the adjusted family report, his death, and the mention in the paper of the donation to the Upjohn Institute. "I wanted to get another copy of the paper, so I tried to go outside. That's how I ended up talking to Sir Gregory." I frown. "If you don't believe me, you could find a copy of it."

"I don't need to."

"Hold on," I say. "You're the one who left it for me, aren't you?"

"No."

There's nothing hidden by her demeanor, so I'm pretty sure she's telling the truth. "Do you know who did?"

Her shrug is less convincing than her no.

"Who do you—"

"Situations such as Mr. Walker's happen all the time," she says, refocusing our discussion. "Though not everyone kills themselves."

I want to push her on the point of who left the newspaper, but I know it'd be a wasted effort, so I say, "Then it *wasn't* a heart attack."

"I don't know for sure," she said. "I haven't looked into this case, but what do you think?"

"Suicide. What I don't understand is, why?"

"What do you think the institute really does?"

The words come automatically out of my mouth. "We trace family histories."

"We *uncover* family histories," she says. "The good and the bad. What the institute usually reports is only the good. The bad is kept for other things."

"Johnston said something similar, that the bad just gets filed away."

"That's the company line, and Johnston is nothing if not a top-flight company man," she says, not hiding her disdain. "Let me tell you how things probably went with Walker. First, Lady Williams presented him with a clean but inaccurate family history. All smiles and thank-yous and respect. A few days later, Sir Wilfred pays Walker a follow-up visit, in which he presents the true facts, ones that could destroy the family's social standing and spell disaster for its business. Several options will be laid out, the important part of each being a 'sizable donation' to the Upjohn Institute."

"Blackmail."

"Yes."

"So they told Walker to kill himself?"

"I'm sure that was one of the possibilities covered. In which case, those who inherit would be brought into the discussion. It doesn't matter to the institute which direction is chosen. Its only concerns are the size of the donation and that the institute never come under any scrutiny."

"So when we receive payment, the bad goes away?"

She shrugs. "Until it's needed again."

"That's . . ." I don't know which word to use—terrible, disgusting, unbelievable. None fully conveys the revulsion I feel. "I can't believe the institute would do something like that."

"Oh, Denny," she says, "you've spent nearly your whole life hovering just above the bottom of society. Surely you realized long ago that everything in the empire is corrupt."

We're taught from a very young age that to degrade the empire is to degrade the king, so saying the words out loud is treasonous. But she's right. I've seen my share of corruption and learned early on to turn a blind eye to it. The difference here is that this is on a scale much grander than the daily graft I've been exposed to.

"You're saying our job is to feed the corruption," I whisper.

"Only if you always follow regulations."

I look at her, apprehensive. "What are you talking about?"

"You and I have spent a lot of time together. I could tell early on you know the difference between right and wrong. We wouldn't be having this discussion otherwise. All I'm saying is that sometimes it's okay to ignore what you've been taught. Maybe you come across something you think the institute might use in ways you're not comfortable with. You can choose not to report it. As you get a sense of those you're tracing, you can decide how much or how little the institute learns."

These words are treason on a slightly smaller, institute-related scale, and would certainly result in her being locked up in some deep, dark dungeon at Upjohn Hall.

She must be reading my mind, because she says, half smiling, "You're free to turn me in if you want, but I would appreciate it if you don't. At the very least, give me some warning."

"Of course I won't turn you in." *How can I, when everything you say makes sense?*

"All I'm really trying to tell you is that when you're unsure of a situation, you should take however long you need and then do what you think is right. If you're not true to yourself, this job will kill you."

The part of me that remembers growing up as the son of a laborer—constantly reminded to "know your place" and "don't make waves" and "do as you're told"—is waging an all-out war with the part of my mind that wants to embrace the path Marie is offering me.

"I'm only telling you to do what you think is right," she says.

"Is that what you've been doing?"

She looks across the meadow, whatever's left of her smile disappearing. "Not as much as I should."

"How am I supposed to know what's right?"

"You'll know."

Will I?

As the sun nears the mountains to our west, the temperature drops noticeably. Marie rubs her arms. "Is there anything else you wanted to know?"

A million things, I think, but what she's already told me has overloaded my mind. "Not right now."

"Then you should head back."

"What about you?" I ask.

"In a bit. Go on. I'll be fine."

Once I'm off the rock, I ask, "If I have more questions, can we meet again?"

"We'll see."

It's not exactly the answer I'm hoping for, but at least she doesn't say no. I turn, intending to put a little distance between us before I travel home.

"It's Roger, by the way," she says.

I pause and look back. "I'm sorry?"

"The student I hadn't met yet who watched Dawson Tower go down. His name's Roger. I'm training him now."

"Is he your last?"

She shrugs. "I don't know. Haven't planned on stopping."

"Maybe you can take future students somewhere else. The roof *is* getting a bit crowded."

"Maybe."

I detect her uncertainty and wonder what she's thinking.

"Go home, Denny," she says before I can ask. "You'll do fine."

CHAPTER TWELVE

As winter becomes spring, Johnston assigns me more and more responsibility on each of our projects. Sometimes it feels like I'm doing all the work while he finds a place to get a drink and wait until I'm done, but I'm not complaining.

I enjoy the work. I enjoy the places we go and the things we see.

So far, I've been lucky in that I haven't found myself needing to decide whether or not I should cover up something. I know I will at some point. When that time comes, I hope I'm not too scared to do what Marie has suggested.

The first time Johnston leaves me completely alone, we're in London, England, 1893, tracking the maternal great-grandfather of a minor industrialist from northern Virginia. According to what we've been able to piece together, today is the day the man will meet his future wife for the first time. This isn't a critical item, exactly, but clients love to know these small details. Our job today is to verify the meeting.

"You ready?" Johnston asks.

"Of course." I assume he's about to go in search of a pub, so I ask, "Where are we meeting up?"

Johnston shakes his head. "No meeting. I have things to do back at the institute. Return when you're done."

My blood goes cold. "You're leaving me here alone?"

"You've been handling everything by yourself just fine for the past several weeks. What does it matter if I'm here or not?"

"But what if something happens?"

"If something happens, you've done something wrong. You're not going to do anything wrong, are you?"

"No. Of course not, but—"

"Just do the job and return to the institute. Got it?"

Reflexively I nod, while inside I'm shouting, *No, I don't have it! I don't have it at all!*

"Good. I'll see you when you're finished." He strides off, and I soon lose him among the other pedestrians on the walkway.

I'm hoping he's only trying to fool me and isn't really leaving, but I know in my gut that the moment he gets someplace private, he'll be gone.

I take several deep breaths to calm down.

"Are you all right?" A man has stopped nearby and is looking at me, concerned.

"I'm fine, thank you. Just . . . a little winded."

"If you're sure."

"I am."

With a nod he moves on.

I look across the street at the target house just in time to see the man I'm supposed to be following turn onto the sidewalk. I almost missed him. This realization nearly spins me into another near panic attack, but I keep my head and take up pursuit.

It turns out that our information's correct, and at precisely 1:43 p.m. on July 2, 1893, Harold Radcliff runs into an old friend named David Wallis, who introduces Harold to his sister, Elizabeth Wallis. In exactly eight months and seven days, Harold and Elizabeth would wed.

I note all the pertinent information and even snap several pho-
tographs with the camera built into my jacket—the latter strictly
for institute records.

As soon as the meeting ends, I find a deserted space between
two buildings and send myself home.

For two more weeks, Johnston and I repeat this pattern. We jump
to our specified location together, Johnston makes sure I'm set on what
to do, and then he returns to the institute while I do the work alone.

On the fifteenth day, I enter the prep room and begin pulling
on the outfit that's waiting for me. When Johnston enters several
minutes later, he sits on the bench.

"Have we been canceled?" I ask.

"Not that I know of," he says.

"Are you . . . going to wear that?" His clothes are distinctly
twenty-first century and would definitely stand out in 1824.

He gives himself a quick look. "You don't like this?"

"It's fine, but—never mind."

He snorts a laugh. "Hurry up."

I button my shirt, pull on my shoes, and follow him out the
door.

As we walk to the departure hall, Johnston quizzes me about
our assignment. Like with all our projects, I've memorized the brief,
so I answer everything quickly and correctly.

"Good," he says as we enter the hall. From him this is the highest of praise.

The room has eight different platforms raised a few feet above
the floor. Checking the board, we see we're assigned to platform
number five. As soon as we get there, I climb on top, and then realize Johnston hasn't joined me.

"You know what to do," he says from below. "Get the information and get back."

"You're not coming?"

"You're more than ready for a solo."

As far as I know, none of the others from my training group have gone solo yet, so the idea of my being the first causes my stomach to flip a few times and threaten to give back my breakfast. "O-okay," I say.

I grasp my chaser in both hands and tell myself, *Just go through the protocol.*

I check the settings and make sure the location number and date and time match those from the briefing.

I turn to the raised dais where the departure officer sits overlooking the platforms. When he turns in my direction, I give him the ready signal—flat palm forward, then curled into a fist.

Over the speaker above my platform comes the voice of Palmer's data observer in the companion center. "Stand by."

Several seconds pass, then the voice says, "Benson, clear."

Trying to project an aura of confidence I don't feel, I raise my finger and depress the button.

There is no reason to have gotten so worked up. The job is the easiest I've had since finishing training—a half hour spent in an abandoned graveyard and another walking through a quiet neighborhood verifying addresses—which was probably why it was chosen for my first solo mission.

Onward I go alone, day after day, each mission taken with less fear but more difficult than the last.

I've got this. I'm truly a rewinder now.

I can do whatever they give me.

I can do it all.

◆ ◆ ◆

One morning, after I've been taking trips on my own for about three weeks, Johnston says, "How are you feeling?"

"Fine," I say.

"Not your health, jackass," he says. "I mean about the job."

I give him the same answer.

"Administration wants to know if you're ready to be cut free," he informs me. "What do *you* think?"

I have to catch myself from blurting out, "Yes, absolutely," and instead ask, "What did you tell them?"

"That you're close. Another week should do it."

I feel a smile grow on my face before I can stop it. That's still a whole three months before my supervised period is supposed to end. "Yeah, a week sounds right."

"You ready for today's mission?"

"Yes." The job today will be challenging—there will be following over physical distance and observation of several locations. It should be interesting, though, because unlike most of our missions, it revolves around a tiny bit of history.

"Then let's get to it."

We walk side by side to the departure hall. As always, several of the platforms are in use. We are on number seven this time. As I take the short staircase up, I spot Lidia on platform one with her supervisor. Though I've seen her several times since the conversation we had in the dining hall months ago, we've never talked again. When she notices I'm standing on my platform alone, she gawks for a moment before turning away, tight-lipped, and then she and her supervisor, Bernard Swanson, disappear into the past. I can't deny her annoyance gives me pleasure, but I unfortunately don't have any time to enjoy it.

I take my position, check the settings, and give the departure officer the signal. When I receive the "clear" announcement, I press the button.

Since I'm going nearly 250 years back, I'm using the hop method. For most of the journey, everything seems fine—2015 fades, the gray mist appears, and 1963 winks in for a second before the next jump initiates. Back I go, through the early twentieth century and across the nineteenth. Every time I'm in the gray mist, I feel the connection with Palmer and sense the same hint of jealousy I've picked up each time since I started going solo.

It's on the final hop, though, that everything changes. As I leave 1839, the gray once more surrounds me, but then suddenly it's like someone has started flipping a switch back and forth, the gray turning black then gray then black before settling on gray again. And that's not the only weirdness. I don't feel Palmer at all.

Finally I'm deposited into the dark of night as a splitting headache doubles me over.

Nearly thirty minutes pass before I feel well enough to function again. I check my chaser screen first to verify I've arrived in 1775. I then take a look around and find that I am, as planned, in a farm field, standing between rows of some kind of grain.

I've made it, and now it's time to go to work.

I reset my chaser for sixteen hours in the future and jump.

CHAPTER THIRTEEN

I do what I was trained to do.

First, I witness the event from afar, in this case from a copse of trees across the dusty road from the Three Swans Tavern near Cambridge, Massachusetts. Tied to the rail in front of the establishment are several horses, while in the field next to the building, two wagons sit waiting. Lantern light flickers in the windows, and I can hear voices now and then. Calls for more drink and food, I assume.

Carefully I record arrivals and departures, describing each man—they're all men—by the clothes they wear, their height, and whatever else makes them stand out. At fourteen minutes and fifty-three seconds after 8:00 p.m., I watch myself walk into the tavern. This I also enter into the log as I make a mental note that I could use a haircut.

The person I'm most interested in arrives six minutes later. Young Richard Cahill. I know it's him because I've seen him when he's older, on the trip I made the day before. He's considerably thinner here, but the eyes and nose and mouth are the same.

I celebrate the moment by drawing a box around his name and time of arrival. My job isn't done, though. It's only beginning. I remain where I am until Cahill leaves the tavern at 8:47 p.m. and twenty-one seconds. After I witness my own departure at 8:51 and eleven seconds, there's no more reason for me to stay.

The hop I make is not a long one, merely thirty minutes back in time and a half mile east into the woods, where no one else is. There I refresh myself with a food bar from my satchel as I study my notes. When I've committed all the necessary times and descriptions to memory, I hop forward again, arriving near the empty wagons beside the Three Swans. I reach the tavern's door at 8:14 and fifty-three seconds.

The room is lit by several lanterns and large enough for three long tables but not much else. Seven men are scattered around, most with enough space between them to indicate they're alone. Only two men are obviously together. They sit opposite one another and are leaning forward so they can talk in low voices.

I have a quick choice to make. Somewhere in this room is the person Cahill will meet with, and though I'll be using my directional recorder to pick up the conversation, I'd like to be close enough to hear it for myself. It's the way Marie taught me.

The patrons are largely weary farmers or businessmen who only want to eat their meal and be on their way. So after writing most of them off, I settle on two possibilities for the person Cahill will meet—the man who's looked at me twice as if wondering whether or not I'm someone he should know, or one of the two men who are together.

Not wanting to narrow it down further, I take a spot midway between my targets. Moments after I sit, the back door opens, and a thin woman who looks older than she probably is enters carrying two bowls of something steaming. She acknowledges my presence with the barest of nods before setting the bowls in front of the two men who are together.

"You're eating?" she says to me a moment later.

"Yes, please."

Without another word she turns and exits the way she came in.

The things that always surprise me when I travel are the smells. It doesn't matter how far I go back—a decade, a century, or the nearly two and a half I went this time—the smells are unique. Spices and sweat and sewage and perfumes and God only knows what else. Some make me cock my head in wonder, while others cause the bile in my stomach to rise to my throat.

Unfortunately, the smells in the tavern are much closer to the latter than the former, so I reach into my pocket and pull out my tiny savior. Pretending to cough, I cover my nose with my hand and break the capsule, releasing the chemical blend that will dull my sense of smell for the next several hours. I should've taken it before coming in, but I always forget.

As I'm slipping the spent capsule back into my pocket, the outer door opens, and in walks Richard Cahill, exactly on time. He stands just inside the room, much like I did, and surveys those present. When he spots the two men sitting together, he walks toward them.

My mission today is to confirm the small part Cahill plays in the history of the empire, giving his descendants in House Cahill the official certification they seek.

One would not think upon first seeing Richard Cahill at this time that he'd be so important. He's nineteen and rail-thin, and while he seems to be putting on a brave face, I can tell from where I sit that he's nervous. But if the history we've learned is correct, he's a linchpin—albeit a minor one—in the development of the North American portion of the empire. His actions on this very night will put a quick end to a nuisance that might have otherwise troubled the kingdom for a few more years.

At first Cahill sits quietly, far enough away from the duo to give the illusion he's alone. While he waits for the servingwoman, he looks around the room. When his gaze turns in my direction, I make sure I'm looking down so I don't come off as a threat.

Once I sense his attention's no longer on me, I remove a worn-looking wooden box from my pocket. If anyone were to open the top, they would find tobacco and a pipe. I leave the top down, however, and instead touch the edge that activates the built-in recorder, then I position the box so that the microphone is pointing at Cahill and his friends.

It's not until after the woman returns with my stew and leaves to get Cahill his that the larger of the two men says, "Now is not the time for nerves."

"I'm not nervous," Cahill answers, his voice shaky. "But this is all—"

"Calm yourself," the big man's partner says.

Their voices are so low that I strain to hear every word. Their caution is understandable. They are, after all, in territory largely infiltrated by the rebels. If they're caught, they'd likely be dragged into the woods and shot. I know that won't happen, but they don't. For them this is real, this is now. For me, it's like the first time seeing a performance of a play I've read many times. Cahill is destined to die at the ripe old age of fifty-four, after being gifted land and title for his service to the king. I've seen this already. Today I'm seeing the making of the man.

I lift a spoonful of stew to my lips but am careful to not ingest any. I've received all the inoculations to protect me from parasites, but to be safe, I seldom eat anything other than food I've brought with me. Instead of putting the spoon back in the bowl, I move it under the table and let the contents dribble onto the floor.

"So," the large man whispers, "did you find out?"

Cahill nods. "There's a meeting tonight at eleven."

"Where?"

"At the Hensons' farm. In the barn."

"Will you be there?" the smaller man asks.

Another nod. "I'm to be on standby in case a message needs to go out."

"You need to get in close enough to hear what they say."

"I'll try."

"No. You'll do it," the large man says. "We need to know their plans."

"I . . . I—"

"Is there a problem?"

Though I'm not looking at him, I imagine Cahill's lip trembling as he says, "No, sir."

I can't help but feel a sense of accomplishment. Not only does this confirm that Richard Cahill was indeed a British agent working undercover as a messenger for the rebels during the American incident, but this meeting at eleven has to be the same one where he learns of the traitor George Washington's whereabouts. This he will pass on to his contacts before the sun rises, and by twenty-four hours real time from now, Washington will be dead, and the ill-fated rebellion squashed. As I said, it's but a minor point in the history of the kingdom, but it's fascinating to witness.

The woman enters the room again, this time with Cahill's meal. The young spy and his companions exchange few words as they eat. My work here is basically done. The only task I have left is to witness Cahill's predawn arrival at British headquarters with news of what he's learned. But I know from my previous observations that I don't depart until after Cahill leaves the tavern, so I busy myself pushing my stew around and pretending to eat more.

The two men finish off their bowls first. The larger man pulls a small cloth pouch from his pocket. As he sets it in front of Cahill, I hear the distinct jangle of coins.

"As promised," the man says.

Cahill peeks inside the bag and then looks at the men, confused. Forgetting to whisper, he says, "This isn't all."

"Hush," the short one says.

I turn my head away just as he looks over his shoulder.

"You'll get the rest *after* you report on the meeting," the large man says.

"That wasn't our agreement," Cahill counters, anger seeping into his voice.

"I caution you, sir, to remember whom you are speaking with," the short one tells him. "Would you rather we take you in and lock you up as a traitor?"

The tension is as thick as fog. Casually I sweep my gaze across the room, like anyone sitting alone might do. I expect to see Cahill's cheeks red with anger, but instead, the fear is back in his eyes, and I start to think he's not quite the willing spy my pre-mission research has led me to believe.

Do these men have something on him and he's being coerced? If so, that would be the opposite of what the client expects to hear.

When Cahill gets up to leave, I put a coin on the table and pick up my wooden box. At the same moment, the servingwoman reaches around me for the money, bumping my elbow and causing me to lose my grip on the box. It falls to the table with a loud clack.

Cahill, nearing the door, stops and looks back. When he sees what's caused the noise, he turns to continue on his way, but the strap of his bag catches the corner of the nearby table, stopping him again. After he frees the strap, he exits the tavern. As is my habit, I reach into my satchel and push the button that will mark the time of his departure on my chaser.

The woman doesn't even give me so much as a grunt as she heads to another table. I put the box away and open the satchel just wide enough for me to see the chaser's screen and double-check my exit time. My attention, however, is drawn to the time marked as Cahill's departure.

Certain I'm remembering incorrectly, I check my notebook. The time I've written down is 8:47:21. The problem is that the time marker on my chaser indicates the door was opened at 8:47:33. I know I may not have hit the button at the exact moment he left, but there is no way I was twelve seconds off.

I find it suddenly hard to swallow.

I've caused a change.

It's okay. It's only twelve seconds. It won't affect anything.

This is what I tell myself over and over as I head for the exit. I don't even think to check my own time until I've already pushed the door open. I'm early. A full two *minutes* early.

Again I tell myself that's okay. I matter even less than Cahill's discrepancy.

As I step across the threshold, I trip. Not enough to fall to the ground, but more than enough to prove that the time line I witnessed earlier from the trees is no longer valid.

I rush around the building and into the dark, deserted meadow where the wagons are. I set my device to take me to 3:00 a.m. near the British military headquarters, where Cahill will report his findings.

The trip is so short I never even see the gray mist. I do experience a short headache, though, which has never happened for a trip of this distance. Once my chaser is stowed, I head toward the fort.

All is quiet when the British garrison comes into view. The only bit of light is the dull flicker of a lantern leaking over the top of the wall.

It's possible Cahill has already arrived. The records I found on the matter indicated only that he comes before sunrise. But the distance between the fort and the farm where the rebels meet means it's highly unlikely he'd get here before 4:00 a.m. The other factor supporting this argument is that if he's made his report already, I'd see activity at the fort. There is none.

I settle in to wait.

Four a.m. passes without even the sound of a footstep. It's still quiet at four thirty. At five, I begin to hear soldiers starting their day inside the fort. This is followed soon by the smell of cooking meat wafting into the woods where I'm hiding. And yet the gate remains closed.

At twenty to six, I hear the pounding of a horse's hooves on the road leading up to the fort.

Thank God, I think. He's finally here.

But my sense of relief vanishes when the horse that appears is carrying not Cahill but a British soldier. He hails one of the sentries at the fence, and the gate parts for him to enter.

An hour past sunrise, there's still no Cahill.

Perhaps the historical records have it wrong. Perhaps Cahill came later. Even as I cling to this thought, I fear the truth is something far different.

There's no dispute about when and how George Washington is ambushed. The event is well documented as taking place just after 3:00 p.m. on this very day, by soldiers from the garrison I'm spying on. But to be in position to take advantage of that situation, the British troops would need to begin organizing almost immediately.

I wait, my panic growing with each passing minute.

It was only twelve seconds, I tell myself. *How could that have changed anything?*

During one of the training lectures, we were taught that even a change of only a fraction of a second could ripple out to cause a much larger change. This is why it was stressed over and over again that we are observers, not participants. Yes, we would, on occasion, interfere in some lives, but those instances are to be kept short and as noninvasive as possible. Those who belong to the lineages of princes and dukes and lords are to remain untouched at all costs. Violating this rule would bring the severest of punishments.

A voice in my head says, "Go back to last evening and stop yourself from going inside." This is the fix that should put everything back as it should be. At least, I think it is. Then again, what if my not being there causes Cahill to leave sooner? Maybe the woman serves him faster, or . . . or . . .

God, nothing messes with your head more than messing with time.

"If you get hung up on paradoxes, you'll end up huddled in a corner as your sanity sprays out of your ears," Marie told me during training. "The truth is, they exist. You can be in two places at once, or even three—or a dozen. You can interact with yourself, like I did on the roof in Chicago. Hell, you can even shake hands with yourself, and you won't implode. It's your particular moment in time that's important. If something changes, it's what comes after that's affected. You are the constant."

So I can change things back.

Probably.

Before I go meddling again, though, I should gather more information, starting with finding out what happened to Cahill. I can go back and stop myself from entering the tavern later. That point will always be there for me to fix.

Calmer now, I pop back to the tavern on the evening before, but remain in the shadows so my other selves don't see me. There's no sense creating more confusion at this point.

When Cahill comes out, I glance at my chaser—8:47:33. The same twelve-second variation from the natural timeline.

Once I see which way he's going, I take a tiny hop in both time and distance along the road, arriving several seconds before he does. After he goes by, I hop forward again. I do this until he doesn't appear where I expect him to. Backtracking both physically and in time, I find him turning down a road that leads west.

I've memorized a partial map of the area in anticipation of this trip, but his destination falls outside this region. My guess is this is the way to the Hensons' farm. Keeping my trips even shorter in distance so I don't lose him again, I track him through the countryside.

After we've been traveling for a good thirty minutes in real time, he turns down a rutted path that leads to a dark farmhouse. If this is the Henson farm, he's over an hour early.

I watch from the cover of an outbuilding as he gets off his horse and approaches one of the windows of the main house. Quietly he taps on the pane.

The window opens, but it's too dark inside for me to see anything. I can hear whispered words but am too far away to make them out. After several moments a hand juts out of the window, and Cahill puts something in it.

Frustrated, I study the house and see some shrubs not far from where Cahill is standing. I pop behind the brush and back in time thirty seconds before Cahill first arrives at the house.

Again, Cahill gets off his horse and taps on the windowpane. When it opens this time, I can see a shadowy figure inside, but it's still too dark to make out the face.

"Richard?" The voice sounds surprised, and though it's high enough in pitch to be a woman's, I get the distinct impression it belongs to a boy.

"I need you to do something," Cahill whispers.

"What?"

"Take this."

The boy reaches out, and Cahill puts what I can now see is the pouch of coins from the tavern in the kid's hand.

"Is this—" the boy starts to say.

"Give it to Father. Tell him I'll bring more later, but that should help."

"He'll want to know where you got it."

"Tell him it doesn't matter. It's money." Cahill pauses. "You can tell him I didn't steal it." He backs away.

"Where are you going?"

"I have to do something."

"What?"

"I'll see you later."

Cahill sprints back onto his horse and rides away.

This can't be where the change has occurred. With or without the twelve-second delay, he must have always planned on stopping here.

Confused, I take up pursuit again and trace him as he stays to the roads outside of town, passing nothing along the way but the sleeping silhouettes of other farmhouses.

Given that it's less than fifteen minutes before the meeting is supposed to start, he can't be more than a mile from the farm when I see two British soldiers riding toward town on a road from the east. They reach the junction with the road Cahill is on a mere five and a half seconds after the reluctant spy passes by.

"Stop!" one of the men calls out.

Cahill rides on, apparently not hearing the command over the thuds of his horse's hooves.

The soldier who spoke motions at his companion, and they take off in pursuit.

As they close in, the first soldier shouts again. This time Cahill looks over his shoulder, startled. I see hesitation on his face as he races past another of my positions, and I know he's contemplating whether or not he should try to outrun them.

"In the name of the king, you are ordered to halt," the first soldier shouts.

The mention of the king finally causes Cahill to stop his horse. As the two soldiers approach, the one who's been silent raises a Brown Bess rifle to his shoulder and stops a dozen feet away, while his partner rides in closer.

"Awfully late to be in such a hurry," the soldier says.

Cahill's eyes dart back and forth from the soldier to the muzzle of the other man's rifle. "I . . . I'm, um, trying to get home."

"Home? And where would that be?"

Cahill takes a moment before saying, "My family's farm. North of town."

Even if I didn't already know it, I can see Cahill is lying.

The soldier can see it, too. "And which family would that be?"

Again, Cahill doesn't answer right away. He probably wants to tell them he's on important business for the British, but he's smart enough to know they won't likely believe him and will bring him to their commanders, causing him to miss the meeting, to the displeasure of his contacts. "Please, I only want to get home."

The soldier's face tenses. "Which family?"

I watch what happens next from so many different vantage points that there must be nearly a dozen of me in the bushes surrounding the road by the end. If all the versions of me were to step out in unison, we would be more than enough to overpower the soldiers. But that would be far too much involvement.

Cahill's mouth opens, but instead of answering, he yells his horse's name and kicks its hindquarters, spurring it into motion.

The boom of the musket is accompanied by a cloud of smoke, but the shot comes too late and flies through the empty air where Cahill was a second ago.

The first time I witness this, I'm sure he's going to get away, but the thought barely passes through my mind before the sound of a second musket rips through the air, and I see that the first soldier is now also shouldering a rifle.

I pop backward twenty seconds, and this time watch from as close as I can as the soldier raises his Brown Bess and fires at the departing Cahill. The musket ball slams into Cahill's back, a direct hit to the spine.

There will be no attending the eleven o'clock meeting, no delivery of the information to the British on the rebel Washington's whereabouts.

I stay there in my final hiding place long after the soldiers have hauled Richard Cahill's body away.

He was only a minor spy for hire, I tell myself. Even with him gone, not much will have changed. The insurgency might have continued for a bit longer, but the redcoats would still have snuffed it out.

Sure, House Cahill will likely be affected in some way, but otherwise everything should be much the same.

Right?

I have two options.

The obvious is to fix things now before returning home. No one would be the wiser, and I could go on breathing. What stops me is the fear of making another mistake that would compound the problem.

The other choice is to return to 2015, kneeling with my head bowed in repentance. This should at least allow me to explain what has occurred, and then a more experienced rewinder could fix things properly. Perhaps it won't prevent me from being punished, but it may result in a bit of leniency.

I know the second option is what I must choose, and I decide to take the trip in a single leap, the pain I'll experience being the symbolic start of my punishment.

I take one last look around at the deserted road, thinking in all probability this has been my last trip to the past, and then I tap the home button.

CHAPTER FOURTEEN

At first all I know is the pain.

It's the worst I have ever felt; it feels as if a red-hot spike is being hammered through the center of my brain. Pulsating waves of torture surge through every nerve in my body as I stagger forward.

In a half-second pause between onslaughts, I realize something's wrong. If not for the wall I just ran into, I would be on the ground. But the arrival hall at the institute is a large space, fifty feet across in either direction. There should be no wall for me to run into. Besides, the institute's walls are cool marble, while the one my shoulder leans against feels as if it might break if I hit it too hard.

I force my eyelids apart enough so I can take a look around. I am *definitely* not in the arrival hall. This space can't be more than fifteen feet across at its widest, and windows are on three sides. There are no windows in the arrival area at the institute.

Out front I can see bushes and grass and a road with several odd-looking carriages parked along it. The wall without windows contains an arched entry into another room and a brick fireplace.

A home, I think.

I cringe and fall to my knees in another fit of agony, and all thoughts of where I am momentarily disappear. When I open my eyes again, I see my chaser lying several feet away on the wood-slat floor.

Through the fire in my head, my training struggles to be heard. *Protect your device.*

I turn, intending to crawl over to it, but as I set my hand down, my stomach retches, and the protein bar I ate before entering the tavern spills onto the floor.

Out of habit I murmur, "I'm sorry," as I crawl around it.

When I reach my chaser, I try to put it in my bag, but the satchel isn't at my side. I can feel the strap across my chest, but in my haze and confusion, I can't seem to move the bag from where it lies against my back.

Protect your device.

Yes, yes, I know!

A wave of nausea passes through me as I scan the room, but thankfully I'm able to keep down whatever's left in my stomach.

There, I think. *I can hide it there.*

I crawl across the floor to the hearth and shove my device up the chimney. I half expect it to fall when I pull my hand back out, but it doesn't.

My head begins to swim so I close my eyes. When I open them, I realize I must've blacked out, because I'm sitting with my back to the fireplace and have no idea why I'm here.

When the smell of vomit hits me, I push to my feet and inch forward, using the wall as a crutch. Gray begins to appear around the edges of my vision as the rod of pain in my head refuses to ease.

Feeling like I'm about to pass out again, I will myself to stay alert. I need to know where I am. I need to assess my situation.

I don't notice the door until it's only a few feet in front of me. I struggle with the knob, and when it opens, I feel the touch of a breeze.

Unsure where the exit leads but wanting desperately to be outside, I stagger over the threshold and don't see the two steps leading down. With a groan of surprise, I tumble face-first, landing half on grass, half on concrete walkway.

I feel blood running out of my nose, but whatever agony the fall might have caused is masked by the excruciating pain of my time trip.

I hear what I think is a voice, but it seems so far away. And then running steps.

And then . . .

. . . nothing.

◆ ◆ ◆

Four days. That's what the nurse tells me.

Four days since I arrived at the hospital. The missing time is unnerving, but it's the hospital itself that really scares me.

Brooklyn Hospital Center, the nurse called it.

I've heard the name Brooklyn before. It's the city next to New York. But it's not the name that's a problem. The facility's too modern, both in equipment and approach, to fit any era but my home time. Granted, the facilities for those in the upper castes are off-limits to Eights like me, a point I know well from the lack of treatment my sister received. But I've seen pictures of those medical centers. They were impressive, to say the least, but none was comparable to where I am now.

One of the things Marie taught me was that traveling past my home time and into the future is impossible. According to her the future is an impenetrable barrier. The institute has conducted exhaustive tests, but no one has ever traveled beyond his or her home time. Have I somehow done that?

It's the only explanation I can think of, but the idea falls apart when the nurse returns and I ask the date.

"March 28," she tells me.

"What year?"

"Still a little groggy, are we? It's 2015." I must look surprised, because she asks, "What year did you think it was?"

"I . . . forgot for a moment, that's all. It's what I thought."

She smiles. "Maybe you can answer something for me."

"Um, sure."

"You want to tell me your name?"

I hesitate. Once my name is entered into the data system, the institute will be notified, and someone would come for me. So far, I seem to have extended my freedom by at least four days, but I'd like to experience a few more while conscious.

"Do you remember it?" she asks, her smile slipping.

"Denny," I say. It's a common enough name, so it shouldn't ring any bells. For my surname, though, I choose one from a book my mother used to read me. "Denny Wicks."

"Denny? Like the restaurant?"

I have no idea what she's talking about, but I nod.

"Is that a nickname for Dennis?"

It's not a nickname for anything, but erring on the side of caution, I nod again.

She writes my name down on the large pad she's carrying. "Nice to meet you, Denny Wicks. I'm Clara. I'm your afternoon nurse today." She adjusts the sheet covering my chest. "Someone will bring you some food in a bit. For now, try to rest. I have a feeling the police will be back to talk to you soon."

"Police?"

As if she's telling me a secret, she whispers, "They want to know why you were in that house."

I stare at her. "What house?"

"The one you were found in front of," she says.

It takes me a moment, but then I remember. The one with wooden floors and no furniture. The one where I threw up.

The police officers come as I'm finishing a meal of bland meat and a fluffy white dollop of potato. The men's uniforms are unfamiliar to me, the material so dark blue it's almost black. Strapped around each man's waist is a belt lined with compartments and holders, one of which carries a pistol. Pinned to the shirt on each man's chest is a miniature silver shield that reads NEW YORK CITY POLICE and has its own unique number.

The badge confuses me.

New York City?

It can't be.

Upjohn Hall is in the city called New York. Though I've seen very little of the metropolis, it *is* where I live.

When I realize both men are looking at me expectantly, I clear my throat and whisper, "I'm sorry?"

The man closest to me looks a bit put out. "You told the nurse your name is Dennis Wicks. Is that correct or not?"

"Yes," I say.

"All right, Mr. Wicks. Can you tell us where you live?"

"Live?"

Again he's not pleased. "Your address."

"I'm . . . not . . . sure."

"You remember your name but not where you live?"

From a book I read, I know that head trauma sometimes causes memory problems, so I say as sincerely as possible, "I'm sorry. I don't."

"Do you at least remember if you're from the city? Or just visiting?"

"Which city?"

He grimaces. "New York."

I pretend to think for a moment before shrugging. "I wish I knew."

The other man asks, "How about the house? Why were you there?"

"I don't know."

"You *do* remember the house, right? Two forty-four Rosemary Avenue?"

"Not really."

"Did you break in so you could sleep there?"

"I'm not a squatter," I say.

"So you don't remember the house, but you do remember you weren't crashing there for the night?"

The phrase is strange, but I get the gist and realize my words are getting me into trouble. I sink into my pillow and close my eyes. "I don't know. Maybe, I guess. It just doesn't feel like something I would do."

Clara, who's been standing across the room, approaches the bed and says, "I think maybe he's had enough for now."

The police don't look happy, but the main one says, "Sure. Mr. Wicks, we'll come back when you've had a little rest."

I keep my eyes closed until everyone's gone.

I stare at the ceiling, my heart racing in my chest. I'm not concerned about the policemen specifically, but rather what they represent, what this hospital represents, and the new potential explanation for what's happened.

It isn't long before Clara returns and checks some of the wires that run from me to nearby instruments. "Are you okay?" she asks as she grabs my wrist and glances at her watch.

"I'm fine."

She lets go of my hand, and I see she doesn't believe me. "Your heart rate's a little elevated. I'm going to go grab something to help you relax. I'll be right back."

"I'll be fine," I say to no avail. She's already out the door.

I don't want to take something that will put me back to sleep. I need to think. I need to figure out what the hell is going on.

More than anything, I really need to get out of here.

I reach up to scratch the side of my neck and feel a tug on my arm. I glance down and see the wires and tubes attached to me. They must've alerted Clara to come check on me. If I'm going to leave, I'll need to yank everything off and get out in a hurry. This thought leads me to another problem. Clothes. No way can I go anywhere in the thin covering I'm wearing.

I look around. There's only one cabinet, so if my clothes are here, that's where they'd be. Is my leather satchel in there, too?

My breath catches in my throat.

Oh, God. My chaser.

I would've been holding it when I arrived at the house. Is it stored with my other things? Or do the police have it?

My escape from this place is now even more pressing.

I look at the machines around my bed again, and notice that most of them are on wheels. If I'm careful, I might be able to roll them far enough for me to reach the cabinet without setting off an alarm.

Before I can test the theory, the door opens and Clara returns. In her hands is a tray holding two cups. One contains water, and the other contains two pills.

"Pop them in your mouth," she says as she dumps the pills in my hand. "They'll help you sleep."

I try to fake taking them, but one falls out of my hand as my fingers hit my lips.

"Let me," she says. She takes the pills and pushes them into my mouth.

As she raises the water to my lips, the only thing I can do is shove the pills between my cheek and teeth with my tongue and hope they don't slip free as I drink. One of the pills cooperates, but the other doesn't.

"There," she says, lowering my head back to the pillow. "The best thing you can do right now is rest. I'll check on you later."

The moment her back is to me, I pull the remaining pill out of my mouth and slip it under the covers. I hope to God the one that went down isn't enough to knock me out, but in my condition, who knows?

Clara dims the lights and leaves.

As soon as the door is completely closed, I set about trying to lower the railing on the side of my bed. I spend more time than I should on it, but finally get it to swing downward. I scoot toward the side of the bed so I can move my legs over the edge, but I feel a tug below my waist. I stop and look under the sheet.

What I see is disturbing, to say the least. There's a tube running between my legs that appears to be carrying away my urine and is connected to me in a way I'm not at all excited about. If I'm going to leave, though, it can't stay there. I grab the tube with one hand and where it's attached to me with the other.

Silently I count down from five and then pull. I'm prepared for searing agony, but what I feel is more pressure than pain.

Freed, I swing my legs off the bed. Most of the machines I'm plugged into are on one side, but one apparatus is not, and its cords aren't long enough to swing around the end of the bed. I have no choice but to unhook myself from it.

I hurry over to the cabinet, the other machines rolling along most of the way there. I find my clothes in the large upper section. They're designed to be worn in 1775 colonial North America, but they're better than the open-back hospital smock. I pull on my pants and shoes. My shirt and jacket can't go on until I'm unplugged. Before that, though, I look for my bag.

I pull open the lower drawers and finally find the satchel in the bottom one. When I open the flap, I tense. My chaser isn't there. I look around the room, thinking maybe I've missed a cabinet, but spot nothing.

The police? Please, no.

I close my eyes and try to remember my arrival four days earlier. Bits and pieces come to me—flashes of the house, the windows, the floor.

Then a flash of my chaser, lying several feet away. Another flash, and it's gone.

Did I put it in my bag or not?

Concentrating harder I think about my satchel until I can almost feel it flopped across my back. What I sense, though, is that it's not where I put the chaser.

Hurry! I tell myself, sure that Clara will return at any moment.

A flash of another window, then a wall, and then—

—a fireplace.

Yes. I remember now. I stuck it in the chimney.

My eyes shoot open, and I yank off the tubes and wires. Clutching jacket and satchel in one hand while pulling my shirt on with the other, I hurry to the door and open it enough to peek out. Beyond is a wide, well-lit corridor. There are several closed doors along the other side that I guess lead to other rooms like mine. Here and there, rolling equipment sits against the wall. Though I can hear someone walking in the distance, I see no one.

I widen the opening and slip out.

I hoped to find an empty hall, but to the left are several people walking in both directions. Some are wearing white like the nurse who's been helping me, while others are dressed in clothing that again looks odd to me. To the right, the hall is less occupied, but about fifty feet down is an open area with a counter where several nurses sit.

I decide my best bet is to go left, away from where the nurses are gathered. I don my jacket and pull my satchel over my shoulder as I move into the hallway. I feel the urge to run but resist it and turn down the first intersection I reach. Now that there are more walls between me and the room I was in, I feel a bit better, but I know I'm not out of trouble yet.

Ahead I hear a bell, followed by a whooshing sound. The hall soon widens to accommodate a row of metal doors. One is open, revealing a small room where several people are standing.

A lift, I realize.

The door starts to shut, but a hand juts out from inside and stops it.

"You going down?" the man whose hand it is asks me.

"Yes, thank you," I say as I dart into the compartment.

"Lobby or somewhere else?" The man's outstretched finger is hovering near a panel with numbered buttons on it.

"Lobby," I say.

The lift is larger than any I've ever been on and could hold at least twenty people. At the moment there are only four others besides myself—the man who held the door, a young couple, and a female nurse. The nurse is the one who worries me most, but she doesn't seem to have any interest in me. The other three, however, do.

"Nice getup," the male half of the couple says.

"Excuse me?"

"Is it Fashion Week already?" the woman asks.

"Fashion Week?" I ask, then realize her question was triggered by my clothes.

"No. I bet you're an actor, right?"

"Right. An actor."

"You're in a play?"

"Uh-huh."

"Which one?"

I'm backed into a corner. Theater is a subject I have paid little attention to. It wasn't an extravagance my family could afford. But I do know a few titles. "*As You Like It.*"

The woman cocks her head. "Shakespeare? Which theater?"

I'm saved from answering by the ding of the bell and the doors opening. I start to step off, but the man by the panel says, "Not the lobby yet, buddy."

I move back in and press against the wall as several more people enter the lift, separating me from the inquisitive couple. One of those closest to me takes a long look at my clothes but says nothing.

Thankfully the rest of the journey is made in silence. When the doors open again, I wait until I see the light in the L button turn off before I join the other passengers filing out.

Following signs marked EXIT, I pass through a door into a large room with dozens of chairs, most of which are occupied. At the far end of the room are several glass doors. Through them I see fading daylight. Before I can feel any relief, I notice the police officers who visited me standing off to the side, one of them holding something to his ear that he appears to be talking into. It looks like a com-phone, but it's smaller than any I've ever seen.

I slow my pace so I can hide behind a group headed toward the exit, and arrive outside unseen.

As I move away from the entrance, I look around. A parking area full of strange vehicles stretches out from the medical facility's entrance. I'm surprised by how different they are from the carriages I know, but it's the variety that's the most shocking. Dozens of different colors and shapes and sizes. Where did they all come from?

One of the vehicles drives by me, its motor humming in an unfamiliar way. There's only one person inside, which at first makes me think he must be no lower than a Four, but the vehicle itself is dented and scratched in a way no one of that social standing would be caught in.

"Either move out of the way or walk," a man says as he steps around me, his shoulder brushing roughly against my arm.

I look around and realize he's not the only one who's had to alter his course to avoid bumping into me. But before I can step to the edge of the walkway, a voice shouts, "Hey! You!"

I turn toward it and see one of the police officers has exited the medical facility and is looking in my direction.

When we lock eyes, he yells, "Stay where you are!"

A rush of adrenaline shoots through my body. I ignore his command and sprint in the opposite direction.

"Hey! Stop!"

For a few seconds, I weave in and out of the other pedestrians, then it dawns on me that I can make better time if I cut into the street. A horn blares from one of the vehicles and the driver shouts something through his window, but I don't even look in his direction as I keep running. A few more drivers honk, but most don't seem to care that I'm in the middle of the street.

"Where the hell do you think you're going?" The police officer again.

His voice sounds farther away, so I chance a look. He, too, is in the street, but he's older than I am and fatter, so he's already slowing.

Instead of easing up, I increase my speed. Ahead is an intersection with a traffic-control system that's both familiar and not. The ones I'm used to are mounted horizontally, and the lights are green, orange, and red. The one ahead of me is vertical, with red on top, *yellow* in the middle, and green at the bottom.

Red still seems to mean stop, though, so when the light turns that color, I cut across the road and continue down the new street. After a block my breaths start feeling heavy, and my days spent unconscious begin to catch up to me.

My run becomes a jog, then a walk, and then a shuffle before I finally stop.

Panting, I glance back. No police.

I rest my hands on my hips and try to catch my breath. What I'd really like to do is find someplace I can lie down for a while, but I know that's the effect of the pill and I need to fight it.

Once my breathing is under control, I take a better look around. Both sides of the street are lined with shops—restaurants with signs that read ITALIAN and DELI and COFFEE and ESPRESSO, something called 7-Eleven, several clothing stores, and others I can't identify.

Have I stumbled into an area reserved for the upper castes? I could almost believe that, if not for the makeup of the crowd sharing the walkway with me, not to mention the trio of vagabonds I can see from where I'm standing.

What the hell is going on here? Where in God's name am I?

One of Marie's lessons forces its way through my growing confusion. We were in Rome, somewhere in the 1700s, surrounded by so much history that I couldn't hide my excitement.

"It's easy to get overwhelmed," she said. "But that's when mistakes are made. Stay within yourself. Take in everything step-by-step."

Step-by-step, I tell myself. *Get the chaser, and then figure out what's going on.*

I close my eyes and concentrate until one thing rises above the others: 244 Rosemary Avenue.

CHAPTER FIFTEEN

The store called 7-Eleven turns out to be a kind of prepackaged food market. The sheer number of items the place carries would be enough to distract me if I didn't force myself to stay on mission and approach the counter, where a clerk is finishing up with a customer.

From the turban the clerk's wearing and the color of his skin, I guess he is Indian. There are many from the India region of the empire in New Cardiff, too, so this man's presence is not a distraction to me. But his customer is. Though her skin is lighter than the clerk's, there's no question in my mind she's African. When she speaks I expect to hear a heavy accent, but the one she has is similar to that of my nurse, Clara.

The woman must have sensed I've been staring because as she leaves, she glances at me and says, "What's your problem?"

"I'm sorry. No problem. I didn't—"

"Yeah, you'd better be sorry," she says as she pushes open the door.

I take her place at the counter, and the clerk says, "Can I help you?"

"Do you carry maps?"

"A map of what?"

"Brooklyn."

He turns, pulls something out of a holder on the wall behind him, and sets it on the counter. "With tax, eight ninety-three."

I reach to pick it up, but he puts a finger on it, holding it down. "Pay first."

"I just need to take a quick look at it."

"Eight dollars and ninety-three cents, or it goes back on the wall."

The only money I have is what I was given to use on my mission. Since it's two hundred years old, I doubt the clerk would honor it. Besides, I don't know what kind of dollars he's talking about. In New Cardiff we use the pound, and I'm not sure why they aren't doing the same here.

"I'm looking for a street. Rosemary Avenue. Can you just help me with that?"

"Buy the map, find the street. If not, go. I have other customers."

The answer I need is inches away, but it might as well be on the other side of the ocean. "Thank you for your time," I say and make a quick exit.

Stepping outside, I have no idea what to do. As I turn left, I see the customer who was inside the store earlier. She's standing on the sidewalk, pulling disks of food out of a hand-size yellow and white bag.

She raises both eyebrows and says, "Why do you keep looking at me? Who the hell do you think you are?

"I'm sorry. I'm not staring," I say quickly. "I was actually wondering if you could help me."

"Huh. Right."

She turns and starts walking away.

"Please, wait. I . . . I'm looking for a map. You wouldn't happen to have one I could look at, would you?"

"And have you run off with my phone? Not going to happen."

"I didn't say anything about a com-phone."

She stops and looks back at me. "A what?"

"I'm trying to find out where Rosemary Avenue is."

"You don't need any map to find Rosemary Avenue."

"You can tell me where it is?" I ask.

"Yeah, but it'll cost you."

My shoulders sag. "I don't have any money."

"Of course you don't." She looks me over. "You don't look homeless."

Another new term, but one with a meaning easy enough to figure out. "I'm not." I reach into my satchel and pull out a Spanish dollar. "You can have this."

"What is that? A quarter?"

I toss it to her.

"This isn't American," she said, turning it in her hand.

"No. It's Spanish. An antique. I'm sure it's worth something."

She looks at me, her eyes narrow. "You're going to give me an antique coin for directions? This is a fake."

"It's not." I'm tempted to give her another, but think that might reinforce her belief that the coin isn't real.

"That's a pretty nice bag," she says.

I drop a hand over my satchel. "I can't give this to you. I need it."

She laughs. "I'm just messing with you. I don't want your bag, but I'll keep your stupid coin."

Night has fallen by the time I reach Rosemary Avenue. I follow the numbers until I arrive at 244. There's a sign out front that proclaims FOR SALE. Under this is a person's name and phone number.

So far I recognize nothing, and wonder if I misheard the address from the policeman. But then again, the only memories I have of the house are from inside, so that's where I need to check. I sneak around the side of the house to search for a way in where I won't be noticed, but the windows and back door are locked.

The thought of slamming it open crosses my mind, but I doubt my weakened body could get the door to budge. Instead, I wrap my jacket around a brick and use that to break a basement window. Once the glass is cleared away, I drop inside.

The basement is as unfamiliar to me as the outside, so I assume I never made it down here. The stairs take me up into a small hallway on the ground floor. From there I pass through the kitchen to the room at the front of the house, and suddenly I know I'm in the right place.

This is the room that flashed through my mind, and I finally feel like everything is going to be okay.

But as I take the first step toward the fireplace, I hear a voice just outside the front door.

I look across the room in time to see the knob turn, but the door does not move. Whoever's outside apparently doesn't have the key.

I tiptoe as close as I dare.

"Told you it was a long shot," a male voice says. "Face it, we're never going to see him again. We already wasted enough time searching for him around the hospital. I say we go back to the station."

"Stop whining," a second man says. I recognize this voice immediately. It belongs to the policeman who chased me outside the hospital. The other voice must be his partner's. "We're here, so we might as well check around back. *Then* we can go. Okay?"

A sigh is followed by a resigned "Fine."

I freeze. They're going to find the broken window and come after me. As I hear them descend the front steps, I whip back around and hurry quietly to the fireplace. Kneeling, I stick a hand up the chimney.

"Hey, check this out!" The shout comes from the back of the house, and a moment later, I hear the crunch of glass as someone lands on the shards in the basement.

I feel around, searching for my chaser, until my fingers finally brush against its familiar shape. I hear creaks from the basement stairway and shoot a sideways glance toward the back of the house as I tease the device off the ledge it's perched on. When I try to pull it out, it catches on the vent. Panicked, I twist it one way and then the other before it falls free.

After activating the screen, I see that the date and time are both still set to my previous trip, here, four days before. There's no time to change both, so I leave the date as is and input the only location I've ever memorized. One I thought I would never use.

"Police! Hands in the air!"

The two officers are standing in the doorway to the kitchen, each holding a gun pointed in my direction.

"Hands in the air!" the first one repeats as I disappear.

◆　◆　◆

The mist of the trip starts out silent, but right before the end, I get the hint of a companion, only it doesn't "feel" like Palmer.

The gray is soon replaced by my good friend—the darkness of 3:00 a.m. My headache is considerable for a four-day trip but not debilitating, so I'm able to assess my surroundings right away. The location I used is the cemetery where my mother and sister are buried, nearly three thousand miles to the west of New York, at the eastern edge of the Shallows. I memorized it the first night after receiving my chaser. But as I look around, I'm not at the cemetery.

It's close, though. I can tell from the almost-but-not-quite-right silhouette of the hills. I'm probably no more than a mile away. I write it off as a lack of a companion, but still, I should be closer than this.

I can see several lamps down the hill from me, lighting up empty streets. Other lights scattered among the hills look like they belong to houses. Though I can't see any of the buildings well, they appear to be fairly large and would have to belong to a caste well above mine. If such an enclave is located near the cemetery, I don't recall it.

Looking east, I can see the glow of New Cardiff rising above the darkened hills. It seems more intense than I remember it.

I reinput the location of my mother's grave. Since I'm close now, the jump should be accurate.

Where I end up, though, is inside a house. I double-check the coordinates. According to my chaser, I'm within a few feet of where my mother and sister are buried.

A low growl emanates from a room to my right, and a large dog appears, moving slowly as if stalking its next meal. I shove the recall button and instantly return to the hill.

The problem must be with my chaser. Either it's taking me to incorrect locations or to incorrect times. Maybe both.

But this is something I can check. I just need to go to a location I know well. Someplace I can use to recalibrate the chaser.

Home.

I need to go home.

◆ ◆ ◆

Taking a series of small jumps, I head for the house I once shared with my father in the heart of the Shallows.

Over 30 percent of New Cardiff's working and tradesman class live in this part of the city. It's an area of apartment blocks and tiny homes—almost none owned by the people who live in them—where the streets are narrow and the only personal carriages one sees are pieced-together jobs that look as if they may fall apart at any moment.

I finish my final jump and look around. I'm in a residential area, but the homes are much nicer than those in the neighborhood I grew up in. Because of an abundance of tall trees, I can see no visual landmarks to confirm my location.

Instead of taking another jump, I decide to walk until my view is no longer obscured.

As I pass through the neighborhood, I see more of the same kind of strange vehicles I saw in New York. Most have names on the back that I've never seen on a carriage before—Honda and LaCrosse and Forrester and Chevrolet and Ford and Caravan.

I lock away the new information one bit at a time so that it doesn't overwhelm me and make me lose sight of what I'm doing. But then I reach a wide road that allows me a better view of the area. The hills to the west and north are exactly the same hills I saw from my home every day growing up.

My chaser isn't broken.

I *am* in the Shallows.

I *am* home.

The date function, then. Perhaps that's where the device has failed.

I seize on this possibility out of desperation.

The nurse in New York lied to me. I wasn't unconscious for four days. I must have been in a coma that lasted much, much longer. Years, maybe. So, in a way, I've traveled into the future. I did it by sleeping my way there.

My theory is riddled with holes, such as how long would I have to be out for so much change to occur? Or why would the cemetery be replaced by houses? But I shut these out of my mind and try to convince myself that I'm right.

What I need is proof, something that will ease my mind.

I walk several blocks until I spot a sign I've seen before.

7-ELEVEN.

At the one in New York, I remember seeing newspapers in a stack near the front counter. The store down the street would likely contain the same.

Sure enough, upon entering, I see a rack near the door with a sign across the top reading LOS ANGELES TIMES. It's not a paper I've heard of, but it probably comes from the downtown district. Unfortunately, the rack is empty.

I look over at the clerk, a Spanish-looking man in his midforties. "Are there any more newspapers?"

"Today's are here. Just haven't put them out yet. If you want a copy, you'll have to pull it out of the bundle by the back door." He nods his chin toward the rear of the store.

"Thank you," I say, and head back.

The stack is sitting on the floor, held together by several clear straps. I have to move one to the side to see the date: MARCH 24, 2015.

It has to be a misprint.

I hurry back to the front of the store.

"You didn't find 'em?" the clerk asks.

"What's the date?"

"Uh, the twenty-fourth."

"Of March?"

"Yeah.

"Two thousand fifteen?"

He looks at me through narrowing eyes. "What else would it be?"

I leave the store in a state of shock. The honk of a horn is all that keeps me from stepping onto the road and being hit. Moments later, there's a part of me that wishes I didn't heed the warning.

I can no longer hide the truth from myself. There's only one answer for what happened, and it has nothing to do with a faulty chaser.

Something in the past has changed, and the ripple has led to this.

Two words repeat over and over in my mind.

Twelve seconds.

CHAPTER SIXTEEN

Exhausted, I use a trick Johnston taught me: find an out-of-the-way, quiet spot that shows no signs of anything having been there in a while, then jump back to 11:00 p.m. and stretch out. By the time my eyes crack open again, it's already after 9:00 a.m.

The hours spent asleep were not gentle ones. I was bombarded by dreams of my world unraveling and being replaced by different versions of what I can only describe as hell. I also saw people I know—Marie, Sir Gregory, Palmer, my mother, my father—fall past me, calling my name as they grabbed for my hand, but always slipping away before I could close my fingers.

And Ellie.

For a moment upon waking, I feel relief, but it quickly fades. I don't know if the world I'm in now is hell or not, but I do know the world I'm *from* is gone.

One other thing I know.

I'm the one who did it.

I can't afford to make another mistake, so it's imperative that I know for sure the change occurred at the Three Swans Tavern.

I need to find a library.

Pushing myself to my feet, I catch sight of my old-fashioned shirt. Before I do anything else, I should clean up, get some new clothes, and find something to eat. And money. I'm going to need some of that, too.

Using the chaser, I skip into a series of back gardens until I find a place where the occupants aren't home. One more time hop, and I'm inside.

The house I grew up in had only a tub for washing. In this place I find a bathroom off the largest bedroom upstairs that has not only a tub twice as big as my family's, but also a roomy shower.

I have no idea how long it will be before the people who live here return, but I'm a mess so I strip off my clothes and step inside.

Once I figure out how to balance the temperature of the water, the shower is amazing. I don't think I ever want to take a bath again. I look around for soap but find only several plastic bottles. One is labeled "Shampoo" and another "Bodywash." I know what shampoo is, and though the phrasing is odd, I can guess what bodywash means.

Five minutes later I'm dripping wet but clean. I grab a large towel hanging from a nearby rack and dry off. In the bedroom I search for clothing. I don't like the idea of stealing, but I don't have much of a choice.

From what I find, I know a man and a woman share this room. It's shocking to me how much clothing the woman has. Dresses and blouses and skirts of various lengths fill most of the closet. They've got to be Threes for sure to be able to afford this much. And shoes. My lord. Who would ever need so many shoes?

The man's clothes are limited to a handful of jackets and pants and shirts. I pull out a shirt but immediately see it won't fit me. The man, though probably around the same height as I am, clearly has a much larger girth.

I decide to check the other bedrooms. One of the rooms belongs to a girl, but boys live in the other two, one of whom, it turns out, is about the same size I am. I pull on a pair of pants made of a blue, rugged material, but when I zip and snap up, I find that the waist rides low, exposing the top of my butt. I search through the boy's cabinet for a pair that has a higher waist, but all the pants are the same.

I realize I'll have to make do, for now, with the pants I have on, as uncomfortable as they make me feel. I go in search of a shirt. In an upper drawer, I find a pullover of a thin soft fabric that feels like cotton. It's dark gray and has a silhouette of a stylized bat printed on the front. It's long enough to cover the top of the pants so I won't be exposing the crack of my butt to the whole world.

In the closet I find shoes. Not nearly as many as the woman has, but several times more than the single pair I had growing up. The ones I try on are a bit large, but they'll do.

After dressing and collecting my things, I head down to the kitchen. There I take two apples from a bowl on a counter and several slices of bread out of a clear bag, and then turn on the faucet and take a long drink of water. I want to look through the cupboards, but I've already taken enough from this house, so I set a new destination on my chaser and leave.

Though I still don't have any money, I feel less conspicuous now. As I walk down some busy streets, I see larger vehicles that appear to be for transportation of large groups, similar to the Pub Cs—public carriages—I'm familiar with. They stop every few blocks at locations marked by signs. These usually have overhead coverings and a bench where people can wait for the next ride.

It's at one of these that I find an older woman who points me in the direction of a library.

◆　◆　◆

The sign outside reads: LOS ANGELES PUBLIC LIBRARY—WOODLAND HILLS BRANCH.

Los Angeles again. Still no mention of New Cardiff.

Inside the library is laid out not too differently from those I have known. In the history section, I decide to work my way backward through time, so I start by choosing volumes that will give me an overview of the twentieth century.

After finding an empty table hidden among the shelves, I crack the book open and begin to read. It's not long before my heart starts to race. With the exception of location names—though not even all of those—nothing's familiar here. It tells of "world wars"—two of them—and more individual nations than I can fathom. The British Empire is nonexistent, at least in the way I know it. Instead, a "Commonwealth of Nations" encompasses many of the territories I know as being under direct rule of the king. According to the book, those territories are now mostly independent nations.

What surprises me is that the only part of North America that belongs to the group is Canada. The part of the continent that's always been my home is its own nation, with no direct political ties to the kingdom at all. It calls itself the United States of America.

When I come to the section about the 1970s, I feel the weight of my actions closing in on me again. In the year 1976, the US—as the book often refers to it—celebrated its bicentennial.

Two hundred years of existence means the nation was started in 1776, one year after the twelve-second error at the Three Swans Tavern.

Leaving the book unfinished, I hurry to the shelves and select a text specifically on the history of the United States of America. I don't even make it past the table of contents before I know the truth.

A chapter entitled "George Washington" includes subsections with the titles: "The War Years 1775–1783" and "The First President 1789–1797."

The Washington I'm familiar with was captured and executed, thanks to information provided by Richard Cahill. In this new time line, Cahill died before he could fulfill his role, and Washington not only lived but thrived.

How do I describe how it feels to confirm I'm both the annihilator of my world and the creator of this one? That in a single slip of my hand, I've changed the paths of millions—maybe billions—of people and likely killed more human beings than all the tyrants in history combined?

Perhaps *kill* isn't the right word. To be killed a person would have to exist and then have his or her life taken away, right?

It's not murder. It's not genocide.

My crime is taking the lives of those who now have never been. There's no word for that.

I begin reading the book, but this is merely out of habit. My mind is so numb that the words might as well be in a foreign language. My eyes are following the patterns while my fingers automatically turn the page when I reach the end, that's all.

"Excuse me, sir." The voice comes from somewhere behind me, but I pay it no attention. "Excuse me. Sir?"

A hand touches my shoulder and then pulls away. I turn my head and find a smartly dressed woman standing behind me.

"The library's closing in ten minutes," she says. "If you want to check that book out, you'll need to do so now."

"Oh, okay. Thank you."

She walks off without another word.

I look down at the book that has confirmed my crime. I've gone through nearly three-quarters of it and can't recall a single word. I do need to hold on to it so I can really read it, but borrowing it the traditional way would likely require identification I don't have. Luckily I'm not limited to the traditional route.

I look around to make sure no one can see me, and then use my chaser to hop back to the middle of the previous night at the library.

There are fewer lights on than during operating hours, but it's more than bright enough for my needs. After retrieving the book I was reading and slipping it into my satchel, I hunt around for a biography on George Washington. When I locate the right area, I'm surprised by the number of choices I have. The man who was no more than a footnote in the history of my world is clearly a legend here. I pick one at random and add it to my bag.

I have no intention of stealing these books. When I'm done I'll return to this very night and replace them on the shelves so no one will be the wiser.

Before I leave, my stomach starts growling, so I reach into the satchel for one of the apples, but they're all gone. There's no bread left, either. I don't remember eating, but I must've done so during the lost hours I sat staring at the book.

Another growl lets me know I need to find some food fast. Since I still haven't figured out the money situation here, I can't just walk into a store and buy what I want. I could hop around until I find a place that's closed, but that might take some time. So I decide to search the library first, hoping those who work here keep food someplace.

I discover a room for employees only that has a few large, box-like machines that dispense food. Here again I need money. Thankfully, in the next room I find a refrigeration cabinet, much nicer than any I have ever seen. Inside are several bags and containers. Most have names on them, but there's half a sandwich wrapped in plastic sitting on a lower shelf, unmarked.

I feel a tinge of guilt as I pull the wrapper off, but I'm too hungry to let it stop me. After I shove the last bit into my mouth, I look in the cold cabinet again, this time for something to drink. Several metal cylinders of various colors with names like Coke and Sprite and Dr. Pepper are spread around, some additionally marked Diet.

I pick up one of the red Coke cans. The mechanism for opening it is new to me but only takes a few seconds to figure out. A hiss and a pop greet the pull of the tab, followed by a sizzling sound from inside. The can is cold, but the sound makes me think the liquid is hot. Perhaps it heated up when I pulled the tab. Careful so I don't burn anything, I take a very small sip.

Cold.

And sweet.

I take a longer drink.

And good.

Tipping the can back, I let the liquid run down my throat. I'm able to finish only half before I need to stop. The sweet flavor is wonderful but almost too much.

With my stomach no longer complaining, I decide to take advantage of the location. I sit at the table and start reading. But things don't always go as planned, and before I can get a handful of pages in, the words begin to swim, and I lay my head down and fall asleep.

◆ ◆ ◆

I'm aware of voices behind me, but am still in that zone between dreams and reality, so I don't realize the significance until someone grabs my shoulder and shakes me.

"Hey. Wake up!" The voice is sharp, female.

I blink, and for a second have no idea where I am. Upjohn Hall? My father's house?

No. There is no Upjohn Hall, I remember, and it's highly likely my father is among those who have never existed.

I'm in a now that shouldn't be.

"What are you doing here?" My inquisitor is a short, thin woman in a brown skirt and beige blouse.

I part my lips, but don't know what answer to give.

"Do you speak English?" she asks.

Finally finding my voice, I say, "Yes. I'm, uh, sorry. I didn't, um—"

"How did you get in here? Did you break in? Or were you hiding when the library closed last night?"

"No, neither," I tell her, which is true.

"Maybe he was accidentally locked in." This comes from a different woman standing back by the door. She's younger, maybe even as young as I am, with long auburn hair and suntanned skin. She's wearing blue workman's pants like mine and a black button-up sweater that matches her black-framed glasses. Her tone is considerably more sympathetic than her friend's.

The older woman glares at me. "Is that what happened?"

I nod. "Yes. I was, um, locked in. I didn't know what to do."

"So where were you when the staff closed up?"

"Um . . ."

The woman frowns and glances back at her colleague. "Ms. Davis, call the police. I'll keep an eye on him."

"The police?" I say. "But I didn't do anything."

"And what do you call trespassing?"

"Maybe we should cut him a break," Ms. Davis suggests. "He was just sleeping. He didn't hurt anything."

"And how do you know that? Have you searched the building yet? Who knows what he's done?"

"I haven't done anything." Out of the corner of my eye, I can see my satchel sitting on the table, less than an arm's length away. If I can get my hand inside, I can press the button combination that will take me fifteen minutes back and ten feet to the side.

Ms. Davis points past me, and I'm momentarily afraid she's going to tell the older woman to take my bag. But what she says is, "You really think he went around destroying things, then came in here to read a book about . . ." She looks at me. "What were you reading?"

"It's a history book," I reply. "About the . . . United States of America." It's the first time I've said the phrase aloud, and it feels odd on my tongue.

"A history book, Ms. Hendricks."

"I don't care what he's reading. Call the police."

Reluctantly Ms. Davis walks over to a wall-mounted com-phone. In that moment neither woman is looking in my direction, so I slip one hand into my satchel and grab the strap with my other. Once my fingers find the correct buttons, I pull the bag to me and push the emergency-escape combination.

Both women disappear as my perspective shifts ten feet and I'm dumped on the ground. I can only imagine the librarians' reactions. At least they weren't looking at me when I winked out. They'll probably find some rational way to explain what happened to me.

I pull my satchel's strap over my head and get to my feet. At the table my earlier self is slumped on top of the book, sound asleep. I'm tempted to wake him up and tell him to get out of here, but I've already made my escape so it makes sense to let things play out.

The book, which I would dearly like to grab and take with me, has to stay, or else it would change the things that are about to happen. I could come back for it later, but I think it best to avoid this library from now on. I set the chaser to take me just outside the building at dawn, but before I press "Go," a poster on the wall catches my eye. It's an announcement of an upcoming "continuing education" seminar at the "Central Library."

A central library sounds like a place that would have all the information I need. I hastily write the address on a piece of paper. As I finish I hear footsteps in the hallway, soft and distant, but heading in this direction.

It's time for me to leave.

CHAPTER SEVENTEEN

My priorities are simple: survive, learn, fix.

I focus first on survival.

Several blocks from the library, I spot another 7-Eleven. The red, green, and white sign has become comforting and familiar in a world full of the unknown.

Upon entering I find many customers waiting in a line to pay for the items they've selected. My first step is to get an understanding of the money used here in the United States of America, so I pretend to be interested in some of the goods around the front end of the counter. From there I have a perfect view of the clerk and each customer he helps.

The money seems to come in three different forms—paper, coins, and some kind of plastic card. The first two are just like money from home, only instead of the colorful notes we have, the type in use here seems to be uniformly green and white. I see denominations of one and five and what I think is twenty, though the last passes quickly between hands so I can't be sure. The coins are too small for me to see their designations, but they probably won't be too hard to figure out. The type I don't fully understand is the plastic card. When used, it isn't given to the clerk but run through a machine on the counter, and then kept by the customer. The cards also seem to come in a wide variety of colors. I decide to avoid them for now. Sticking with the less complicated notes and coins should be enough to get me through.

I leave before I overstay my welcome, wondering where I can get my hands on some money.

A bank is a possibility. If it works here like the ones I've known, it'll have a vault where currency is kept. I'm suddenly thinking like a master criminal. I don't like it, but it's the only choice I have at the moment. Besides, when I fix everything, none of this will matter.

I walk around until I find a building with a sign on it reading BANK OF AMERICA. I peek through the windows but can't see the vault. I need to visit during business hours, so I find a quiet alley, set my chaser for 9:15 a.m., and huddle down next to a large rubbish bin as I jump.

A loud whining greets me on arrival and is quickly joined by a low rumble and the sound of feet. I don't even have time to get up before a man wearing gloves comes around the side of the bin.

He jerks to a stop when he sees me, then barks something in Spanish and waves his arm, making it clear he wants me to move. As I get out of the way, he pulls the bin from the wall and turns it at a ninety-degree angle. A large vehicle approaches from the other side and lifts the bin into the air.

I don't stay to see what happens next.

Upon entering the bank, I note the similarities between this facility and the few I visited growing up, but there are differences as well. First among them is a wall of thick glass or plastic that sits above the counter where the clerks work, physically dividing them from the patrons. Holes are cut into these panels for speaking and passing information. It's an obvious deterrent to robbery and makes me wonder how many this bank has experienced.

I walk over to the line of patrons but don't join it. I take a casual look around through the clear wall until I spot the vault. After placing my satchel on a counter, I pull my chaser out just enough so that I can see the screen, and then use the destination calculator to figure out the location address for the vault.

I make the jump from behind the building the moment no one is around, timing my arrival for the middle of the previous night.

The vault is pitch-black. The only light comes from the chaser screen, and it's barely strong enough for me to see a few feet at a time. Most of the room is lined with tiny numbered doors, each having two separate keyholes.

I walk around, but all I find are more doors. Some are larger and require only a single key, but it all adds up to the same thing—no money out in the open that I can grab.

Taking cash from a bank is something that feels anonymous to me and won't trouble my soul, but with that option closed, I'm forced into a less desirable choice.

I find a store-packed street called Ventura Boulevard—again, the quantity and variety of establishments astound me. I jump from closed store to closed store, hunting for money. Many have their own safes, and those that don't seem to have had their tills emptied at closing time. That said, I'm able to find a few notes and coins hidden in desks and under counters. To temper my guilt, I limit my take to no more than ten United States of America dollars at each stop.

I've amassed sixty-three dollars in paper bills and seventy-two cents in coins—which, as I assumed, were easy to figure out—when a loud, repetitive alarm begins blaring in the store I've just entered. Not having come through a door, I'm not sure how I set it off, but I hop out immediately and decide to get by with what I have for now.

At a coffee shop about an hour after the sun comes up, I go in search of food and walk into a place called The Homegrown Café.

I'm shown to a table and given a menu that immediately confuses me. The items listed are things like: tofurky and tofu scramble wrap, seitan and cashew cheese omelet, and wheatgrass shake.

The waitress approaches a few moments later. "What can I get you?"

"Uh . . ." Hopelessly lost, I set down the menu. "Do you have coffee?"

"Sure. Milk?"

"Yes, please."

"Soy or rice?"

"I'm sorry?"

"Milk. Soy or rice?"

Milk from soy or rice? How is that even possible? "I'd prefer cow."

She frowns. "This is a *vegan* restaurant."

Not seeing how that's an answer to my question, I wait for her to say more. But when she doesn't, I say, "Vegan?"

She closes her eyes in annoyance, then opens them again and points out the window. "I think what you're looking for is over there."

◆　◆　◆

The new restaurant is called Starbucks Coffee.

When it's my turn to order, I point at the glass cabinet and say, "May I please have one of those muffins and a cup of coffee?"

"House blend?" the clerk asks.

"Um, okay."

"Black or with milk?"

"Is it from a cow?"

"As far as I know," he says with a smile. "We also have soy, if you'd prefer that."

"No, the cow's milk is fine. Thank you."

I consume my meal at one of the tables, then ask a clerk who's cleaning the area if he could tell me how to get to the central library. The guy, while kind, is unsure.

"No car?" an older customer sitting alone at a nearby table asks me after the clerk moves on.

"Car?" I say, not sure what he's talking about.

He laughs. "Yeah, I know what you mean. Got rid of my last one four years ago. You got a bus pass, then?"

Am I to be hopelessly lost in my own language? *No* seems to be the safest answer, so that's what I say.

"You a tourist?"

Realizing it's a good cover, I say, "I am."

"Where are you from?"

It's amazing how simple conversations aren't so simple when you have much to hide. "East."

"East Coast?"

There's a hopefulness in his voice that worries me. "Not quite."

"Ah. Well, I got a sister up in Boston is all. You ever been?"

"No."

"So you're looking for the central library?"

I nod.

"Here's what you want to do."

The bus turns out to be the same public transportation vehicle I noticed earlier. According to Isaac, my new friend, I'm to take the express to "Universal City," and then something called "the metro" to "downtown." He explains the details of paying and riding, and then I'm off.

Even though the bus is an express, it takes nearly an hour to reach Universal City. What amazes me during the journey is the sheer amount of land that's been taken over by the city. While New Cardiff is not (was not/never existed as) a small city, parts of the valley the bus now takes me through are (were/never were) still used as farmland.

There's something else I notice. I'm no engineer, but even to my untrained eyes, I can tell that the buildings I'm passing—especially those more than two or three stories tall—are considerably better built than those of the world I know.

I'm also finding it hard to pick out the caste differences of the people I see. This is something I could do in my sleep growing up, but here it's not so easy. There are a few on the bus I'd categorize as belonging to one of the lower castes, but I'm not sure where the others fit.

The metro is similar to the tram system of New Cardiff. In fact, if I squint just right, I almost feel like I'm back home.

When I reach my stop, I take a moving stairway up from the station to ground level—downtown. If I was awed by the sights before, I'm struck silent now. Here buildings rise dozens of stories into the sky. I've seen pictures and films of structures as high as these, but those buildings were all in London or Hamburg or Peking or Shanghai. There are none in the North America I'm from.

I get lost once, but with the help of a passing pedestrian, I finally find the library. After I enter I can't keep the grin from my face. Outside the facility looks as if it has only three floors. Upon entering I discover that's an illusion. The library is huge, four floors aboveground and—accessed via more moving stairways—four floors below.

According to the map I find, the history section is on the very bottom, so down I go.

◆ ◆ ◆

When it's announced that the library is closing, I give in to my pleading stomach and go in search of something to eat, fully intending once I finish to pop straight to the next morning when the library would open again. But as my hunger is sated, exhaustion takes its place.

The first hotel I find requires—for one night—five times the amount of money I have and something called a credit card, which I'm guessing is one of the plastic cards I saw at 7-Eleven.

Several blocks away I find a rundown place where the cost is only a fraction of the other amount, and if I'm willing to leave an extra twenty dollars, a credit card is not needed. I get to my third-floor room via a dirty, narrow lift. The few other residents I see I immediately identify as Nines, or maybe even unclassified drifters. This gives me an odd sense of comfort.

My room is small, thin-walled, and dusty, but I'm too tired to care. As I start to drift off, I hear a faint triple beep, but before I can figure out where it came from, I'm out.

The next morning I'm at the doors of the library several minutes before they open at 10:00 a.m. There are others waiting, too. After a few minutes, I get the sense I'm being watched, so I cautiously look around. There's a group of older people and a few others closer to my age, but if any of them was looking at me, none is now.

A triple beep causes me to look at my satchel, and I remember the same noise from the previous evening. I lift the flap and see a message glowing on my chaser's screen. I move over to the side where no one can see into the bag, then open it wide enough for me to read the message.

POWER LEVEL 10%

I've never received a power message before. Usually my chaser is charged between missions. But I've made a lot of trips since it was last plugged in, and since I don't have a charger with me, I'll have to be careful from now on and take no unnecessary trips.

I hear the door lock turn, so I hurriedly close my bag, and soon I'm back in the basement of the library.

As my research takes me from one book to the next, time begins to have little meaning. One of the first things I learn is that there's no mention anywhere about the day Washington was supposed to have been captured. There are other references to close escapes, but the rebellion leader proves to be elusive and is never apprehended.

Though I take no pride or credit for what he has done, I know that all he's accomplished since that night in 1775 has only been possible because of my ineptitude. I'm thoroughly convinced now that if I stop myself from entering the Three Swans Tavern, all will return to normal.

This is the moment I should go back to and fix, so those I have unintentionally erased will live again and the empire will be restored.

But I don't leave. I don't even attempt to move my chair back. This world I have unwittingly created has started to fascinate me, and I want to learn more before I banish it.

I read about the Declaration of Independence and the Constitution. I learn of a second war with the British in 1812, and that slavery continued in America until the 1860s, ending only after a deadly civil war engulfed the nation. I learn of assassinations and innovations and the rights of women. I find out that America and the United Kingdom are allies now, fighting on the same side in the world wars I learned about in the other library.

There are more wars for America, smaller in scale, in Asia and in what I know as Arabia but they call the Middle East. And internal struggles that often revolve around something referred to as civil rights—the idea that everyone in a society should have the same rights. It's a concept I wish were true in my world, but I fear would never even be considered.

Then there's this thing called the American Dream. While it's a simple concept, it's difficult for me to accept at first. By the standards of this "dream," it doesn't matter where you start out in life, you can rise as high as you want if you put your mind to it and really work for it. To me "dream" seems the right word at first, but as I read on, I find it's more than wishful thinking. There are stories about rulers of this country coming from humble beginnings, leaders of industry starting with next to nothing, and others fighting against the life they were born into to become doctors and writers and professors and community leaders.

For everyone who has achieved this American Dream, there are probably many more who have tried and failed, but this concept is still a million times better than the entrenched social structure I know.

Every night when the library closes, I purchase the cheapest food I can find before returning to my hotel, and every morning at 10:00 a.m., I'm with the first group in. Not a day passes without me experiencing the sensation of being watched, but when I look around, I never catch anyone. It's unsettling. Other than that, though, I lose myself in a past that should not be.

The shocks keep coming. In Great Britain, instead of reigning for less than two years, Queen Victoria remained on the throne for over sixty-three. All the subsequent kings and queens I was forced to memorize as a schoolboy never wore the crown. Then there were the political parties: Labour and Conservative. Labour doesn't exist in my world, and the Conservative Party may share common Tory beginnings with the North Party, but its ideology is nowhere near as extreme. The Norths don't exist at all in this new world, and as far as I can tell, they never did.

On Fridays and Saturdays the library closes at 5:30 p.m., so I spend those evenings walking around downtown, trying to absorb all I've learned. It's an impossible task. My head swims with historical events that seem like fiction to me.

On Sunday, I arrive at 10:00 a.m. again, only to realize on this day the library doesn't open for another three hours. I curse myself for not reading the sign and curse again at the library for having reduced Sunday hours. I'm anxious to get back in. The previous afternoon, after guidance from one of the librarians, I moved up one level to the social science section and began learning more about current culture. The amount of information available is overwhelming but so very fascinating, and I can't wait to pick up where I left off.

"They open late on Sundays."

I turn to find a girl about my age, with short black hair and pale skin, standing a dozen feet away. Peeking out from the collar of her black cotton shirt—*T-shirt*, I have learned—is a tattoo of several tiny birds. Her pants are blue jeans—another phrase I've picked up—ripped in a few places that would've made me think she was poor, but I've seen others wearing this style who, from their jewelry and other accessories, are clearly well-off, so I can't tell what her status is. There's something vaguely familiar about her, so I figure I must have seen her around the library.

"Thank you. I know," I say, and then turn back toward the door. I've been very careful to keep all conversations to a minimum so that I don't get tripped up.

But apparently she's not ready to end our talk. "You a student or something?"

I nod without looking back.

"I thought so."

Not wanting to give her the chance to ask anything more, I adjust my satchel's strap and walk off down the sidewalk. I might as well get something to eat. I used up the last of my cash on dinner last night, so first thing this morning, I made another circuit of stores, using the same rules from before. I came back with nearly two hundred dollars and an eighth of a percent less power on my chaser.

I go to a little café down the street where I've eaten a couple times before, and take my food and coffee to a table by the window. I've taken only a bite of my croissant when the door opens and the girl from the library walks in.

"You're not using both these chairs, are you?" she asks, approaching my table.

I want to say yes but am unsure of the proper etiquette, so I remove my satchel from the second chair and put it on the floor next to me. "You may have it."

I hope she'll take it somewhere else, but she removes the bag she's carrying from her back and sits down.

I busy myself with my meal, hoping she gets the hint I want to be alone.

She doesn't. "That looks good."

"It is," I tell her between bites.

"Kind of makes me wish I hadn't already eaten."

I respond with a noncommittal grunt.

For a few moments, she says nothing, and I'm thinking maybe I can finish and get out of here before she opens her mouth again.

"You *are* a student, right?" she asks. "I mean, why would you be spending all day every day for a week in the library?"

I put another piece of croissant in my mouth, wondering how the hell she knows this.

"I'm guessing since you spent most of your time in the basement, you're a history major. Me, I'm premed . . . well, I will be when I get into a university. I'm going to LACC right now."

I don't know what that is, nor do I care.

"Actually, I'm not *in* school this semester," she says. "I'm taking it off. A little break . . . okay, a forced break. One of my teachers and

I didn't agree on the grade I got last semester, and he apparently was unable to appreciate the way I expressed my dissatisfaction. They call it a semester suspension. I call it a miscarriage of justice."

The half cup of coffee I have left I'm happy to leave behind, but I need the nutrition the croissant provides. Two more bites, and I'll be done.

She holds out her hand. "My name's Iffy."

As much as I want to ignore her, I can't. I give her hand a quick shake and say, "Hi."

"Is that your name?"

I frown. "It's Denny."

As I glance at her, I'm struck again by the feeling of familiarity. I know I've never met her before, but there is something about her. Something more than maybe having glimpsed her across the lobby of the library.

"Uh, hello? You okay there, Denny?"

I blink and realize I've been staring at her. "Sorry. I'm, um . . . it's just . . ." I push my chair back and stand up. "Nice meeting you."

"You're going already?" she asks as I start to walk away. "You haven't finished your coffee."

"It's yours if you want it," I tell her, and then leave the shop.

◆ ◆ ◆

I am back at the library at 1:00 p.m. sharp and am deep in a book about the "rise of social media" on the "Internet" when someone sits down on the other side of the table. Enthralled as I am by a computer network that connects people from around the world, I register the person's presence only on a subconscious level.

In my time line, we have our version of computers, but the network through which data can be obtained is tightly controlled and, as far as I know, does not extend beyond the borders of the empire.

Here you can witness live events happening half a world away, and read "posts" by anyone affected by revolt and protest or by people just discussing their lives.

It's hard to explain how this makes me feel. I know from my research that the people of this reality are not free to do whatever they want. Some are close to achieving that, while many others are restricted by heavy-handed political rule or sheer poverty. Or both. But in my world, almost everyone lives under heavy-handed rules, and there are at least as many poor as there are here.

"If you're writing a research paper, why aren't you taking any notes?"

I glance up and am surprised to find Iffy sitting across from me.

"I don't mean to be rude, but I'm busy," I tell her.

"I can see you're busy. I've seen you be busy for several days now."

So, I *was* being watched.

"That probably sounded a little creepy, didn't it?" she says, then pushes her chair away from the table. "Sorry I bothered you."

With that, she's gone.

I know I should be troubled by the fact she's been watching me, but the sense that I somehow know her stays with me and makes me almost wish she didn't leave. It takes several minutes, but I'm finally able to get back to work.

Unfortunately, not only does the library open late on Sundays, but it also closes early, so at 5:00 p.m., I'm forced to leave with the rest of the afternoon crowd. When I walk outside, Iffy is standing there.

"That croissant was a long time ago," she says as she falls in step beside me. "I bet you're hungry."

Though a part of me is secretly glad to see her, I need to keep to myself. "I don't know what you want, but you've got the wrong person."

"Guy," she says.

"What?"

"Wrong guy. That sounds more natural."

Frowning, I say, "Whichever way, the statement still applies."

"You have an interesting way of speaking. Where are you from?"

"Please, leave me alone."

I pick up my pace, but she matches me stride for stride.

"Okay, maybe that was prying too much," she says. "But you've got to eat. Do you like Peruvian?"

"I'm not hungry, thank you."

"Aw, come on. Now you're straight-out lying. That's not nice."

I make the mistake of glancing at her, and for half a second lose myself in her eyes. "I'm sorry," I say as I pull my gaze away.

"Then make it up to me by buying me dinner. It's not expensive, trust me."

I stop and turn to her. "Why are you doing this?"

"We both need to eat, don't we?"

"No, I mean, why are you talking to me?"

She hesitates and then looks at the ground as she says, "You seem interesting."

"Now you're the one who's lying."

"I'm not. You *do* seem interesting. And we do both need to eat."

She tents her eyebrows and smiles in a way that pushes her left cheek up. I stare at her, telling myself I need to walk away, but I don't. "Okay. I'll buy you dinner."

CHAPTER EIGHTEEN

When she leads me into the metro station, I almost back out.

"You wanted Peruvian, right?" she says. Before I can point out that was her choice, not mine, she continues, "The best place I know is in Hollywood."

"Hollywood?" This is a name I've read quite a bit since I shifted into researching popular culture. Despite my reservations, I'm intrigued. "How far?"

"Just a few stops."

I relent, and we board the next westbound train.

"You have been to Hollywood before, haven't you?" she asks after we take seats next to the door in the nearly empty car.

"No." There's no Hollywood in New Cardiff.

"So I'm right. You're not from here. Where, then?"

"Far from here."

She smirks. "Never heard of that place."

I shrug, but don't give her any more.

Neither of us says anything until after the train makes its first stop. When the doors close again, Iffy says, "Okay, so Hollywood's probably not what you think it is. The one you see on TV or read about is more up here." She taps her head. "The physical Hollywood is a little rougher around the edges than you tourist types are expecting."

"I'm not a tourist."

"You know what I mean. The city's trying to make it more like what people are hoping to see and they're getting there, but there's still a lot of real Hollywood around." The way she says this makes me think she prefers this *real* Hollywood. "You'll see what I mean."

We get off at the Hollywood/Vine station and surface to a crowded walkway. The main part of the sidewalk is black with red stars set into it, each containing a different name written in gold. Across the street there are even more people gathered under the wide awning of a building.

"Pantages Theatre," she tells me. "*Newsies* this month. You seen it?"

I shake my head.

"Yeah, neither have I. Come on."

She grabs my hand and pulls me through the throngs of pedestrians past a building with a big red W in front. At the corner she turns left. Here the sidewalk is less crowded, but it doesn't seem like she'll let go of my hand so I do it for her.

She glances at me with those tented eyebrows again and begins to sprint. "Hurry up," she yells. "It's only a couple of blocks, and I'm starving."

It feels good to run down the sidewalk, weaving between people, with this strange girl leading me. For a few moments, all thoughts of what I've done are pushed miles away, and I almost feel happy.

As promised, the restaurant isn't far. Several of the employees greet Iffy as we walk in and take a table along the wall. She does the ordering and then excuses herself to use the toilet.

Leave, a tiny voice in my head whispers. *Get out of here.* I try to shove it away, but before I'm able to do so, it says, *The last thing you need is to make a connection with anyone here.*

This makes me pause. The voice is right. At some point I'll be returning to 1775 to fix the mistake I committed, which will then wipe out this world. The only reason I haven't gone yet is my fascination with this place, but as soon as I finish my research, I'll make the trip.

That's what I've been telling myself, at least.

Leave her here and go. You've already learned all you need to know.

I almost give in to the command, but then I see her walking back across the restaurant. I see her easy smile. I see her intelligent yet guarded eyes. And I don't move.

The food is as good as she said it would be. We talk as we eat. Well, she does most of the talking, telling me of things I should see while I'm in town, of her classes at college, of the job she recently quit or was fired from—I'm still not clear which.

After we finish and I've put enough money on the table to cover the bill, she says, "You know, if you need a place to stay, there's a room at the house I live in. The lady who owns it rents them out. It's not too far from here."

The offer catches me off guard. "That's okay. I, uh, have someplace already."

"Trust me, the house is a hell of a lot better than that rundown hotel you've been crashing in."

The smile slips from my face, and I slowly lean back. "You followed me to my hotel?"

"That doesn't sound good, does it?" she says. "I really need to work on my phrasing."

Get out of here. Run. Go!

I fight the urge to launch myself from the table. "Why are you following me?"

"I told you, you're interesting."

"And I told you you're lying."

When I see the hesitation in her eyes again, I know I'm right.

I lean forward. "Did someone put you up to this? Are you a police officer?"

"Police? Why? Did you commit a crime?"

I did. I committed the biggest crime ever.

This is getting me nowhere, and the best thing I can do is leave. I pull on my satchel as I shove up from the table.

"You won't believe me if I tell you," she says.

I stop. "You won't know that unless you try."

She looks down at her hands and takes a deep breath. "We're connected, okay? I don't know how or why, but we just are. About a week ago, I had this . . . episode, followed by a terrible headache. When it finally went away, I knew you were out there. In fact, I seem to always know exactly where you are." She looks up at me again. "I told you you wouldn't believe me."

The problem is, I do believe her. No, not just believe her. I *know* she's right.

Somehow, someway, my chaser has turned Iffy into my companion.

But this is way too much for me to deal with. I stumble forward and race out of the restaurant.

That night as I lie in my hotel bed, desperate for sleep, Iffy's voice keeps me awake as she says over and over in my head, "I knew you were out there . . . I seem to always know where you are."

My time with Iffy has unnerved me, so the next morning I avoid the library and get out of downtown for a few hours.

From the metro station, I catch what's called the Purple Line as far west as it goes, to a station called Wilshire/Western. As I approach the top of the moving stairway—the escalator, I've now learned—I think I must still be in downtown. The buildings here are like those in the center of the city, tall and sleek. But after walking a few blocks, I realize that these merely line Wilshire Boulevard, and none go quite as high as those in the city center.

The area is full of signs written in symbols I don't recognize. Some include English, and I deduce from the multiple times I see the word *Korea* that the symbols are from the language of that country. Research from the past week flashes in my mind: Korea. Asian peninsula west of Japan, bordering China and a very tiny strip of Russia. Split into two countries, North and South. The divide was created when the Korean War in the 1950s reached a stalemate. The South is more aligned with the commerce culture of what is called "the West." The North is ruled by a totalitarian regime handed down from father to son and is largely cut off from the rest of the world.

In my time line, Korea is part of a different China and seldom mentioned.

I wander around until I spot a coffee shop and go in. I'm still too uncertain to try one of the fancy-named drinks these places offer—not to mention they'd deplete most of my cash reserves—so I order a simple coffee. Once I have my cup, I look around for an open chair.

Iffy sits at a small round table along the wall. She's looking at me, her smile tentative and a bit worried. Me? I'm having a full-on panic attack—racing heart, cold sweats, and the sudden inability to catch my breath.

I head toward the door, my attention more on the danger behind me than where I'm going.

"Excuse me!"

I jerk to a stop just in time to avoid spilling my coffee on an older Asian woman.

"Watch where you're going," she says.

"I'm so sorry," I tell her.

As I step past her toward the exit, I toss my untouched drink in the trash bin and rush outside.

A few seconds later, I hear Iffy shout, "Denny!"

"Leave me alone!" I yell back.

"I'm not following you. I've been here for twenty minutes. I . . . I knew you'd come."

I don't want to hear this. I don't want to even think about what her words mean, so I pick up my pace until I'm running. Behind me I can hear her sprinting after me, but I know I'm faster.

Finally her pounding steps stop. "Be careful, Denny! Something's coming!"

I look toward the street, thinking she's warning me about a vehicle headed toward me, but there's only stopped traffic on the road. So I race on, not slowing until I'm blocks and blocks away.

The rest of the day is spent wandering around in a partial daze. Each time I turn a corner, I expect to see Iffy waiting for me, but she doesn't reappear. When darkness falls, I return to my hotel.

The next morning I wake early, gasping for air. Whatever dream I was having is lost, but the anxiety it induced still surges under my skin.

I check the time. I plan to return to the library that morning. If Iffy can find me at a random coffee shop miles away, what's the use in hiding? But according to the clock, it's just shy of 5:30 a.m. The library won't be open for another four and a half hours.

As I roll on my side, I notice something's been shoved under the door to my room. Assuming it's a note from the proprietor, I close my eyes and try to go back to sleep. It's a futile effort. There's still too much adrenaline coursing through me for sleep to return anytime soon, so I shower and dress in another set of the cheap clothes I've purchased, and then decide I might as well head out.

The note is still waiting for me when I reach the door. I pick it up and unfold it. The message starts with an address, and below it:

> That room's still available.
> Iffy
>
> P.S. I wasn't following you.
> P.P.S. I know you're going back to the library today, but don't worry. I'll leave you alone.

I ball up the paper and toss it at the bin by the bathroom door. It hits the edge but falls onto the floor. I'm tempted to leave it there, but my mother taught me to clean up after myself and I can feel her staring at me, waiting. I pick up the note and start to drop it in the can, but stop.

The eyes I see now are not my mother's but Iffy's, and I know I can't throw the note away. I press out the wrinkles, slip it into my pocket, and leave.

I start the day reading about television—what my world calls a broadset—but a line in a paragraph about a "medical documentary" sends my mind reeling.

No, you're just dreaming. It's not worth even thinking about it. It's not like you could do anything with the knowledge.

But I can't let it go, and soon find myself in the biology section of the library, where I spend the rest of the day.

As I walk out into the night after closing, the idea sparked by the documentary's description has turned into a blazing fire. I know what I'm thinking is only a fantasy, but I could make it happen. A part of me even thinks I *should* make it happen. *Screw everything else*, it tells me. *What's really most important?*

Rising above the noise of a passing bus, a voice calls, "Denny!"

I stop, my eyes closing as my chin drops to my chest. Iffy again. I don't have the energy to run or argue.

"What do you want?" I say as I turn around.

But the girl standing there isn't Iffy.

It's Lidia.

CHAPTER NINETEEN

I stare at her, unable to move.

Lidia.

From *my* time line.

The world that is no more.

It takes everything I have to squeeze out the words. "Are you real?"

Without warning she flies forward and throws her arms around me. This breaks my trance, though it takes me another few seconds before I hug her back. This is Lidia, after all, the girl who's only shown me scorn until now.

"How did you find me?" I ask.

She lets go and takes a step back.

"Bernard," she says, naming her supervisor. "He showed me how to tune my chaser to locate other devices. It's not perfect and I never know who I'm going to find, but . . ." She looks me up and down. "It led me to you."

"Bernard, is he . . . ?"

"He's okay. We split up to see if we could find others."

"Have you?"

She nods. "Last we checked with each other, Bernard had found four. I've found two. Well, three with you." She pauses. "You were a little tougher to locate, actually. For a while there were conflicting signals for your device. They seemed to be coming from both coasts and were strong enough to mask each other. I figured it was an error, so I spent my time looking for others. When I checked your signal again, there was just the one."

It was no error. It was my other self, the one lying unconscious in a New York hospital for four days—the same days I relived out here after I escaped.

She looks around. Though only a handful of people are on the sidewalk, it's apparently too crowded for her. "Do you have someplace we can talk? Private?"

"I have a room."

"Great. Let's go."

Upon entering my room, Lidia looks around with disdain. "This is the best you can do?"

This is the version of her I know.

"They didn't ask for an ID or credit card," I say in my defense.

"So what? I have a whole pocketful of credit cards now. I stay anywhere I want. You want me to get you a better room?"

I turn my back so she doesn't see my annoyance. "This works for me."

The bed squeaks as she lowers herself onto it. "Suit yourself, I guess. More your caste level anyway."

There's no disdain in her tone. She's only stating the facts as she knows them, which makes me see them even more than I would if she were trying to goad me. But I bottle it up as I pull over the rickety wooden chair that normally sits near the window.

"What have you been doing this whole time?" Lidia asks.

If her supervisor had come to find me, I'd confess that this whole new world is my fault, but I can't say it to Lidia. The person I really wish for is Marie. If my old instructor were sitting here with me, we could figure this out together. We could—

"Marie. Did you find her?"

Lidia looks confused. "Your old trainer?"

"Yes."

"Not that I know of. Was she on a mission?"

"I . . . I don't know."

"Well, if she was, she'd have to have been pretty far back to still be around."

"What do you mean?"

"So far everyone we've found was at least as far back as the eighteenth century when things went wrong. I think the most recent rewinder was in 1769. Bernard and I were in 1648. When were you?"

I lie without hesitation. "Seventeen fifty-one."

"See what I mean?" She begins to pace, which in my room means a four-step loop between the front door and the bathroom. "Unless we find someone who was on assignment more recently than 1769, then whatever happened must have occurred within a few years either side of that point. Bernard says that since society moved slower back then, it's possible the change event happened before 1769." She snaps around and looks at me. "Nothing weird going on where you were, was there?"

I dive even deeper into my lie. "I wasn't there more than an hour. Just checking grave markers. Didn't even talk to anyone." This is a standard step when rewinding a family history.

"Where were you?"

The last cemetery I checked pops immediately to mind. "England. Outside Southhampton."

"With your supervisor?"

"No. I do solo missions now."

Her eyes narrow. "Oh, really. How nice for you."

After a few seconds, she resumes carving a path across my floor.

I let her make a couple of passes before I ask, "Do you really think a rewinder did this?"

She looks at me as if I'm the stupidest person on the planet. "Look around you. *Everything's* changed! History shifted! Who the hell else could have done it?" She takes a deep breath. Her tone's more controlled when she speaks again, but it's still infused with anger. "Bernard and I are going to find whoever it is, and once that person has fixed this mess, they're going to pay for what they've done."

"What if you can't find them?"

"Oh, we'll find them." She looks at me. "And you're going to help us."

"Me? How?"

"By finding out exactly when the break occurred."

"That might be impossible."

"Of course it's possible. No one knows history better than us. The others are already working on it, so one of you will track it down. When we know where the point is, we'll go back and fix it ourselves if we have to."

She's right. Someone's going to figure it out, and when that happens, I'll be exposed.

"We could end up making it worse," I say, trying to come up with anything that will delay the inevitable.

She stares at me as if trying to read my thoughts. "Are you saying you like it here?"

"No, I'm not saying that at all. This isn't home. It's a mistake." To me every word that comes out of my mouth sounds fake, and I'm sure my attempt to deflect attention is doing the exact opposite.

But her face relaxes as she says, "You're right. It is a mistake. That's why we need to fix it."

"I'll, um, do all I can."

"Yes, you will." She pulls open the drawer of the narrow nightstand by my bed, shifts the Bible that's inside, and then shoves the drawer shut. "Isn't there any paper in this place?"

I pull a sheet from my satchel. "Here."

She takes it and stares at me. "Not going to do me any good without something to write with."

"Of course." I give her my pen.

Using the nightstand she scribbles something on the paper and then hands it and the pen back to me. She's written a location number and the date May 12, 1702.

"When you have something, report here. The point is well before when we think the change occurred. We'll use it for our safe zone when we change everything back."

"It may take me a little while to figure out."

"You have four days."

"That might not be enough."

"If it isn't, we'll reassess. But I'll be leaving right at the deadline, so if someone does find the answer, then whoever's not at the meeting point when I arrive will be left behind. I don't have to tell you what will happen if you're still *here* when we fix the problem."

No, she didn't.

"You have until Friday at noon, East Coast time," she says. "What is that? Eight o'clock here?"

"Nine," I say.

"All right. Nine a.m., then. Are we clear on everything?"

"Yes. Very clear."

"Good. Then I'll let you get to work. See you in the past." She whips out her chaser and winks out of my room.

I sit in my chair, staring at the space where she was, half expecting her to reappear and point an accusatory finger at me.

The sudden desire to be anywhere but this room is what finally gets me to push off my chair. I fold Lidia's note and shove it in my pocket. My fingers touch another scrap of paper. When I pull it out, I see it's the message Iffy left me.

Her address.

A place that's not here.

Something's coming! Iffy's words.

Something came, all right.

I shove my few possessions into my satchel, pull it over my shoulder, and leave my dingy hotel room for the last time.

CHAPTER TWENTY

Using a map I purchase near my hotel, I make my way to the address in Hollywood from Iffy's note. There I find a three-story house with green wooden siding and a large, dimly lit stone porch.

As I walk up to the door, I wonder if I'm making a mistake. Maybe I should find another hotel and lock myself away until I can figure out what to do. But I can't stop myself from knocking.

A beautiful woman of African descent opens the door. "Hello," she says with mild surprise. "Something I can help you with?"

"I'm sorry to bother you. I think I might be at the wrong place," I say.

"Who are you looking for?"

"A girl. Her name's Iffy."

"Not the wrong place. What's your name?"

"Denny."

"Of course it is." Turning slightly she calls, "Carl, can you tell Iffy her guest is here?"

From somewhere inside, a male voice says, "Sure."

The woman opens the door wider. "Come in, Denny."

She leads me into a large living room that features a wide stone fireplace. The couch and chairs are leather, while the small tables are stained dark brown. A blonde woman is sitting in one of the chairs, probably ten years younger than the woman who answered the door.

"Catherine, this is Denny. Iffy's friend."

The woman smiles as she rises from her chair and holds out her hand. "Nice to meet you, Denny."

We shake.

"And I'm Marilyn," the first woman says. "Please have a seat."

I sit on the couch but perch near the edge.

Marilyn takes one of the overstuffed chairs. "So, you're Denny?"

"Uh, yes."

"She described you well."

"She what?"

Marilyn smiles as she reaches forward and pats my hand. "It was all very innocent. Don't worry."

"She told you about me?"

"Only that she made a new friend and that you'd be stopping by tonight."

"What do you do, Denny?" Catherine asks.

"Do?" I say.

"Your profession."

"I'm a . . . student."

"Oh. Which school?"

The only answer I can think of is one I saw on a sign at the library. "University of Southern California."

That garners raised eyebrows from both Marilyn and Catherine.

"My, USC. You must be a smart one," Marilyn says.

"Or rich," Catherine throws in. "Let me guess—business school?"

My lies have been coming so fast and thick that I feel the need to say something closer to the truth. "History."

"That's . . . interesting," Marilyn says. "What do you plan to do with that?"

"What do you mean?"

"When you graduate. What kind of job do you get with a degree in history? Teacher?"

I'm saved from burying myself under even more lies by the arrival of Iffy and a man I assume is Carl.

"Hi," she says as I shoot to my feet.

"Hi."

The awkward silence that follows is broken by Marilyn. "Perhaps we should give you two the living room."

"That's okay," Iffy says. "We'll go to my room." She waves for me to follow her.

As we leave, Catherine says, "He's cute, Iffy. Nice catch."

"Leave them be," Marilyn chides.

Once we're out of the living room, Iffy grabs my hand and guides me up a set of stairs, all the way to the single room at the top of the house on the third floor.

The ceiling slants in either direction from the high point in the middle, convincing me this was once an attic. The shortened walls to either side are lined with bookcases stuffed to overflowing. A mattress lies on the floor at the far end under an open window, the only other piece of furniture being a dresser near the stairs.

She leads me to the mattress. "We can sit here."

As I lower myself, I say, "So I guess you knew I was coming."

An uncomfortable nod.

"It's okay," I tell her. "You're not crazy."

"You don't know me very well."

She's right about that.

"The something I warned you about happened, didn't it?" she asks.

Instead of answering I say, "I came because you said there was a room."

Her lower lip slips between her teeth, and she looks away.

"There is a room, right?"

She half nods, half shrugs.

"Can I use it? Who do I need to talk to? Marilyn?"

"Uh . . ."

"What?"

"Well, um . . ."

"There isn't a room, is there?"

She shoots me a worried glance that tells me everything I need to know.

"Dammit," I mutter and push myself to my feet.

She jumps up and puts a hand on my arm. "There was one, I swear. Marilyn rented it out to a couple of guys this morning. They've been moving their stuff in all day."

I start walking toward the stairs.

"Where are you going?"

"To find a place to stay."

"You can stay here. I'll sleep downstairs on the couch. I've done it before."

I shake my head. "I'm not kicking you out of your room."

"Please don't go. Not yet at least. Just . . ." She rubs a hand across her eyes. "I don't know what's happening."

I stop and turn to her. "I told you, you're not crazy."

"Then what's going on?" she says, looking as if she's on the verge of a breakdown. "Why do I know where you're going to be? Why do I know you're in trouble? Why do I *feel* you?"

My training demands that I say nothing, but in reality, what will it hurt? Once the twelve-second gap is eliminated and Richard Cahill is allowed to report Washington's position, Iffy will either be entirely erased or live a life under empire rule in which she never meets me. As I think this, other thoughts begin stirring in my mind, the ones I was having at the library earlier today. I shove them away before I have time to acknowledge them.

I walk back to her. "I know why."

"Tell me, then. Please!" Whatever she's been using to hold herself together crumbles, and she begins to cry. "I want to understand."

I shouldn't do it. I shouldn't even be thinking about doing it. I should be turning around and walking out. I should already be on the stairs.

I pull her into my arms. I can't think about what I *should* be doing, I can only think about what a bastard I've been. All this time I've been focused on how our connection affects *me*, not what it's doing to her.

When her body begins to relax, I lower us to the mattress again. She sniffles a few times and then looks at me through watery eyes, waiting.

"You're not going to believe me," I tell her.

· "I will."

"You won't."

"I'll believe anything you say."

She's probably telling the truth, but I need to ease her into it. I need to ease *myself* into talking about it. "Tell me about your name first."

"My name?"

"Are there a lot of others named Iffy?"

That gets a laugh out of her. "I got it in high school, from someone who used to be a friend."

"Not your parents?"

"My given name is Pamela."

"That's pretty."

"For a soccer mom, maybe."

179

I'm not sure what a soccer mom is, but I get the larger point. "So, why Iffy?"

She thinks for a moment. "My friend and I had been in school together since third or fourth grade. One day she blew up at me, said she'd had enough of my waffling."

"Waffling?"

"Yeah, said she was sick of me not being able to make a decision, that I was iffy on everything. She started calling me that, and it wasn't long before others did the same. It used to make me so mad. I couldn't wait to go to college where no one knew me and I could be Pamela or Pam or anything else."

She pauses. "The thing is, the bitch was right. I was horrible at making decisions. By the time I left home after high school, I was so used to hearing the name that I kept it. Decided to use it to help me be better."

"And has it?"

"Still a work in progress, but getting there." She tilts her head and looks at me. "The old me would have never come looking for you. She would've hidden in her room, hoping the feeling would go away. Your turn. Why is this happening? Why you?"

❖ ❖ ❖

How do you tell someone you're a time traveler? Not from the future, but from the now? Only the now you're from is real, and the one the other person knows is an imposter.

I start at the beginning, with my selection to join the Upjohn Institute, and lay it all out from there.

Iffy is so quiet that I think, contrary to what she said earlier, she doesn't believe a word. Why should she? If someone had come up to me before I joined the institute and said the same, I would've thought the person was insane.

After a while she begins asking questions, having me fill in gaps in my story. When I come to my encounter with Cahill, I carefully explain what should have happened and then what did. She falls silent again, and I take this to mean she's having a hard time following, so I start explaining it again.

"I got it," she says, stopping me. "You created a delay that resulted in him being killed and Washington being allowed to live. That's when everything changed."

"Yes."

I tell her of my mostly unconscious time in New York and my escape to what I thought would be New Cardiff.

"I didn't want to believe at first that I'd caused the change, so that's why I went to the library, hoping to find it was something else."

"You must have figured it out fairly quickly, though," she says.

I nod.

"Then why didn't you go back and fix it at that point? I mean, all you have to do is keep yourself from entering the tavern, right?"

I nod. She's understood it all perfectly.

"Then why haven't you gone yet?"

"I . . . I guess I want to know more about this world first. It's so different than where I'm from. I want to know it better." I take a moment and then say, "Do you believe me?"

"You still haven't told me why we're connected," she says.

I hesitate, then pull my satchel over. From inside I remove my chaser. "This is what you're really connected to."

"What is it?"

"A chaser. It's what allows us to travel through time."

As if fearing it'd shock her, she carefully touches it before taking it from me. She turns it every which way until she's inspected the whole thing. "Why would I be connected to this?"

I tell her about how the chasers work, about companions, the sharing of the pain of travel, and the subtle mental connection between the machine and both of the users. "When my original companion disappeared, it chose you for some reason."

"But why?"

"I've been thinking about that. I'm not a scientist or an engineer, so I don't really know the details on how all of this works, but I do know the link between machine and companion is made, from the human side, on a cellular level. You call it DNA here, I think. You know what that is?"

"Sure. Everyone does."

"My theory is that you and Palmer Benson share, um, I guess, common relatives."

"You mean like we're cousins?"

"In an odd way, I guess. If I'm right, then the device linked with you because you were the closest match to what it knew. How it figured it out . . ." I shrug. We're already way beyond my areas of expertise and into pure speculation. I let her live with this for a minute before I say, "You haven't answered my question."

She looks at me, eyebrows raised.

"Do you believe me?"

"It doesn't matter if I believe you. You can just prove it to me." She hands me back the chaser. "If I give you a date and time and place, you can go there?"

I smile at the thought of performing the same demonstration Marie used on me. "I can."

"All right. February 13, 2012, 7:00 p.m." She gives me an address in a city called San Diego. "That's my mom's house. I was still in high school. Oh, probably not a good idea to just appear in the living room."

Despite the fact that the trip will use up precious power, I owe her this. "All right," I tell her. "But you should know that as companion, even though the trip isn't far, it'll be painful for you."

"Yeah, I've experienced a bit of that already."

My short trips around the city. "I'm sorry. I didn't know."

"It's all right. Now get going."

"What am I looking for?"

"Take a slow walk along the other side of the street from my house, right at seven. You'll know."

"Fine. But I need a map to figure out the location. The chaser doesn't understand your addresses."

"No problem. I'll bring it up on Google."

◆ ◆ ◆

If there is a difference between 2012 and 2015, I'm not tuned into the culture enough to perceive it. To me it looks like I could have hopped a couple minutes into the past to another part of Los Angeles.

I arrive early in the morning of February 14. Since the computer map Iffy showed me uses satellite images of the neighborhood, I'm able to coordinate this with my chaser and pinpoint my arrival to a narrow space behind several retail shops a few blocks away from Iffy's mom's house. Since the space hasn't been paved over, I can check for footprints in the sand. There are shallow depressions that look at least several days old, but nothing indicating anyone has walked between the buildings since then.

Confident my arrival will go unnoticed, I set the Chaser for 6:30 p.m. the previous day and jump back.

The evening is cool but not unpleasant. I note the addresses and keep track of time as I walk casually through Iffy's neighborhood. Her house comes into view a minute before 7:00 p.m.

A car has just pulled up in front of her house. A baby-faced teenager straightens his hair and runs a hand down his nice shirt before heading up to the front door. I'm still not directly in front of the house when the door opens, but I'm able to see the large man standing inside. A conversation ensues. The only thing I can understand is when the man yells into the house, "Pamela!"

When Iffy appears at the door, I slow. She looks young enough to pass for a preteen. While her skin is pale as ever, her hair has yet to be reduced to her current boyish style and is pulled into a long ponytail. She's wearing roomy pink pants and a matching bulky top.

The look on her face when she sees the boy is one of surprise, and judging by his demeanor—though I can't see his face at the moment—he's surprised, too.

Words float across the street . . .

"Ready" and "dance" and "I thought" and "way."

The large man says something to Iffy. She looks reluctant, but he continues talking until she steps outside with the boy. The man closes the door, and the two kids walk slowly toward the boy's vehicle.

I cross the street, angling my path so that I'll reach the sidewalk at the far edge of Iffy's property. It crosses my mind that this could interfere with their conversation, but it soon becomes apparent that they're so wrapped up in each other, they don't even notice me.

". . . talk about it," the boy is saying when I'm finally able to hear them.

"That was two months ago. I thought you were kidding. You should have checked with me again."

"I didn't . . . I thought . . ."

"Ryan, you're a nice guy and all. I'm just not a dance kind of person, okay?"

"But you said yes."

"Because I thought you were *joking.*"

"I wasn't."

"I'm sorry, all right? I'm so sorry."

She turns back to the house. When I reach the sidewalk, I continue past a couple houses before looking back. The boy is still standing by his car, staring at Iffy's house. I turn away, feeling like I'm adding to his embarrassment.

◆ ◆ ◆

Iffy gasps as I reappear in her room. She's lying on her bed, her hands pressing against her temples.

"Are you all right?" I ask.

She blinks multiple times as she breathes deeply. When the tension finally leaves her face, I know the worst of the pain is over.

"How do the companions stand it?" she asks, propping herself up on an elbow.

"They're sedated and don't feel much, I think."

"They'd have to be if they do this all the time."

I help her sit all the way up.

"So . . . what did you see?" she asks.

"The fact that I vanished from your room and your nerve endings caught on fire isn't enough to sway you?"

"Could be that's just a teleportation device. Which, I admit, would be *very* cool. But it's not time travel."

"You're a tough one, aren't you?" I know I shouldn't let this happen, but I'm enjoying our banter.

"Tough enough to survive a bout of crippling pain." A pause. "Well?"

I tell her about the boy.

Her eyes are wide as I describe him. When I finish she nods and whispers, "Ryan Smith. We'd known each other for years."

"And the man who answered the door? Was he your father?"

"Stepfather." Her voice is stronger now. "He made me go out and talk to Ryan."

"The boy asked you to go with him somewhere, but you didn't want to, right?"

"To the high school Valentine's Day dance. He asked me, like, months before. I didn't think he was serious, especially since he never mentioned it again."

"He must've been afraid you'd back out."

"Yeah. I figured that out eventually."

"Why did you pick that for me to see?"

She looks down at her hands. "In May, before school ended that year, Ryan and his mother were killed in an accident. A truck driver dozed off and crossed the centerline, right into their sedan." She looks at me. "Same car you saw. I'm positive I'm the only girl he ever asked out, ever *would* ask out, and I turned him down in the worst possible way. So that night's kind of stuck with me. Talk about selfish. What would it have hurt to give him one night?"

I could say it wasn't her fault he never asked anyone else out, but I know it won't do any good.

"I believe you," she says, and then leans against me, her head on my shoulder. "I believe you."

I don't realize how much tension I've been holding until it breaks at that moment. My secret is now a shared one.

Without any forethought I slip my arms around her. Our faces turn toward each other, and our lips meet in a kiss initiated by both of us. It's my first, and it's impossible to believe there will ever be a better one.

We lie back on her bed at some point, and I tell her the part of my story I left out earlier—the part that triggered my coming to find her.

A shiver runs through her when I finish, so I pull her close.

"You're telling me in four days everything will go away," she says.

"I wish it were different."

"It could be."

I know what she's thinking, because I've spent the whole day at the library thinking it, too, but I say, "Your world shouldn't be here. It's a mistake."

"Which means I'm a mistake."

"That's not what I meant."

"But it's true."

I say nothing.

"If you change things back," she says a few moments later, "you'll only be replacing one genocide with another."

This, too, I know. It's part of what's been brewing in the back of my mind, haunting me. "No matter what I do now, I will always be responsible for one."

She lays her head against my chest. "And you think it should be the one I'm part of?"

I run my hand over her hair and onto her back.

I don't know what the answer is.

CHAPTER TWENTY-ONE

The creaking of the floorboards wakes me.

I open my eyes to a sunlit room and the sound of birds. What's missing is the press of Iffy's body against mine.

From across the room, I hear a faucet turn, followed by the spray of water. A few moments later, I can see steam building in the bathroom through the partially open doorway. I lay my head back against the pillow and stare at the ceiling.

How is she going to feel about me this morning? How is she going to feel about the man who, in now three days' time, will help erase her world?

If I were her, how would I feel? What would I do?

In all honesty it's a wonder she hasn't called the police and had me locked up, in hopes that would stop what's coming. But of course she's smarter than that. If I don't make the change, the other rewinders will, so she knows there's nothing she can do.

The water cuts off, and soon Iffy exits the bathroom wrapped in a towel and running a toothbrush through her mouth. For the first time, I can see her tattoo is more than just birds flying over her clavicle. It extends down her side, the birds turning into a tiger's tail that continues under the towel.

"Good," she slurs through a mouth full of foam. "You're up. Take a shower and get ready. We've got things to do."

"What things?" I ask.

"No time for questions. Get moving."

Thankful that she's even talking to me, I make my way into the bathroom and do as she asks. When I finish, I find her already dressed, wearing blue jeans and a black top held up only by thin straps over her shoulders.

After I pull my clothes on, she picks up a small backpack and says, "All right. Come on."

"Where are we going?"

She smiles, then heads down the stairs without answering. I grab my satchel and follow.

In the kitchen we find Marilyn sitting at a round table with a man I haven't met yet. She wears a silky red robe and holds a steaming cup of coffee near her lips. In contrast, the man is dressed in a business suit, his hair perfectly combed.

"Look who's up early," Marilyn says. "Or is it you've not slept yet?" She looks at me, a coy smile on her face. "Hi, Denny. Nice to see you're still here."

"Good morning," I say awkwardly.

"Is this one of the new guys?" Iffy asks, nodding at the man.

He extends a hand. "I'm Reece."

"Iffy," she says, shaking with him. "Attic dweller."

"Nice to meet you. My partner, Stephen, probably won't be up for a while. He's a late sleeper." He turns to me and holds out his hand. "Reece."

"Denny."

"You an attic dweller, too?"

"Just, um, visiting."

Raising an eyebrow he looks me up and down, then turns back to Iffy. "Not bad. You should have him visit more often."

"Still to be determined," she replies. "Marilyn, I'm wondering if we could borrow your car."

"Sure. I'm not going anywhere today."

"Actually, I was hoping to keep it for a few days. Need to go on a small trip."

"Something wrong?"

Iffy shakes her head. "Just something I need to take care of."

"Well, as long as I have it back by the weekend, I guess that would be okay."

"Friday afternoon works," Iffy says, not adding that Friday afternoon will never come.

With a nod Marilyn says, "You know where the keys are."

"Thanks." Iffy grabs my hand. "Let's go."

"Have fun," Marilyn calls after us.

"Nice meeting you," Reece says.

This is my first time inside one of this world's personal motor carriages. Iffy tells me it's called a Prius and that it's a hybrid, running on both electricity and oil-based fuel she calls gas. The word is an odd choice, as I soon learn the gas is liquid and not, well, gas. In my world we call it petrol, which I'm pretty sure is the same thing.

"What are we doing?" I ask as we drive west on Hollywood Boulevard.

"Hold on. I need to concentrate."

She studies the numerous vehicles around us. Given that it's about seven in the morning, I assume the abundance of traffic is due to people heading to work. Iffy gives the wheel a sudden jerk, and we enter the lane next to us, which seems to be traveling marginally faster than the one we were in.

"I hate rush hour," she says.

Yet another term to add to my vocabulary list. "You were going to tell me what we're doing."

She checks the traffic once more before saying, "You've spent most of your time here sitting in a library. So I was thinking, if there are only three days of this left, then you should spend it actually experiencing my world. That way somebody will remember it."

The full weight of what she's proposing falls onto my already overburdened shoulders. To be both the eraser of her world and the one who remembers it—dear God, how will I ever be able to handle that?

A part of me wants to tell her to let me out now, to scream, "Please, no! I don't want to see any of it!" And grab my chaser and jump back to the meeting point in 1702. But I already know too much about her world, and there's no going back from that. Anything more I learn won't keep away the pain I'll feel when it disappears. That torture is already guaranteed.

"Okay," I say. "Show me."

◆ ◆ ◆

We stop at a place called Runyon Canyon and hike up a trail that was once a road. A lot of others are also doing this—some in groups, some alone, some with dogs, and some with baby carriages.

Iffy sets a fast pace but says little. After a particularly steep part, the road begins to level, but instead of continuing along it, she leads me onto a dirt path that takes us out on a bluff above the canyon. From here we can see the road as it winds back down the hillside. But that's nothing compared to the view we have of the city.

Los Angeles spreads out as wide and far as I can see, stopping only in the far west, where it meets the grayish-blue Pacific Ocean. I can see the buildings that make up downtown and smaller clusters of similar structures spread across the city.

"Does New Cardiff look like this?" Iffy asks.

"I've never been in these hills before, but no, it's not this large."

"I've only been here since last summer, but this is my home, Denny. This is where I live."

We stand in silence and watch the city for nearly half an hour before Iffy touches my arm and says, "Remember it."

"I will." *How can I not?*

We drive from Runyon to the beach area she says is called Santa Monica, where we park on a large pier and walk out over the ocean. There's an amusement park in the middle with rides and games, but all are closed until later in the day. We go out as far as we can and look back at the coast. From this vantage point, everything seems peaceful.

Around the edges of the pier, fishermen tend their lines. Most, though not all, have the darker skin and hair of those coming from the former Spanish possession in the Americas.

Iffy sees I'm looking at them. "Some come out every day. It's how they feed their families."

The same thing is true in my world. There might not be a state-sanctioned societal structure here, but there are certainly economic divides that serve some of the same functions.

We eat breakfast at a restaurant on the pier near the beach end, and then Iffy drives us down the coast a few miles before stopping again.

"We should really come here on a weekend afternoon when it's packed with people," she tells me as we get out, "but since there won't be any more weekends, now will have to do."

The day has grown warmer as noon approaches, and I have to squint to keep from being blinded by the sun.

"Welcome to the Venice Boardwalk," she says when we reach the beach.

The wide, concrete walkway runs along the edge of the sand, paralleling the ocean several hundred feet away. On the opposite side are all sorts of stores. Several are already open, while many others have yet to unlock their doors.

"On weekends you can't walk without knocking into someone."

I'm amused by a man and woman rolling by on shoes with wheels. Iffy tells me the footwear is called Rollerblades. Scattered along the beachside, people set up stalls where they sell oils and candles and paintings and other things.

"What's wrong?" Iffy asks when I stop in the middle of the walkway.

"Don't you have decency laws here?"

"What are you talking about?"

Trying not to be obvious, I nod toward a man and woman walking in our direction. The only difference in what they're wearing is the skimpy brassiere-like top the woman has on. The bright gold covering between their legs is barely big enough to hide anything.

Iffy snickers and says, "Don't stare."

I force myself to pull my gaze away.

"Thongs," she says.

"What's a thong?"

"Just wait."

As soon as the couple passes our position, Iffy turns to watch them walk away, so I do, too. The cloth in the front is only connected to a string in the back traveling up the crack of their butts. Their cheeks are out for all to see.

"That's legal?" I ask.

She shrugs. "In most states."

Once we continue walking again, Iffy nods toward a woman sitting at a portable table, a deck of tarot cards spread in front of her. "Want your future told?"

"No, thanks," I reply. I'm trying to forget the future for the moment.

"When it gets busier, street performers come out. Comedians, singers, contor—"

She stops midsentence and runs inside one of the stores. When I get there, she's purchasing a T-shirt from the clerk. When they're done with the transaction, Iffy shoves the shirt into my hands and says with barely controlled glee, "Put it on."

I start to unfold it so I can get a better look, but she stops me.

"No, no. Just put it on."

So I do. The shirt is dark gray, and when I look down at the front, I see a white cartoon dog wearing black glasses and a red bow tie.

"It's perfect," she says.

"Is it supposed to mean something?"

Her smile is a mile wide. "It's Mr. Peabody!"

"Okay, and . . . ?"

"And it's perfect." She grabs my hand. "Let's go."

At one point Iffy wants to rent Rollerblades and show me how to use them, but this is one idea I veto. As we're walking back to the car, we pass two men holding hands, heading in the other direction. I turn and watch them for a moment.

"Don't tell me you've never seen a gay guy before?" Iffy says.

"Gay?"

"Homosexual."

The word represents a taboo subject in my world. "You mean they're together?"

She shrugs. "Together for the moment, anyway."

"And they're allowed to walk around like that?"

"Not everywhere, but out here in LA, it's fine, and it's getting better elsewhere. The world's becoming more accepting. Why? Does it bother you?"

"It's not that it bothers me; it's just, well, I've never even met a homosexual before. No one I know has, either."

"I doubt that's true, and besides, you met one earlier today. Reece? Back at the house?"

"He's . . . a gay?"

"Just gay, not *a* gay. And yes."

"So his partner"—I try to recall his name—"Stephen. He's not a business partner."

Iffy laughs. "No. His boyfriend."

"And you're okay with that?"

"Who am I to tell someone who they can love?"

It's a good question. I've just never been in a position to consider it before.

Iffy loops her arm through mine. "Don't worry. You'd be fine with it if you were around it long enough."

Our afternoon is spent driving through neighborhoods and business districts. She doesn't tell me, but I know she's doing this to show me how people live. After the sun goes down, she parks along a deserted beach, and we lie against the windshield of Marilyn's vehicle, looking at the night sky.

"Satellite," she says, pointing at a dot of light traveling steadily across the sky. "You have those, right?"

"Of course we do."

She nods to herself. "Then you've put a man on the moon, right? We did it in '69. What year did you do it?"

"Nineteen sixty-nine? You're joking with me."

"Not at all," she says. "Neil Armstrong and Buzz . . . crap, I can't remember his last name." She thinks for a moment. "'One small step for man, one . . . giant . . . leap for mankind.' That's what he said when he put his foot on the surface. When did you all do it?"

I suddenly feel like I'm in a competition, and I haven't only lost but been humiliated. "We tried in '98. There was an accident, so we didn't go again. I think the Russians gave it a shot a few years ago, but as far as I know, they didn't make it, either."

"Huh. Okay. Weird."

Not so weird, I'm coming to realize. More a product of the society I'm from. In a corrupt world, all hands need their payoff. Even the Upjohn Institute, which I at first thought was above this, is driven by greed (*was* driven/might or might not be driven again).

We take a room at a place named Motel 6. According to Iffy we are in the city of Santa Ana in the county of Orange, which is a surprise to me. As far as I can tell, we have yet to leave Los Angeles.

"What do you think?" Iffy asks.

The room has two beds, but we're lying next to each other, neither of us wanting to be apart. "About what?"

"Everything we've seen today. Life."

"Your world's complex."

"And yours isn't?"

"It is. It's just . . . different."

"Is that good or bad?"

That's the big question, isn't it?

"It just is," I tell her.

The quiet that follows lasts for some time, and I begin to suspect she has fallen asleep until she whispers, "I don't want you to leave me."

It takes all of my will not to say, "I don't want to leave you."

I hope she thinks my silence means I've drifted off.

CHAPTER TWENTY-TWO

The next morning Iffy takes me to an amusement park called Disneyland.

I can say without hesitation, it's the most fun I've had on any single day of my life.

All I know are Iffy's laughter and smile. All I feel are her hand in mine and her lips on my lips. All I want is to be a part of . . .

. . . her life.

That thought again, sneaking out of its box. I'm in no mood to shove it back, and instead let it run wild while we race down mountains and splash down waterfalls.

We spend the night in the same Motel 6, falling asleep beside each other, still beaming from the day.

When we wake, only about twenty-four hours are left until Lidia's deadline, and the euphoria of the day before has been replaced by tension.

"You don't have to come with me any longer," Iffy says as we head to the car.

"I thought you want to show me things."

"I *have* shown you things."

"Where are you going?"

"Home," she says. "San Diego. I . . . want to see my family."

I slip my hand into hers and squeeze. "Take me with you."

❖ ❖ ❖

On the drive down the coast, I ask her about her family. She tells me her father left when she was young and her mother remarried a few years later.

"It worked out all right," she says. "My stepfather's not a bad guy." She thinks a moment. "Actually he's a good guy. I'm lucky I had him."

"And your mom?"

"Mom is Mom. A little clueless, but harmless. I could've been better to her. You know, moms and daughters, constantly fighting with each other. I guess it's not always true, but it was in our case."

"Any reason why?"

She shakes her head. "It's just what we always did."

The closer to San Diego we get, the less she says, and when we pass the city-limits sign, her lips seal tight.

After she exits the freeway and turns down a couple of streets, I begin to recognize the area from my trip into her past. When she turns onto her street, I notice that the knuckles on her hands have turned white from gripping the wheel too hard. I touch her shoulder, hoping to relax her, but she jerks away.

From the sideways glance she gives me, I can see she didn't mean to do it but couldn't help herself. I know what's going on. Her fate is becoming real for her, and she's trying to break away from me, trying to sever a bond already too thick to cut.

She parks near the spot where I saw her tear Ryan Smith's heart in two. After turning off the ignition, she stares out the front window before finally looking at me.

"I don't want you coming inside." Her eyes are watery, and her lip trembles slightly.

"If that's what you'd prefer."

"It is." She pauses. "You're sure? Tomorrow it all goes away?"

"That's their plan."

"And they can really do it?"

"Yes."

I sense there's another question she wants to ask, but the moment passes and all she says is, "Remember."

With a quick pull of the handle, she jumps out of the car and runs to the house.

◆ ◆ ◆

Where do I go? I don't know. I just walk.

Homes. Busy streets. An ocean breeze. Loud music drifting out the door of a bar. A couple pressed into a corner, kissing long and deep.

As much as I want to push everything away, I hear and see it all, my conscience not letting me ignore any of it. After all, this is the world that soon will never have been, many of its people the pending victims of my second genocide.

I walk from when the sun has yet to reach midsky to when it disappears behind the buildings to the west.

As the evening grows darker and I hear the distant sound of waves crashing on a beach, I begin to play the game. At least I tell myself that's what it is—a child's game of What-If?

What if I get to choose which world should stay, based not on my personal history but my observations of both?

First, I would admit that my knowledge of the world I'm currently in is woefully lacking. A week in a library and a few days wandering are hardly long enough to judge a whole civilization.

And yet, what if that's what I have to do?

Lists of pros and cons for each world begin writing themselves in my mind, and I compare and contrast. But all this does is confuse me.

Several times I have to remind myself this is just a game, that changing things back is a foregone conclusion.

A bell rings above the door of a tiny food store nearby as a mother and son exit. Heading toward me, the boy, no more than ten years old, opens the small package he's carrying, revealing a dark brown object. He takes a bite, and I see it's ice cream.

"How is it?" the woman asks.

"Great," the boy says. "Thanks, Mom."

My pace falters as a memory of my own mother hits me. My sister and I are in the kitchen, watching our mother make sugar bread. It must be near Christmas, because that's the only time we would have it. I'm seven, I think, and begging her for a taste of the dough.

It's a dance we do every year. She tells me no, that it's best when it's cooked, and I, unrelentingly, argue that the raw dough is better. Ellie eventually gets into the act, siding sometimes with me and other times with Mom. But like always, as my mother forms the loaves, she pinches off a couple small balls and hands one to each of us.

"Shh," she says. "Don't tell anyone."

◆　◆　◆

I reach the beach as the city behind me is falling asleep. I drop to my knees in the sand. My game of What-If is over, and I need to either accept what's coming or . . .

I hear the echo of Marie's voice. "If you're not true to yourself, this will kill you."

Moving down toward the water to where the sand is firmer, I walk parallel to the sea.

"Do what you think is right." Marie's words again, only this time it's my mother's voice.

What does she mean? Put things back the way they were?

"Do what you think is right," Ellie whispers.

"Fix it?" I say out loud. "I should fix it—is that what you mean?"

"What you think is right." My mother again.

I'm running now, hard and fast, my satchel slapping against my back. But I can't outrun the voices.

"What *do* you think is right?"

I stumble to a stop and rest my hands on my knees as I suck in air. I know the voices aren't Marie's or my mother's or my sister's.

They're all only one voice.

Mine.

And there's only one reason they haven't stopped.

As my breath begins to even out, I know what to do. The only question is—

How?

CHAPTER TWENTY-THREE

I don't know what room Iffy is in. I assume she's still at her parents' house because the Prius hasn't moved from where she left it.

Seeing no other choice, I approach the front door and knock. Several moments pass before a light flicks on inside and I hear footsteps heading my way.

The door is opened by an older version of the man I saw in Iffy's past—her stepfather. He's wearing a wrinkled white T-shirt and short pants and doesn't look happy.

"Who the hell are you?" he grumbles.

"Denny. I'm, um, looking for Iffy."

"You mean Pamela?" I take it he's not particularly fond of Iffy's nickname.

"Yes."

"It's a little late, don't you think?"

It is late, though not for the reasons he thinks. I just hope it's not too late. "I'm sorry. I wouldn't have disturbed you if it weren't important."

"You're a friend of hers?"

"Yes. I'm the one who rode down with her from Los Angeles."

His already narrow eyes close some more. "She didn't mention traveling with anyone."

"Oh, well, uh . . ."

"Wait here."

The door closes, and the lock reengages. When I hear someone approaching again, the steps are lighter and hurried.

"It's okay," Iffy says from the other side of the door. "He's a friend."

I hear her stepfather say something from farther back in the house.

"Don't worry," she tells him. "It's fine."

She opens the door wide enough for her to slip outside and then closes it behind her.

"What are you doing here?" she asks.

"I just . . . I . . ." Suddenly all I was going to say to her seems self-serving. I have a plan now, but I'm scared I'll be stopped before I can pull it off. In a way it doesn't matter if I give her hope. She'll either see later I'm telling the truth, or wink out of existence without ever knowing otherwise. The problem is, *I'll* know.

"What is it?" she asks.

"I . . . wanted to see you one more time."

She hesitates before pulling me into her arms. "I'm glad you came back."

We kiss, soft and tender, and hold each other, the world—all worlds—disappearing around us.

Finally I say, "When I travel back, you're going to feel pain again."

"I know. But then it'll all go away."

Again I'm tempted to reveal what I'm planning, but I resist. I tilt her face toward mine and kiss her again. "I'm glad you were chosen as my companion."

"So am I."

◆ ◆ ◆

Nine a.m. is the deadline, so if I stay a second after that and one of the other rewinders has figured out when the break occurred, I'll cease to exist like everyone else. I could leave at any time, but I must go as close to nine as possible to give my plan the best chance of working.

I make it to 8:57 a.m. before my patience runs out. When I pull out my chaser, I don't set it to May 12, 1702, like Lidia instructed, but to several decades later.

More precisely, to 1775.

As I hit the "Go" button, I feel Iffy through the mist. I try to send her a message.

Everything will be fine. Don't worry. I'll make this right.

I can't tell if she hears me, but there is a peacefulness in our connection that wasn't there before. Four hops later, I'm standing in the field behind the Three Swans Tavern. According to the chaser, it's 8:10 p.m. and nine seconds.

I move over to the wagon farthest from the building, hunker down, and scan the area. If one of the other stranded rewinders has discovered when the break in history occurred, then one or more of them would be around, trying to make things right. The road and grounds around the tavern appear exactly the same as on my last visits, so I'm pretty sure I'm safe.

As I wait I keep looking over my shoulder in anticipation, but I remain alone. A check of the local time again shows it's 8:13 and thirty seconds, almost time. I turn my attention to a point only ten feet from my position. For several moments there's nothing but the field and the silhouette of the forest behind it. Then I see me, the me destined to create a twelve-second gap that will bring Iffy's world into existence. Or I should say, would have brought, if not for—

"Denny," I whisper. While I have seen myself before—in fact, this very version of me—I've never spoken to myself.

Other Me turns in surprise, his eyes widening even more when he realizes who called his name.

I wave him over and move to the side so he can crouch next to me. From here, no one can see us, which is especially important given that the scout version of me is still in front of the tavern and must never know what's going on.

Other Me eyes my shoes as he joins me. I've changed back into the same costume he's wearing, but my 1775-era shoes were misplaced somewhere in Iffy's 2015. I'm wearing the black sneakers I picked up while I was there.

"What are, uh, you doing here?" he asks. Here's a fact most people never think about: pronouns are tricky when talking to oneself.

"You can't go in the building," I tell him.

"Why not? It's an observation mission."

"I know. I've done this before. You can't go in there. Something . . . happens."

"What?"

"Everything will be fine if you stay out here. It's better if you don't know."

He looks toward the tavern and then back at me. "Did Johnston send you?"

"No. I . . . *we* figured it out ourselves. You can't talk about this to anyone. Not even Marie. No one must ever know. Trust me."

"Trust you."

We look at each other for a second and then smile the exact same smile.

"All right," he says. "If you're telling me I shouldn't, then I won't. But what about my mission? How am I supposed to verify if Cahill—"

"He's the one," I say. "In a few minutes, he's going to meet with a couple of British agents and receive orders to observe a rebel meeting, and then he'll report what he learns to the British." I pull the wooden box that caused all the problems out of my satchel and hold it out. "Here. Their conversation's recorded on this. You can use it as proof."

He takes it. "You're sure?"

"Would I lie to you?"

"Probably."

"True. But he's the one, all right. No lie."

"Okay. I'd feel better if I can at least reverify his arrival," he says.

"All right. We can do that. But give me your pipe box. You don't want to show up back home with two."

He gives me the box in his satchel. Together we then watch as Cahill rides up on his horse at 8:20 and disappears around the front of the tavern.

"What now?" Other Me asks.

"Now you go back and forget we ever talked."

He pulls out his chaser, but hesitates. "You really can't tell me what's going on?"

"Nothing's going on now. We fixed it."

He looks as if he's unsure, but with a nod, he disappears.

Step one is done. There's no going back now. While I should feel relieved, I only feel more stressed. There is still so much to do, including one more step here before I leave this night.

From my satchel I pull out my notes and check them. These are the same notes that Scout Me is recording right now. When I have memorized the two times I need, I put the notes back and input the appropriate jump into my device.

When I hit "Go," I move approximately twenty feet forward and ten to the left from my position behind the wagon, and travel back in time only a few minutes, to 8:14 and twenty seconds. My stay in the mist is no more than a blip, but even then I know Iffy is no longer there.

From this new position, I can hear the two other Dennys whispering behind the wagon. I check the time to make sure I'm in sync, and then start counting the seconds as I walk toward the front of the tavern.

I'm a little worried about the shoes. Not so much about anyone from the past seeing them, but more about Scout Me seeing them. It's dark, though, and the shoes are black, so I'm hopeful he won't notice. Besides, there's nothing I can do about them.

I reach the tavern door right on cue at 8:14 and fifty-three seconds. Inside I take a seat in the corner as far as possible from where Cahill and his friends will be sitting. I have a moment of panic that I won't be able to pay for my meal, but then find a Spanish dollar at the bottom of my satchel.

For the next half hour, I pretend to eat my stew while ignoring Cahill and his friends. When he finally leaves—at his original time, not after the twelve-second delay—I wait for a few minutes, pay the woman, and leave at 8:51 and eleven seconds.

As far as Scout Me knows, everything is fine.

It's time to move on. But not to 1702. Not yet.

I set my chaser for a series of jumps that will end on the day before I left Iffy's world, at 9:00 p.m. Before I hit "Go," I see that the power level has dropped to nearly 7 percent. Already down 30 percent from what I had in Iffy's world, and I still have a lot of jumps to make. Hoping the battery lasts, I press the button.

The first sign I get that my chaser is trying to reconnect with my companion is on the final hop to my home time. I meant to disconnect before I made the jumps but totally forgot, which means I'm heading for the institute and not for the cemetery in New Cardiff. I'll have to disconnect right there on the return platform as quickly as possible and jump again. If I'm not fast enough, I'm done for, and all my planning will have been for nothing.

But then I realize something's wrong. The connection with Palmer is fading in and out.

For a microsecond, I see a flash of the inside of Upjohn Hall, but then it's gone, and I materialize in the middle of a busy road.

Carriage alarms ring out, and the beams of headlights swing back and forth as drivers swerve around me. The nearest curb is to my left, so I zigzag through the traffic until I reach safety.

Where am I? I wonder as I catch my breath. Obviously not the institute, and not my mother's grave, either.

I definitely am in a city, and from the lamppost banners celebrating the king, I gather I'm somewhere in the Midlands.

Chicago, maybe?

No, it's too warm for late March.

At least I'm far from New York, and that's all that really matters.

I pull out my chaser and physically disconnect it from Palmer. As I do, I realize what must have happened at the end of the jump. There are *two* of me here in 2015, me and the version I stopped from entering the tavern. That means until I just disconnected my chaser, Palmer was being pulled on by two devices. He would've had a full connection to the other before I showed up and wouldn't have been able to fully control us both.

I check the power supply—5.62 percent. It's going to be close. Shoving the chaser in my bag, I take a look around.

Because of the late hour, the only shop I see open is a fueling station down the road. Unlike the one where Iffy and I filled up on our trip to San Diego, the stations in the empire sell few things that aren't vehicle-related.

I head toward it anyway, hopeful I'll find what I need. On the way I pass a carriage parked under one of the streetlamps and am able to read the tax sticker in the window. Printed at the bottom is "Louisiana," which means I'm somewhere in the Gulf region.

Through a break in the traffic, I run across the road. When I reach the far curb, I hear voices behind me and turn to look. Three men are standing in the halo of one of the lights a little more than a block away. I start to swing back around but then freeze.

Where three men were standing a second before, there are now four.

No, five.

Time travelers. But not rewinders.

They're too far away for me to be sure, but they look like they're wearing the institute's security uniforms.

I crouch behind a parked carriage and move around the front end so I can peek at the men.

They must have figured out via Palmer where I diverted to and have come for me. But instead of looking around, they're just standing there in a loose group. The reason soon becomes clear when a sixth man arrives.

Sir Wilfred. Head of security.

He gathers the men around him and begins pointing in several directions, his voice loud enough for me to hear his anger but not his words.

My hand slips inside my satchel and onto my chaser before I realize what I'm doing. When I do, I jerk my hand back out, empty. I can't risk making a jump yet. My device is dangerously low on power, and I still have much to do.

I glance toward the fuel station. It won't be easy, but I think I can get in and out and jump before Sir Wilfred and his men ever catch sight of me.

Staying low I move back to the walkway and hurry to the station. The business is surrounded by a wide, well-lit paved area. When I reach the edge, I pause to check on the security team.

At first I don't see any of them, but then I hear the sound of steps and am able to pick out two shadows down the street on the other side, heading slowly in my direction. I scan for the others but don't spot them.

I move around the corner and hasten down the edge of the lot, away from the street. When I'm directly opposite the fuel station's main building, I take a breath and head across. My instinct is to run, but I know doing so will draw attention so I keep my pace slow and steady.

As I open the door, a bell dings twice. To me it sounds like a giant church bell yanked hard by a dozen men, and I can't help but cringe as I hurry inside.

There's just enough room in the customer area for a few shelves of fluids and replacement parts, and a counter behind which sits an old, bored-looking man.

He eyes me for a second, taking special interest in my centuries-out-of-date clothing. "May I help you?"

"Newspapers?"

He nods across the store. There I find bins for three papers—the *Louisiana Chronicle*, the *St. Louis Sentinel,* and the *American Times.* The two regional papers will provoke unnecessary questions, but the *American Times* is a territory-wide paper and exactly what I need. The problem—its bin is empty.

"Are there more?" I ask, pointing at the bin.

The clerk takes his time looking over. "Any more what?"

"*American Times.* Do you have any more?"

"Not if it's empty."

I walk over. "You're sure? You don't have anything in the back?"

He stares at me, annoyed. "I'm sure."

I look out the front window and see two security men turn onto the fuel-station property and head for this building. Their pace is deliberate as they scan side to side.

I look back at the clerk and notice the door along the back wall on his side of the counter. "Where does that go?"

"What?"

"The door, where—"

I stop myself as I catch sight of the corner of a newspaper sticking out of a rubbish bin against the wall. On the visible part, I see the beginning of a familiar masthead: *Amer . . .*

I point at the bin. "Can I have that paper?"

As he looks to see what I mean, I take a quick glance out the window. The men are halfway across the lot now. I have maybe twenty seconds at most.

"What? That?"

"Yes! Please, can I have it?"

"Hey, settle down."

I feel the seconds ticking off in my head and know I have no time to argue with this idiot. So I hop over the counter, but as I step toward the bin, the clerk blocks my way.

"What the hell do you think you're doing?"

He pushes me back, reaches under the counter, and pulls out a three-foot-long club. Raising it, he says, "Get out of here!"

With the institute's security men only seconds away, I whirl and open the door behind the counter.

"Hey, you can't go back there! That's not a public area!"

Before he finishes speaking, I'm through the door and into a back room that's twice the size of the one out front. There are shelves full of stock but more importantly, another door.

As I reach the exit, I hear the clerk coming into the room behind me. I undo the lock, turn the knob, and rush outside. I know I'm not free yet, but I also know Sir Wilfred and his men will never know I was in the fueling station. If they ever learned that, at least one of them would have made a time jump and been waiting for me as I opened the outside door.

It's a weird cat-and-mouse game that can bend your mind in ways it was never meant to go. A snake eating its tail. But if I don't stay vigilant, they *will* find me.

In the alley off to the left, I see several shadows of varying shapes protruding from the back of the buildings. Hoping one might provide a place to hide, I head in that direction. As I near, I realize the shapes aren't part of the buildings themselves, but the tents and huts of a small vagabond camp. Most of the occupants seem to be asleep, but two men sit by a fire burning in a can off to the side.

I get an idea and work my jacket off.

"Stay warm," I whisper as I walk by, tossing the jacket to the oldest guy. If this delays my pursuers even a few seconds, it's worth it.

I peek over my shoulder and am relieved to see no one has followed me into the alley yet. So far so good, but I don't allow myself to slow down. Not far past the camp, I come to a group of large rubbish bins and decide they'll do the trick. I tuck in behind one of them and wait.

Two minutes pass. Three. Four.

No one comes.

I'm about to continue down the alley when it occurs to me that if there was a copy of the *American Times* in the small bin at the fuel station, there's a very good chance I'll find another copy in one of the much larger bins around me.

The dim light of the alley hinders my search but doesn't prevent me from finally unearthing a copy. It's from two days earlier, and there's a stain on the front corner, but it'll do.

I climb out of the bin and brush myself off. But as I start to lift the flap of my satchel so I can grab my chaser, I hear Sir Wilfred's voice.

"Mr. Younger, you're a long way from the institute."

CHAPTER TWENTY-FOUR

I had no idea until I'm manhandled into the basement of Upjohn Hall that the institute has actual prison cells. Mine is a small stone room barely large enough for the mattress on the floor and the toilet in the corner. The door is constructed of thin plastic, which can be turned either opaque or transparent by the flip of a switch on the other side.

I know this because after shoving me in, the guard watches me through the closed door until I pull myself to my feet. When I do, he touches the outside wall, and the door becomes a solid wall of black.

I stand there, staring at nothing.

I have failed.

Completely and utterly.

The moment the other rewinders who survived the changing of worlds show up here, the institute will know everything, and I will surely be put to death. It's a fitting sentence for erasing two worlds, albeit one was reinstated.

Iffy.

I've taken from her the experience of life, and yet, if I close my eyes, I can still feel her arms around me.

Remember.

The Los Angeles Central Library. Marilyn's house in Hollywood. The pier in Santa Monica. The Venice Boardwalk. Disneyland. Iffy's parents' home in San Diego.

I know it's all gone.

I'm lying on the mattress when the surface of the door clears again, revealing Sir Gregory and several security men standing behind him.

"Good morning, Denny."

Morning? I've been here overnight already? I don't remember sleeping, but then again, I don't remember much of anything since arriving except the horrors playing through my head.

"Please get up and come with me."

I rise, pretending I haven't heard the tone of disappointment in his words.

"I need to use the toilet," I say.

"No one's stopping you."

I wait a second, expecting the door to go opaque again, but it remains clear. So I relieve myself in full view, the humiliation another deserved element of my actions.

The door opens as I approach, and I'm surrounded by security. Sir Gregory leads our group through several basement corridors to a white door with a red light above it.

As he opens it, he says to me, "Go in and take a seat, please."

There are two tables in the room. At the farthest sit Lady Williams and Sir Wilfred, both on the same side. A third chair is next to them, but I know this is not the empty chair I'm supposed to take.

That chair sits at the other table, facing the two institute leaders. There are two empty chairs side by side. Perhaps Sir Gregory is to sit next to me.

My security escort walks me over to the empty chairs, and one of the men indicates I'm to take the chair to the right. As I do, Sir Gregory heads over to join his two colleagues.

After we are all settled, all lights but the ones aimed at my table dim.

The three lean together and whisper among themselves, making me feel as if they've forgotten I'm here, and I think if not for the guards standing a few feet behind me, I could just get up and leave.

I'm entertaining this fantasy when Lady Williams says, "Denny Younger. You have been with us for just under eleven months, is that correct?"

My mouth is suddenly dry. "Correct, Lady Williams." My voice sounds like it's been dragged across the desert and stomped on by a thousand feet.

"You are from . . ." She looks at a paper in front of her. "New Cardiff."

I nod, not sure I can get another word out.

"An Eight." It's hard to see, but I think she shoots a quick look at Sir Gregory.

I nod again.

She studies the paper some more. "You had a remarkable test score. One of the best we've ever seen."

In any other circumstances, I would feel proud, but not here. Not now.

"And your training reports—stellar also."

I remain silent.

"Mr. Johnston reports that your fieldwork has been all we could hope for, and only a week ago, submitted the forms requesting you be promoted from junior status and allowed to work on your own." She leans back. "From all of this, I would assume you're familiar with institute procedure and policies. Am I wrong to think that?"

I spread what saliva I have around my mouth and say, "No, you're not wrong. I'm very familiar."

"Then tell me, why were you outside the walls of the institute?"

"I, uh, I . . ."

Sir Wilfred leans forward. "Was there a problem with your chaser?"

"Um . . ."

"Were you traveling unlinked?" he asks.

"No. No, I wasn't," I reply truthfully.

"So why didn't your companion home you in here?"

The only thing I can think to do is shake my head.

"Could it be because your companion's attention was divided?"

They know the answer, so there's no reason for me to reply.

Sir Wilfred motions to one of the men behind me. I hear the door open, and more people enter. When they're almost to the table, I look over and see three guards and one prisoner.

Me.

I'm not shocked, but my other self clearly is. He freezes next to the empty chair and stares at me. He finally tears his gaze away and looks toward the other table.

"What's going on?" he asks. "What is this?"

"That's what we're trying to figure out," Sir Wilfred says. "Mr. Younger, please take a seat."

As Other Me sits, he keeps glancing in my direction as if I'm a ghost.

"To avoid any confusion," Lady Williams says, "we will refer to you as Younger A." She looks at me, then turns her gaze on Other Me. "And you as Younger B. So, which of you wants to tell me why there are two of you here?"

"I have no idea," Other Me says. "I . . . um, there's no—"

He must realize I'm the Denny who stopped him outside the Three Swans Tavern and sent him back here. I poke his thigh and hold my hand out flat where only he can see, hoping to shut him up. It seems to do the job. For the moment.

My life might be sacrificed, but I still have the chance to save his. It's a long shot, but if he can play the dummy, he might be able to ride it out, and I will have survived. Not the me that knows Iffy and her world, but a version of me nonetheless. That seems worth fighting for.

"I'm waiting," Lady Williams says.

Sir Wilfred growls, "If you don't want to voluntarily tell us what happened, we *will* find out another way."

From the looks on their faces, I can tell they have no idea what occurred. Which means none of the others have returned yet. I can use this to my advantage.

"He doesn't know anything," I say, nodding to my double. "It's my fault. I'm the one who shouldn't be here. I created a break but was able to fix it without him knowing."

Other Me's right leg begins to bounce softly. It's a nervous tick I get sometimes when I'm stressed.

Just hang on. I'll get you out of this.

"Is that right?" Sir Wilfred says. "And what was this *break?*"

I need to be careful. The only power I have is the information in my head, and until I'm sure Other Me will be okay, I need to be judicious about how much I share. "I unintentionally affected the time line of a subject I was observing."

"That's amazingly vague," Sir Wilfred says. "How about you fill in the details?"

"I will, but only under certain conditions," I say with far more confidence than I feel.

"Conditions? This isn't a negotiation. You are in no position to—"

"Sir Wilfred, I'm very clear about my position. I will never leave this level alive." I stare at them, daring them to contradict me, but no one does. "Here are my conditions. One"—I gesture toward Other Me—"he's immediately released. Two, he is in no way to be punished for my actions. He knows absolutely nothing about this and should not pay for something he didn't do. And three, he's given the free choice to either stay here and continue as a rewinder or return to New Cardiff and be placed in a position appropriate for his status as a Five."

For the first time since he retrieved me from my cell, Sir Gregory speaks, his voice surprisingly calm. "You understand, Denny, um, A, that we can't just take your word that he wasn't involved."

"Sir Gregory, those are my conditions. Once they're met, I'll tell you absolutely everything."

"I find your attempt to save what amounts to your own skin comical," Sir Wilfred scoffs. "What you have to tell us will unlikely be worth giving you anything."

I lean back in my chair and look each of them in the eye. "All right. Fair enough. I'll tell you this much. For a while this world vanished. No empire, no institute, no time travel, nothing you know. And then I brought it back. I could make it happen again, too. Good enough for you?" I push my chair back and stand, defiant. "Let him go, and I'll tell you the rest."

Sir Wilfred's face turns red. "You are a prisoner here. You don't tell *us* what—"

Lady Williams places a hand on his arm. "Sir Wilfred, if I may."

"Of course," he says quickly.

When she looks at me, I can see she's trying very hard to hold back whatever it is she's feeling. It's not anger, though, more like . . . excitement. "Younger A, we'd like to discuss the matter among ourselves. If you don't mind, I think it would be best if we pick up this conversation later."

"You're in control," I say.

The corner of her mouth ticks up. "I wonder if that's true."

◆ ◆ ◆

Other Me and I are escorted back to the cellblock. As we walk he whispers a question only I can hear. "It was you at the tavern, wasn't it?"

I see no reason to reply. He knows the answer, just like he knows I'm the key to his survival.

I spend the rest of the day alone in my cell, pacing. Every minute could be the one when Lidia and the others return, ruining everything. When I finish with my dinner, I lie on my mattress, hoping to fall asleep, but it's impossible. I can't stop thinking. Ways on how to ensure that Other Me lives mingle with my now ruined plans. These, in turn, wrap themselves around memories of Iffy and my mother and Ellie and my time as a rewinder before it all went bad.

If I were coming at this fresh, if I were at that tavern and the twelve errant seconds occurred, given the choice of fixing it right then or doing what I've done, which would I choose?

I'm surprised the answer comes so quickly: exactly what I've done.

The only thing I regret since creating the mistake is being caught. Iffy's world, even with all its faults, is so much better than this.

I don't know how long I've been lying here when a voice whispers in my ear, "Don't move."

When I jerk in surprise, a hand touches my chest, not pressing down to confine me but lying softly, comforting me.

"Put your arms around me," the voice says.

Perhaps I should be scared, but I'm not. I wrap my arms around my visitor and find a small body, a woman's shape.

Gray mist, then dim light.

I'm no longer in my cell but in a room three times as large.

219

My visitor peels my arms off her back and pulls away.

Marie.

"Stay here," she says. "I'll be right back."

She vanishes, and returns a few seconds later with someone else in her arms. Other Me, also still wearing the clothes he had on during the interrogation.

After giving each of us a quick look up and down, she focuses on me. "Well, seems like you've been having fun."

"What's going on?" I ask.

"Yeah, what are we doing here?" Other Me says.

She raises an eyebrow. "Dealing with one of you was hard enough. I'm not sure I like this."

"I wasn't that—" I stop, realizing Other Me has been saying the exact same words I am. We look at each other.

"That was kind of creepy," he says.

"Agreed," I reply.

Marie focuses on me again. "Tell me what happened."

I've always been able to trust Marie, but maybe it's my confinement that makes me say, "Why? So you can go back and tell Lady Williams?"

"Do you really think I would do that?"

I don't, but my defense is still up. "Why do you want to know?"

"Because maybe I can help."

"I'm already taking care of it," I say.

"Yeah, by sacrificing yourself to save me," Other Me says.

"I'd love it if I were in the position to save myself, but I don't think that's an option," I tell him.

Other Me looks around. "Well, we're not in our cells now, so it seems to me all options are on the table."

He's right. I turn to Marie. "Where are we? Can we leave? Is there any way I can get my chaser?" Maybe I can actually finish my plan, but I'll need my device to do that. All my location coordinates are stored in it.

"Relax," she says. "We should be safe here. This is a storeroom that hasn't been used in years, out by the stables."

Instead of calming me, this increases my anxiety. "We're still on institute grounds?"

"If I try to take you beyond the walls, chances are greater we'd be discovered. Here I can unlink and hop without anyone knowing. Besides, no one's looking for you yet. We're three days in the past."

"So we *can* leave," Other Me says.

"I want to know what happened first," she says, her eyes on mine. "I'm your friend, Denny. I'm not going to use this information for anything other than helping you. And the last people I would ever tell are Lady Williams and Sir Wilfred."

I believe her, but am still not sure I should say anything.

"I know about the offer you gave them," she says after a few moments. "I know you've said that whatever happened created a whole new history."

"How do you know that?" I ask.

She starts to open her mouth, but the answer comes from behind us.

"Because I told her."

Both Other Me and I turn as Sir Gregory steps out from behind a stack of boxes near the far corner.

Whipping back around to Marie, I say, "You *did* sell me out."

"She did nothing of the kind," Sir Gregory counters as he joins us. "Your little tidbit of erasing this world is something you should have kept to yourself. They're curious now about what took its place."

"Don't you mean *you're* curious?" I say.

"Of course I am," he says, "but not for the same reasons Lady Williams and Sir Wilfred are. Don't you see the potential of what you've handed them? If what you say is true, then you've found a switch. Turn it on and our world is gone; turn it off and it comes back, fully intact." He pauses. "It is intact, isn't it?"

"It's the same," I say. "It has to be."

"So you *have* found a switch."

I don't reply, but the description is accurate.

"Do you see the power that controlling this switch would give someone? He could steal whatever he wants from one world and bring it to the other and be the richest person in both. And you have just planted that seed in the minds of two of the greediest people in the empire. I can't let them have it."

"But you're part of the institute, too," I say. "You're one of the leaders."

"Denny," Marie says.

Sir Gregory raises his hand a few inches. "Your point is taken, Denny. If I'd known the full extent of what they've been doing, I would have never accepted the position."

"And you'd still be in your cells," Marie says.

"I have a question for you," Sir Gregory says to me. He returns to the boxes he was hiding behind and picks something up off the floor. When he comes back, he's carrying my satchel. "What happens if I give this back to you?"

"Is my chaser in there?"

"It is."

I take a few steps toward him and hold out my hand, but he keeps my bag out of my reach.

"Answer my question first."

There's no reason for me to lie. "I'll erase this world and never bring it back."

"I thought as much," he says, still keeping my satchel out of reach. "Is this other place so much better than here?"

"It's not perfect. But, yes, it's better than here."

Sir Gregory tosses the satchel to me.

I look inside. Everything is there. My chaser, my clothes, some money, even the newspaper I pulled out of the bin.

"I think it might be better if we don't know when and where the switch is," Sir Gregory says. "That's something you should always keep to yourself."

"You know what it means if I go," I say.

"I do."

"But why would you—"

"Humanity's been on a downward spiral for over a hundred years," he says. "I and a few others have been fighting as best we can, but we'll never turn the tide. You, though, have found the answer I've been hoping for."

"You mean you've been waiting for something like this to happen?"

"Not waiting, more like dreaming." He pauses. "You're wasting time. You should go."

I look at the other two. Marie nods while Other Me looks scared.

As I retrieve my chaser and activate the screen, I say, "I can give you an hour's cushion before the change takes effect. Use it to jump back before . . ." I pause. Sir Gregory is right—it's better if I'm the only one who knows when the switch is, so a seventy-five-year cushion should be enough to prevent its discovery. "Before 1700. You'll be safe there."

I realize I'm not the only one who knows when the switch is. Other Me might not know the details, but he does know when it happened. But I trust him completely.

Sir Gregory holds out his hand.

"Good luck," he says as we shake. "I'm not sure I'd have the mental strength to do what you're doing."

I walk back to Marie. We hug.

"Will I see you again?" I whisper.

"Count on it," she says.

"Santa Monica Pier. June 20, 2015, at four p.m."

She looks at me funny.

"You'll figure out where that is."

When we release each other, I glance at my chaser's screen. The power level has gone down a couple hundredths of a percent since I last checked. I'm not sure it'll be enough to complete all I need to do. "Do any of you have a charger I can take?"

None of them do, so Marie says, "I'll fetch one and be right back."

But as she retrieves her own chaser, the population of the room suddenly triples. Most are security men, but right in the middle is Sir Wilfred.

"Denny! Go!" Sir Gregory yells.

Sir Wilfred spins around, looking for me, but my fingers are already depressing the emergency-escape combination. I'm now ten feet from where I was and fifteen minutes earlier.

I want to jump to my room and grab Other Me's charger, but I can't be sure Sir Wilfred's men won't already be waiting there. Instead, I quickly adjust the location and time and jump clear across the continent to the cemetery in New Cardiff, an hour and fifteen minutes ahead. This time pad will give Marie, Sir Gregory, and Other Me the extra hour I promised. I hope they're able to escape Sir Wilfred's men and use it.

As much as I don't want to look, I check the power level again and see it's dipped below 5 percent.

One of the functions of my chaser's calculator is to estimate energy use of an upcoming trip. The only other time I've used it was in my instruction room when Marie and I were going over the various functions. I'm scared to use it now, but I need to know if I'm going to have enough power to finish my plan.

Most of the jumps I have planned are of set lengths, so I have little to no margin to play with. I input these first and am shocked to see there's very little power left to work with. I then do calculations for two additional jumps.

The results are heart-wrenching. Making both jumps will be impossible.

I guess I should be happy that at least I don't have to make a choice between them. Only one will fit within the parameters of my remaining power, and even then I won't be able to go as far back as I'd like.

Since this will be my first stop, I enter the location number and set the date back eight years, pushing the time back as much as I dare.

CHAPTER TWENTY-FIVE

It's three in the morning when I appear in the empty lot down the street from my family's house. A few minutes later, I'm at the bottom of the steps that lead up to our door.

The house, like all the others around it, is dark. I can see the window of my room where twelve-year-old me should be sound asleep. There's also the window to my parents' room—well, my father's room, since at this point it's been a year and a half since my mother passed away. Neither of these is the room I'm interested in, though.

I carefully move around the side of the house until I can see the window of my sister's room. Using the location calculator to home in on the hallway outside her door, I make a jump of thirty seconds.

The floor creaks as I appear so I hold my position, fingers hovering over the escape combination in case my father decides to check out the noise. When all remains silent, I pad quietly into Ellie's room.

The strongest memory I have of Ellie is of when she was fifteen, not long before she died, with hair chopped short, her skin ashy-white, and bones showing everywhere. She's asleep on the hospital bed, and I'm sitting on the mattress holding her hand. Father is by the window, looking outside as the doctor finishes his prognosis.

"The truth is, Mr. Younger, there's little else we can do here," he says. "Home would be the best place for her now."

My father says nothing, so I decide to speak up. "But there are treatments. I've read about them in the paper. I even found a book at the library that—"

Looking embarrassed the doctor says to my father, "If you have any questions, you can always contact me."

"I have questions," I say.

"Denny. Quiet," my father orders. "Thank you, Doctor."

After the doctor is gone, I say, "But there *are* treatments. We can—"

"Not for us," Father says. "Pack your sister's things. We're going home."

If we'd been Fives like I am now, it would have been different, but we were Eights, and our options were limited to waiting for her to die.

Tonight that day is well over a year away, and she lies before me with her hair still long and her face full of the promise of the beautiful woman she should have become.

Tears roll down my cheeks as I stare at her.

My God. It's her. My sister, alive.

I ache at the sight of the pills on her nightstand that help her sleep. The illness that will waste her away has started to move in. I hoped to come before that happened, but the chaser's lack of power meant this was as far back as I dare go. Still, the disease is in its early stages. I know from the research I've done on the subject after reading about the medical documentary that there's an excellent chance it can be stopped. But not here. Not in this world.

I grab the pill bottle and shove it in my pocket. After prepping my chaser for the automated series of hops to the next destination,

I kneel next to Ellie, gently wrap her blanket around her, and then climb in beside her. She stirs slightly as I put my arms around her but doesn't wake.

"Everything's going to be fine," I whisper, and then we jump.

◆ ◆ ◆

The last hop takes us into the copse of trees about a hundred yards from the Three Swans Tavern, where everything started.

"What's going on?" Ellie mumbles, her lips barely parting.

Wincing from my post-trip pain, I whisper, "Just sleep."

"Dad, my head hurts."

Dad? Does my voice really sound like his? "Hold on." I remove one of her pills from the bottle and slip it between her lips. "Chew it up, then rest. I'll return soon."

I wait until she drifts back to sleep, then I leap even further back in time.

CHAPTER TWENTY-SIX

Lidia's instructions were to be at the meeting point in 1702 at noon, but wanting to give myself some extra time, I've set my arrival for 10:00 a.m. As an added precaution, I've also adjusted my location to materialize a quarter mile away, just in case any of the others are already there.

Despite my jump-induced migraine, I force myself to look around to make sure I haven't been observed, given that I've arrived in daylight. But I'm in a forest, and the only other living things around are the birds calling to one another.

Satisfied that I'm safe, I allow the pain that's built up over all my hops to run its course. Once it passes, my first order of business is to get out of my colonial outfit and change back into my 2015 clothes. I grab a black T-shirt, but then see the Mr. Peabody shirt Iffy bought me, and I don that instead.

As I start to lose myself in thoughts of her, I force myself to focus. I need to stay sharp, and thoughts of a nonexistent Iffy aren't going to help. Ready now, I sling my bag over my shoulder and head through the woods to the meeting point.

The actual site turns out to be a meadow, not unlike the one Marie met me in, and makes me wonder if choosing places like this is part of some kind of advanced training seasoned rewinders receive.

So far, no one else is here. Instead of walking out into the meadow, though, I choose a spot under the cover of the trees to wait.

Bernard is the first to arrive, appearing at exactly 11:40 a.m. He's a tall man, thin but muscular, and if he's feeling pain from his trip, he's hiding it well as he scans the area. I have never seen him without a serious look on his face. This time is no exception.

At ten minutes to noon, two others show up, both women I don't recognize. Bernard clearly does, though, and comforts them while they work through their trip trauma.

A trainee I know named Cole winks in with his supervisor, a man I believe is called Morris. Then Lidia shows up two minutes later, and I'm happy to see she's as affected by her jump—if not more so—than I was by mine. Her appearance tells me she lied and didn't leave at the deadline like she said she would. Each of those arriving must have left Iffy's 2015 before I did, or they would have been erased when I changed everything back.

As it approaches 11:55, I decide it's time to make my appearance. I adjust the newspaper so that a portion of it sticks out of the flap at the back of my bag. When no one is looking in my direction, I slip out from the trees and stand at the edge of the meadow, my hands to my head.

Bernard sees me first and waves me over. Slowly I walk to the group, making sure the pain I'm projecting is appropriate but less than what Lidia experienced.

When noon hits, there are eleven of us, a few still suffering from the effects of their trips, but most have recovered. Bernard appears concerned as he takes another look around the field.

"They should have been here by now," he says.

"There are others?" someone asks.

Bernard turns back to us. "Four more." His gaze locks on Lidia. "You *did* give them the right time, didn't you?"

This is the first time I've ever seen Lidia look scared. "I did," she says defensively.

"And you stayed until the deadline?"

"Yes."

Liar, I think.

"There are others here I talked to," Lidia says quickly, then glances at me. "Obviously I gave you the right time."

I nod, but keep my mouth shut.

"Then where are they?" Bernard asks.

"I don't know," she replies. "Well, they're traveling without companions, so they could have arrived a little ways away, right?"

Bernard scans the woods. "We'll pair off, do a perimeter search. Lidia, you're with me."

If the missing rewinders left Iffy's world even one second after I did, then they'll never arrive.

"You. Denny, isn't it?"

I look toward the voice and see it belongs to a veteran named Carter. He was the last to arrive.

"Uh-huh," I say.

He waves for me to join him. "Let's go."

If I don't say something now, I will likely lose control of the situation. When I say, "Wait," the first time, there are too many other conversations going on for anyone to hear me, so I repeat it, louder.

This time I have their attention.

"I don't think they're coming."

"What are you talking about?" Carter asks.

"I . . . I . . ." *Come on. Just like you practiced.* "They must've not left on time and were trapped when"—I take a breath—"I fixed everything."

Stunned silence from everyone but Bernard.

He hurries toward me. "When you *what*?"

"I figured out when the change occurred," I said. "So I fixed it. That's what we wanted to do, isn't it?"

"You fixed it?" Morris barks. "You're telling us that everything's back the way it was?"

I nod.

"So you trapped the others back there?" Bernard says. "You erased them."

"I waited until the cutoff time," I lie. "I left right at the hour on the dot. Just like Lidia did. If I left early, she wouldn't be here."

I glance at her and see she's trapped by her lie. When the others look toward her, too, she says, "He must have waited." When they look away, though, the look she gives me is one of suspicion.

"If they didn't leave by the deadline, then it's their own damn fault," one of the women who arrived right after Bernard says.

Morris moves in until his face is only inches away from mine. "I don't care when you left. What I want to know is, who authorized *you* to fix anything?"

His breath is hot and rancid, causing me to take a step back. "I just thought, um, well . . ."

Bernard grabs Morris by the shoulder and pulls him away. At first I'm thankful, but then I see Bernard's anger has kicked in again.

"How did you find out when the problem was?" he asks.

"Lidia said I was supposed to see if I could figure out when it was," I say.

"Figuring it out is not the same as fixing the problem," Morris says over Bernard's shoulder.

"When did it happen?" Bernard asks.

"The problem? Um, it was during the American incident of 1775. One of their leaders was supposed to have been killed. What

I realized was that the man who turned him in was prevented from doing so."

"How?"

It's time for my next lie, one I spent hours thinking through after my last visit with Iffy.

"He was never born." The words sound false, but I hope I'm the only one who picks that up.

"And how did you figure that out?" Morris yells at me.

If Bernard weren't between us, the man's hands would probably be around my neck.

"Answer him," Bernard says.

"The era is kind of my specialty," I explain. "Late eighteenth and early nineteenth century. I've read a lot about it, so I'm very familiar with the period. When we ended up in that other time . . ." I pause, and then clarify, "the time that wasn't supposed to be—"

"We know what you're talking about," Morris says.

"Right. Of course. Well, clearly something happened to break North America from the empire. So I studied its history. The rebel movement is quickly squashed in our time, but here it's referred to as the American Revolution. So I knew that's when the break must have occurred."

"I figured that out, too," another rewinder said. "But I couldn't pinpoint the actual event that changed everything."

Two others added their agreement.

"But *you* found it?" Morris glares at me, as skeptical as ever.

"I told you, I know that part of history," I shoot back. "After Lidia visited me, I spent time writing down what I remembered, and then compared that to what their history was telling me. It took me a while, but I was able to narrow it down to a General George Washington."

"I've seen him," someone says. "He's on their money."

"That's right. He became their first president. But in our history, he's captured and put to death before their revolution can really get started."

"So what did you do?" Lidia asks. "Go back and kill him yourself?"

"Of course not. I'm not going to risk causing a bigger problem by getting directly involved. I'd read about his capture and knew he was turned in to the British Army by a colonist. At first I couldn't remember the man's name, but it finally came back to me. Richard Cahill. But there was no mention of that Richard Cahill during the American Revolution. I used their Internet. You know what that is, right?"

I see a few nods behind Bernard and Morris, but the two men look unsure.

"It's a worldwide digital network," I explain, "accessed through computers. I was able to find birth and death records from the eighteenth century. There was no entry for Cahill's birth. And before you say it, yes, I know, records from that era aren't always complete. What I did find, though, was a death record for a Susanna Cahill, and a note that she was with child at the time of her passing." With each word I speak, I gain confidence in my fabrication. "Her date of death coincides with the approximate time frame Richard Cahill would have been born. So I thought it would be smart to check in person, see if I could confirm she was his mother. Once I knew for sure, my plan was to come here, share what I learned so we could figure out what to do together. I didn't make the trip intending to fix anything."

"I assume you have a good reason for not following through on that," Bernard says.

I nod. "The first thing I did was witness her death. She was run down by a horse-drawn cart that got away from its owner."

"Doesn't sound unusual," Morris said. "How can that—"

"I watched again, this time to see what caused the runaway. What I saw was a rewinder crossing the street at the wrong time."

"What?" Bernard says as others gasp around him. "Which rewinder?"

I make a show of looking around at everyone before saying, "I don't see him here."

"Must be one of those who didn't get back here," someone suggests.

I don't counter this argument. My plan was to blame a fictional rewinder whom Lidia and Bernard were unable to find, but this works even better.

"You talked to them," Morris says, looking over at Lidia. "Did any of them seem suspicious?"

For a moment everyone focuses back on her, allowing me a second to regroup.

"I don't know," she says. "I wasn't with any of them that long."

"Who were they?" Carter asks.

"William Samuels, Brianna Paulson, Todd Meyers, and, um . . ." She pauses, thinking.

"Jared Hendricks," Bernard says.

"Right. Jared Hendricks."

"Meyers is a bastard," Carter says. "I wouldn't put it past him." The attention shifts back in my direction.

"Was it Meyers?" Carter asks.

"I don't know Meyers," I say truthfully. "And I'd never seen the rewinder who crossed the street."

"Then how could you have possibly known he was a rewinder?" Morris asks.

"I couldn't. Not at first. I followed him until he disappeared behind some buildings. When I got there, he was gone. So I time-hopped back a few minutes and hid. When he arrived, he pulled out a chaser and jumped."

Morris looks annoyed, obviously not expecting me to be so thorough.

"Why didn't you just jump here then?" Bernard asked.

"I almost did. But the fix seemed so simple, it didn't make sense not to deal with it. I hopped back to before the accident, bumped into the rewinder as he was about to cross into the road, and delayed him enough so that the cart went by before he continued on his way."

"You didn't tell him who you were?" Morris asked.

"I'm a *junior* rewinder," I remind him. "Would you have listened to me if I tried to stop you from doing something?"

From his expression I know he wouldn't have.

"But how do you know it worked?" someone else—Cole, I think—throws out.

I shrug. "Because I went and checked."

Everyone starts talking at once. Bernard finally gets them quiet and says, "What do you mean? You checked to see that this Washington was captured?"

"I went home, back to 2015. It's our world."

Everyone talks at once again.

"Quiet!" Bernard shouts.

As the murmurs settle, Morris says, "The institute?"

"That's where I went."

"And they sent you back here?" Bernard asks.

I nod. "To retrieve you. After debriefing me, of course." I look around. "If you don't believe me, check your chasers. They should be reconnected to your companions by now."

I pull my satchel around and open the flap as if I'm going to pull out my chaser. Instead, I "accidentally" flop the newspaper onto the ground. Bernard snaps it up and studies the masthead. When he looks back at me, he smiles.

"You *did* do it."

"Let me see that," Morris says, snatching the paper out of Bernard's hands.

Bernard claps a hand on my shoulder. "I'm very impressed. I apologize for doubting you."

"I'll be damned," Morris said. He turns and shows the paper to those behind him. "It's from home. From a couple weeks after we left."

"That's from the first day I was back," I say.

"How long were you there?" someone asks.

"Three days."

Morris turns to me, his anger also gone. "You have my apologies, too."

The paper gets passed around, and I receive thanks from the others. Lidia is the only one who seems less than impressed. Out of everyone here, she's the one most likely to see through me.

I feel a tinge of guilt when Carter says, "There's no reason for us to stay here any longer. I say we go home."

When the others enthusiastically voice their agreement, that guilt grows. But I've made my choice, and this is the only way I can ensure my plan doesn't get unraveled.

As the others pull out their chasers, I do so as well. Without fanfare they begin disappearing.

My finger hovers above mine, as if I'll depress it at any moment, but I'm only waiting for them all to vanish. Since they're all spread out, I don't actually see each person wink out, but within a few seconds, I'm the only one standing in the meadow.

I can't believe it. Two more jumps, and I will have done it. The only thing that can go wrong is if my chaser fails me.

With the power down to 2.23 percent, I enter my next destination.

CHAPTER TWENTY-SEVEN

I've visited the tavern so many times now, it almost seems like a homecoming when I arrive once more in 1775.

This time I hide behind the wagon closest to the tavern. Three minutes later the version of me that was here just over an hour ago in my personal time line sneaks up behind the other wagon, intending to stop the even earlier version of me from causing the twelve-second delay.

I move in behind him. As I know will happen, he looks over his shoulder in anticipation. When he sees me, he smiles.

"They believed you?" he asks.

I nod.

"What about Ellie and Mom?"

I look to the woods where I left my sister and let him draw his own conclusions, quite literally fooling myself.

With a satisfied smile, he pulls out his chaser and hands it to me. I enter the time and location for the same point in 2015 I jumped to after escaping the institute storeroom near the stables.

I hand the device back to him. "All set. Good luck."

"To you, too," he says, then hits the "Go" button and disappears.

The theory is that he will bond with me in transit. In truth I'm unsure what's going to happen to him. I certainly don't feel any different.

I wait until the original Other Me arrives in the field and heads, unhindered, for the tavern door. I don't dwell on the time mechanics behind the fact that I've not only stopped the mistake from happening, but now will stop myself from correcting the error. Going down that road is a sure path to insanity.

After Other Me is inside the tavern, where he'll delay Cahill, I hurry across the field into the copse of trees where I left Ellie. For her it has been less than ten minutes since I left, but for me it seems as if we've been separated a lifetime.

She's lying on the ground, sound asleep.

I want to wake her, tell her what I've done, let her know she's going to be all right, but there will be time enough for talk later. The truth is, she's not all right yet.

I start to crouch beside her, but remember there's something I should do first. I reattach the companion connections on my chaser. I don't know if it will reconnect with Iffy, but if it does, at least she'll know I'm on the way.

I hug Ellie like I did before and place my thumb on the "Go" button.

"Last trip," I whisper to her and press down.

◆ ◆ ◆

I hoped the chaser would link with Iffy, but Ellie and I are traveling rudderless. The last time that happened, I was on this same trip and ended up in the hospital for four days. This time I'm not taking it in a straight shot but three hops. So I don't throw up on arrival, but I am crippled by temporary agony.

Once the pain lessens enough, I take a look around.

I thought I set my location to the alley behind the building near Iffy's house that I'd used before, but we're in the middle of a park. Kids are running around on a playground several hundred feet away, while adults are sitting on benches, watching them. It's a wonder they didn't see Ellie's and my arrival.

I look at the chaser to check the information I entered, but the screen is dark. I press the power button twice before it comes back on, indicating a power level of under 1 percent. Before I can check the location number, the device powers down again.

Ellie sags against me, and I have to grip her around her back to keep her from falling to the ground.

"Ellie?" I say.

No response.

I move her head a few inches and see that her eyes are shut and her face slack. I press my fingers against her neck and check her pulse. Not as strong as I would like, but at least she has one.

I carry her to a nearby bench and lay her down. "Ellie?" I say, rubbing her hand. "Can you hear me?"

I'm so focused on her that a female voice makes me jerk in surprise. "Is she all right?"

I glance over my shoulder and see a woman with a toddler propped on her hip looking at us, concerned.

"I don't know."

"Is she sick?"

I nod.

"You want me to call an ambulance?"

That's exactly what needs to happen, I realize. "Please."

Others gather around as we wait for the ambulance, a few asking questions.

"Who is she?"

"My sister."

"What's wrong with her?"

"She's sick."

"What is it? The flu?"

I pretend I don't hear the question.

After a few moments, another person asks, "How old is she?"

I almost say fifteen, but that's how old she was when she died. "Almost fourteen," I tell them.

Ellie is still unconscious when two fire trucks and an ambulance pull up at the edge of the park. Several uniformed men hurry across the grass, two in front carrying plastic cases and two trailing with something to transport Ellie.

"If we could get everyone to stand back, that would be a big help," the first man to arrive says.

The crowd pulls back but doesn't disperse.

The man crouches down next to me and puts his hand on Ellie's wrist. On his sleeve is a patch that reads SAN DIEGO FIRE RESCUE.

This, more than anything, confirms we really made it.

"Sir, can you tell me what happened?" he asks.

"We were out for a walk, and she collapsed," I say.

"Any reason why that might have happened?"

"She's been sick."

"What kind of sick?"

"I . . . I . . ." I'm not sure how to respond. I think the disease that killed her is called cancer here, but I'd rather a doctor figure that out.

"It's okay," the man says. "Is she a friend?"

"My sister."

"What's her name?"

"Ellie."

The man leans closer to her. "Ellie, can you hear me?" When she doesn't move, he says, "Just hang tight. You're doing fine. We're going to check you out and get you some help."

Another uniformed man puts a hand on my shoulder. "Sir, I need you to back away so we can get her on the gurney."

"Oh, sure."

I watch from several feet away as they work on her before moving her onto the bed. Once she's secure, the man who asked me to move says, "Have you contacted your parents?"

I shake my head. I haven't figured out how to handle that issue yet.

"You can tell them she'll be at Scripps Mercy. I assume you'll want to go with us?"

"Yes. Please."

At the hospital others join us as Ellie is wheeled inside. They get information from the firemen and begin examining her as we move through a hallway and into a room full of medical equipment.

It's not long before I'm asked to step out. My instinct is to refuse, but I know I'll only be in the way so I relocate to the hallway.

A woman dressed all in blue comes out after about thirty minutes. "You're the brother?"

"Yes."

"Are your parents on the way?"

"Our mother's been dead for a while. And our father . . . just passed."

"I'm sorry for your loss." She pauses long enough for me to believe she means it. "You're the guardian, then?"

"Guardian?"

"You're over eighteen?"

"Yes."

"Are you the one in charge of your sister? Or is there another adult?"

Now I get it. "No other adult."

"Okay. There's some paperwork you'll need to—"

Paperwork is out of the question. "How is she?"

"Still unconscious but stable. The EMT said you mentioned she was sick. Do you know what she has?"

After stumbling on the question when the fireman—EMT?—asked me, I thought of an answer on the way to the hospital. "I'm not sure. I know it's not good." I frown. "I haven't been home for a while. Our father was taking care of her until . . ."

"He didn't tell you what she has?"

"He and I didn't really talk much."

She studies me for a moment, a tinge of suspicion entering her eyes. "Can you at least tell me who her doctor is?"

"I can find out."

"That would be helpful," she says. "There's a waiting room down the hall. Why don't you go down there? Someone will come in a few minutes with the forms we need you to fill out."

"Okay," I say.

When I reach the waiting room, though, I pass right through it and follow the signs to the exit. As much as I want to stay with my sister, my presence here will only cause problems. I'll figure out how to check on her later. For now she'll get the help she needs.

I almost expect to see Iffy sitting in Marilyn's Prius at the curb, waiting for me. But neither Iffy nor the car is there.

Using the money I kept in my satchel for when I returned, I take a bus to her neighborhood. It's nearing 2:00 p.m. when I finally turn onto her block. The first thing I notice as I approach her house is that the Prius is gone.

Maybe she did go to find me, and we crossed paths. Or maybe she has no idea I've returned and headed back to Los Angeles, thinking my story about the end of her world was a lunatic's fantasy.

I decide to check anyway.

243

A woman who has to be Iffy's mother answers the door. The eyes, the nose, the cheeks—they're the same as her daughter's. It's only their mouths that are different. Iffy has fuller lips that always seem one step away from a sly smile. Her mother's are thin and cut a flat line below her nose.

"Yes?" the woman asks.

"Is Iffy around?"

"You just missed her. She left about fifteen minutes ago."

"Do you know where she went?"

"I have no idea. Somewhere with her friend, I guess."

"Friend?"

Her eyes narrow slightly. "I didn't get your name."

"I'm Denny."

"Oh, *you're* Denny," she says as she reassesses me. "Hold on."

She disappears inside and returns a few seconds later with a slip of paper. "Her friend said to give you this. Said you'd know what it means."

I take the paper from her. On it is written a time, 4:00 p.m., and a location number—a *chaser* location number. I feel my skin go cold as I realize the handwriting matches that of the note Lidia gave me for the 1702 meeting.

I think back to the field as everyone was popping out to return to the institute and realize I didn't actually see Lidia leave.

The suspicion in her eyes—did she know I was lying and follow me somehow?

"They'll be back at some point," Iffy's mom says. "I'd invite you in, but I'm leaving to run errands soon, so . . ."

"It's okay. I'll find them." I try to look as relaxed as possible, but that's the last thing I feel.

As soon as she closes the door, I run down the street until I reach a small strip of land next to the road that's been turned into a minipark. A man is playing with his dog at the other end, but the rest of the area is empty. I sit on a bench that faces the road and pull out my chaser.

When I push the power button, nothing happens. It takes four more tries before the screen reluctantly comes to life. I bring up the location calculator and enter the number Lidia left for me. A map appears, pinpointing the spot. Unfortunately it's a map of my old world, so I can see the spot is right on the beach, but I can't tell how it relates to this reality.

Making my best guess at the coordinates, I try to make the jump, but the power shuts off again.

I swear under my breath, then jog over to the man with the dog. "Do you know the time?"

At the sound of my voice, the dog begins to run toward me.

"Jasper, come," the man says.

The dog halts between us, its eyes on me.

When the man repeats, "Come," Jasper returns to him. The owner then looks at his watch. "It's 3:05 p.m."

"Thanks."

I have less than sixty minutes.

I don't know what Lidia's plans are, but I can guess.

CHAPTER TWENTY-EIGHT

My plan is to catch a bus, but when I find one of the stops and ask a woman waiting there if I'm in the right place, she laughs.

"The only place this bus'll take you is north," she says. "You need to go west. To do that from here, you'll have to go south first, then transfer to the one going to the beach. Not sure of the number."

"How long do you think that will take?" I ask.

"Depends on how quickly the bus arrives. Maybe forty minutes. Could be an hour."

An hour? I need to find a different way. "Thank you," I say, and move off.

Half a block away, I see some people sitting in the patio area of a restaurant. I run up to the wooden railing that separates the patio from the parking area and yell, "I'm sorry to bother you, but can any of you give me a ride to the beach?"

Several people look over and then just as quickly return to their drinks.

"Please. It's an emergency."

A guy sitting at a table about ten feet away looks at me and raises an eyebrow. "The beach is an emergency?"

"I have to meet someone there at four. It's . . ."

As the man laughs, I realize no one here is going to help me.

I run down the street and spot a large parking area in front of a big store with a sign reading HOME DEPOT. There's a lot of traffic going in and out.

I concentrate on those walking back to their vehicles. The first person I ask looks at me as if I were crazy and hurries off before I can even offer what cash I have. Three more people react the same way.

Why won't anyone help me?

I whirl around, looking for my next target.

"Please," I say to a couple of guys who aren't much older than I am, "are you headed to the beach? I need a ride."

"Get lost," one of them says.

I'm about to turn away when the other guy says, "Which beach?"

"Straight west of here." I don't know what it's called, but that's where the point on the map was.

"PB?" he asks.

"Maybe. I'm not from here."

"Come on, Jerry. Let's get out of here," the first one says.

The other one—Jerry—still looks at me. "We can get you most of the way there. You'll have to ride in the back of the truck, though."

"I'm fine with that. Thank you."

His friend looks upset, and they fall into a whispered conversation as I follow them to their vehicle. Then Jerry nods at the open rear cargo area of a vehicle and says, "Get in."

I pull my cash out of my pocket. "Here. It's all I've got. Fifteen dollars. For your trouble."

"Keep it," Jerry says. "We're going that way anyway."

I sit with my back against the passenger cabin, sharing space with several boards, some round cans with thin metal handles, and a cloth tarp.

As the two guys deposit their bags next to the boards, Jerry says, "You'll have to lie down. If the police catch you back there, we're both going to be in trouble."

"No problem," I say.

I stretch out as best I can as they climb into the cab, and then we're on our way.

The vehicle seems to be in a constant state of agitation, and I feel every bump. Turns are another problem. If I don't brace my arm against the side, I'll slide around, something I learned quickly when my shoulder smacked into one of the cans.

All I can see are the tops of buildings and blue sky, but nothing can keep away the feeling that I'll be too late.

I don't know how Lidia got her hands on Iffy, but there's no question about why she took her.

To control me. And it's working.

The truck has stopped so many times that I don't even notice anymore, so I'm surprised when I hear one of the doors open.

Jerry peeks into the back. "This is as close as we can get you." He points to the left. "That way three blocks and you'll be there."

I hop to my feet. "Thank you so much."

My satchel bounces against my hip as I move to the edge. Before I climb out, I grab one of the coins I have inside and hand it to him. "Take this, at least. It's not much, but—"

"What is this?" he asks, turning it around.

I jump onto the street. "Eighteenth-century Spanish dollar."

"Are you serious?"

I nod. "Thank you again."

Before he can say anything more, I run off in the direction he pointed.

I don't stop until I reach the walkway at the landside edge of the beach. The location Lidia left for me can't be far. I look around, hoping something will stand out, but to the south there is only sand and more sand.

The view north is not quite the same. A couple hundred yards away, a pier sticks out into the ocean. Could that be it?

"Excuse me," I say to a man heading down the path. "Can you tell me the time?"

He pulls a phone out and looks at the screen. "A few minutes until four."

As he starts to put it back, I say, "How many exactly?"

"Um, six."

"Thank you."

Six minutes. Whether it's the pier or not, that's the direction I run in.

As the path nears the pier, it jogs to the right and slopes upward between two buildings. But I'm not paying attention to either structure. My eyes are locked on the arched entrance to the pier ahead. That's why I don't notice Lidia race out from in front of the building on the left until she throws an arm around me and jerks me to a stop.

"Hello, Denny," she says.

Before I can get a word out, the world disappears, and we're surrounded by the familiar gray mist. This lasts barely two seconds before we're on firm ground again.

Wherever we are, it's night, and given that nothing hurts, I know we haven't gone far in time. Probably only a few hours back to the previous evening.

I widen my eyes to help them adjust, but with only stars and no other lights around, it's taking some time for me to focus. The crashing waves tell me we're still near the ocean, but the ground is not sand, nor is it concrete like the path I was on. Grass, I think, or something similar.

Lidia removes her arm and yanks my satchel off me.

"Hey!" I say, twisting around and trying to grab it back. "That's mine."

"Shut up. You speak only if I ask you a question."

"Where are we? Where's Iffy?"

I see her hand a split second before it smacks into the side of my face.

"I told you to shut up!"

My cheek stings, but I refrain from rubbing it. "And I asked you where Iffy is."

I brace myself, ready to grab her arm if she tries to hit me again, but she doesn't. Instead, I hear the flap of my satchel open, then Lidia saying, "Huh. Well, that explains it. I was wondering why you didn't jump to where I was. You're out of power. Which means you've been doing a lot of hopping around."

I lunge at her, grabbing for the bag, but she whips it out of the way as she turns sideways. Unfortunately for her, this puts her rib cage in the direct path of my forearm. I ram it into her, and she stumbles backward with a loud grunt.

I realize too late I should have kept going and completely sub-dued her, but thinking that way doesn't come naturally to me.

Lidia, on the other hand, doesn't have that problem. As soon as she steadies herself, she kicks me squarely in the stomach. Doubling over I trip on something and land hard.

My hip aches, and I'm pretty sure I've scraped a chunk of skin off my arm, but I ignore the pain. I roll onto my side and tuck into a ball in case she lashes out again.

"Get up!" she orders.

I don't move.

"I said, get up!"

Her foot slams into the small of my back, shooting a whole new blaze of pain through me.

"On your feet, dammit!"

I don't want to feel her shoe a third time, so I gingerly move into a sitting position. As I put my hands down to push myself up, one of them hits the thing I tripped on. My chaser. It must have dropped out of Lidia's hand when I hit her.

"Hurry up," she says.

I start to pick up the device as I stand, but she steps forward and knocks it away.

She then wraps a hand around my neck, and I feel a knife press against the skin just below my ear. "Where are the others?"

"The others?"

"Bernard and everyone who was with us. Where are they?"

"I don't know."

She tightens her grip, and I start to choke. "Don't lie to me! You said you knew when the break occurred and you fixed it. But you never fixed it, did you?"

"I . . . can't . . . breathe."

She stares at me for another few seconds before easing her grip enough for me to suck in air again.

"Where are they?" she asks again.

"They went home."

"You're lying. You obviously never changed the world back. Where are they?"

I keep my mouth shut.

The metal tip pushes into my skin just enough to break the surface. "I know you know what's going on. I could see you were lying when we all met. That's why I only jumped into the woods. I wanted to see what you were going to do. When I realized that you waited to be last, I knew I was right. *What* happened to them?"

I counter with a raspy, "Where's Iffy?"

"Answer my question!"

I shake my head, not an easy thing to do with her fingers pressed against the bottom of my jaw. "I don't see her, you don't learn anything."

Neither of us moves. Finally Lidia lets go of me and takes a step back. "All right. I'll let you see her, and then you tell me what happened. If you don't, she's dead. Do we understand each other?"

I nod.

"Say it," she orders me.

"Yes."

"Good. Now don't move."

She circles behind me, and as she starts to put her arm around my waist, I realize we're about to jump.

"Wait!" I yell. "My chaser. We can't just leave it here."

Her arm hovers over my stomach for a second before she pulls it back. "Get it. But don't try anything. If you do I'll leave you here, and you'll never see your little girlfriend again."

Her warning is unnecessary. I'm not going to try anything, not yet, anyway. Seeing that Iffy's all right is the only important thing right now.

I retrieve my chaser and say, "I'm ready."

◆　◆　◆

It's still night, and like before, I feel no pain.

My eyes, having already adjusted to the lower light, have no problem seeing my surroundings now. There is no ocean here, only a wide plain of dirt and brush, with distant mountains on all sides.

The desert, I think, though I might be wrong. Though I lived close to it when I was in New Cardiff, I never visited it.

I listen for the sound of vehicles, but the only thing I hear is Lidia's footsteps as she backs away from me.

Motioning with her knife, she says, "This way."

I follow her across the dirt into a dry riverbed. Lying on the sand, pushed up against the bank, is Iffy, her hands and feet tied.

I sling off my satchel and set it and my chaser on the ground as I drop beside her. "Are you all right?" I shake her shoulder. "Iffy?"

Her eyes remain closed, and for a moment I think Lidia might have already killed her. It's only the rise and fall of her chest that eases my panic.

I twist around and glare at Lidia. "What did you do to her?"

Her lip arches in a sneer. "Just like I thought. You've lost yourself." She grunts in revulsion.

"How did you find her?"

"I didn't find her. She found me. Thought I would be you for some reason."

Lidia's chaser, I realize. Somehow it connected to Iffy. Now I know why mine didn't link with her when I came back.

Lidia raises her knife a few inches. "Where are the others, Denny?"

"They're gone," I say.

"Gone where?"

"I told you. They went home."

It takes a moment before the reality of my words hit her. When they do she rushes toward me like she's going to grab my throat again, but I jump to my feet and shove her back.

"What did you do?" she asks, her teeth clenched.

"I didn't lie when I told everyone I'd changed things back. What I left out was that I wasn't done yet."

Her expression darkens. "You bastard! You let them go back home, and then you, you changed it all to . . ." She looks around as if she's never seen anything so disgusting in her life. "To this?" Her gaze shifts past me to Iffy. "All because of *her*?"

My guilt feels like a set of clothes two sizes too small. I sent the others to the equivalent of their deaths. But I would do it again. It was the only way I could ensure my sister's and Iffy's survival. "I did what I had to do."

Those seven words push her over the edge. She leaps at me, knife flashing. Her anger has gotten the best of her, so her attack is uncontrolled. I'm able to push her weapon to the side and wrap my arms around her. In a heap we fall to the ground.

As soon as we hit, I roll to the side, but she pins me down with her knees. The knife is gone, but that doesn't stop her rage. Her hands seem to come at me from all directions—hitting, slapping, pulling.

"You're going to change it back, dammit! You're going to bring our world back!"

Her palm slaps against my ear, and suddenly all I can hear is ringing.

This actually helps me focus. When one of her hands races toward me again, I knock it away and shove her with all my strength.

She flies off me and lands in a heap.

I hop to my feet and move back to Iffy, intending to pick her up, but my eyes are drawn to a light nearby. The screen on my chaser is on. In the tumble one of us must have hit the power button, and it hasn't shut down again. When I see the power level at .88 percent, an idea comes to me.

Instead of grabbing Iffy, I grab the device and twist back around just as Lidia pulls herself to her feet. She twirls left and right, searching the ground before reaching down and snatching up the knife.

With a roar she starts toward me.

I shove my chaser out in front of me and yell, "Stop, or I'll smash it to pieces, and we'll never be able to change anything!"

Her steps falter, but she says, "Go ahead. I've still got mine."

"Does yours have the exact coordinates of the change? It's a very precise moment and location."

"You know the date and time and basic area. We can figure it out from there."

"And blunder around? Risking an even bigger error? Is that what you want to do?"

Getting the location from me is a possibility, but I could make it very difficult. It would be a hell of a lot easier to use the data stored in the chaser, and I can see she realizes this.

"Have you really looked at this world?" I ask.

She snorts. "What does that have to do with anything?"

"What happens if you go back? You live the rest of your life inside the walls of the institute? That's prison, Lidia. Do you really want that? Here you could live free, go where you want, be whoever you want to be."

"You think I should just stay here?"

"It's not a terrible idea. In fact, it's a pretty damn good one. Drop your knife, give me your chaser, and we'll go our separate ways."

"That easy, huh?"

"That easy."

She looks like she's actually considering the idea before she laughs loudly. "You really think I'd go for that? Here's what's going to happen. You're going to give me *your* chaser, Denny."

I knew she wouldn't take me up on my offer, but I had to give her a chance. Alternating my gaze between her and my chaser, I start working the menu, praying it doesn't shut down again.

"What are you doing?" she asks.

I don't answer.

"Denny, what are you doing?"

She takes a step toward me, so I raise the chaser into the air like I'm going to throw it into the ground. When she stops I pull it back down and pick up where I left off.

"What are you doing?" she asks again.

Again I say nothing.

On the screen is a list of jumps stored in the device's memory. I begin erasing them one at a time.

"Denny! Stop!"

When I get to the entry for the cemetery where my mother is buried, I pause. Though there is no cemetery at that location in this world, erasing it feels like forgetting. My finger hovers above "Delete" for several seconds before it finally taps the button.

"Listen to me," she says. "We'll go back and fix things together, okay? When we get back to the institute, I won't tell anyone it was you."

She takes another step toward me.

"Back off!" I shout.

I'm almost there. There's only one location left on my screen—the meadow where we gathered in 1702. I leave the location the same, but change the date to one in 1743, hoping that will be enough. I'm just finishing up when Lidia charges.

I twist sideways and hug the chaser to my chest, expecting her to smash into me, but instead of heading in my direction, she goes left and kneels next to her bag, where she dropped it when we first arrived.

She pulls out her chaser and smiles at me. As she moves her fingers over the control buttons, I hold out my device and say, "Here. You can have it!"

She pauses.

"The location's there," I say. "I was just getting rid of everything else."

She eyes me suspiciously. "Why?"

"Because . . . because I'm not going with you."

"Oh, no. You need to show me what needs to be done."

"It's easy. You'll see me there. Just stop me from entering the building. That's it."

"That's it?"

"Yes."

It takes a moment, but I can see she's decided I'm not lying to her. And I'm not, at least not completely. "If you stay here . . ."

"I get erased," I say. "What do you think my life's going to be like when I go back? I'd rather it end here."

She looks past me at Iffy. "You should've never left whatever slum it is you came from, *Eight*. You were always playing over your head with us."

My jaw tenses. "Are you going to take this or not? Because my offer expires in ten seconds."

She slips her own chaser back in her bag and gets to her feet. Pulling the strap over her shoulder, she walks toward me. "All right. Let me see it."

When she nears, I give it to her, but not the way she's expecting. I whip it into the side of her head, and she drops to the ground, blood oozing from her temple.

I check her pulse. It's strong, so I probably have only a few seconds. I work her satchel off her shoulders and confirm her chaser is in there.

As I toss the bag to the side, she starts to moan. I scan the immediate area, looking for something long and sturdy. The best I can find is a withered branch about a foot and a half in length. I'm not sure it's enough, but it'll have to do.

I pick up my chaser and see the screen has gone blank again.

No, no, no! I tap the power button. When it comes back to life, I whisper, "Stay on, stay on, stay on," and set the device on Lidia's stomach.

Stick in hand, I stand.

"Hey, what the hell? What's this . . . ?" Lidia fumbles the chaser as she tries to tilt her head up.

I jab the branch into the "Go" button.

257

CHAPTER TWENTY-NINE

I untie Iffy and coax her back to consciousness.

"You came back," she says.

"Of course I did. How do you feel?"

"Like someone tossed me off a building." She looks around. "The girl."

"Lidia," I say.

She nods.

"She's gone."

Wincing, she pushes her torso off the ground. "Is she coming back?"

"No. She's not."

I don't know if there was enough power in my chaser to get Lidia all the way back to 1743, but I do know there won't be enough left for her to leave once she gets there. And since both Iffy and I are still here, Lidia didn't do anything that changed history back or in any obvious way.

"Not ever?" Iffy asks.

"Not ever. It's over."

She looks at me. "So you've decided to let my world hang around for a while?"

I smile. "Don't you mean our world?"

Ellie still hasn't completely accepted what's going on. Who would in her position? Instead of being two years younger than she is, I'm now five years older, and the world she knows and understands is gone.

Iffy has helped me get an apartment in San Diego, where I live with my sister while she's getting treatments. It is cancer, after all. But the doctors have caught it early and feel confident about a full recovery. It all costs money, of course. Let's just say with Lidia's chaser (after I figured out how to link to it) and Iffy's native knowledge, there are plenty of places to find cash. The illegal drug business is one of my favorites. It's ugly yet lucrative, so I have no moral problem taking from drug merchants. My only criterion is that those I "visit" must be thousands of miles away from San Diego.

I'm thinking about using some of the cash to attend college soon. Not sure what I'll study. History would be the natural subject, but, well, I should probably branch out a little. We'll see.

The other thing I've used Lidia's chaser for is to create identities for Ellie and me. After a bit of research, I've even planted records in the court system, officially making myself my sister's guardian.

Iffy is in San Diego, too, living again at her parents'. She and Ellie have become good friends, and sometimes when the three of us are together, it almost feels like this world is the only one that's ever been, and I can, for a little while, forget what I've done.

On June 20, Iffy and I drive back to Los Angeles. The traffic is horrible and I'm worried we'll be late, but we reach Santa Monica Pier by a quarter to four.

"Do you want to do this alone, or . . . ?" she asks after we get out of the car.

I take her hand. "I want you to come with me."

We walk on the wooden boards high above the ocean. Unlike the last time we were here, the amusement park is open. Bells and music and laughter all but drown out the crashing waves below us. I scan those we pass, looking for faces I know, but see none.

We reach the end of the pier two minutes before four o'clock. I lean against the railing again, searching the crowd, certain that at any moment Marie will appear. But the top of the hour passes without her or Sir Gregory or Other Me showing up.

"Maybe she forgot," Iffy says.

"Could be," I say, but I know Marie would have never forgotten. My fear is that they were unable to get away.

We wait another thirty minutes before we start walking back. Halfway down the pier, someone walking about fifty feet in front of us glances back in our direction. I slow in surprise, thinking it's Marie. She's walking with a man who, from the back, looks a lot like me.

Within moments they disappear into the larger crowd in front of the amusement park.

I rush forward, pulling Iffy along behind me, but though we look everywhere, we don't find them. I insist we wait until dark, but still the others don't show up. With much reluctance we head to the car.

As we climb in, Iffy says, "How about some dinner?"

"Why not?" I say, though I have no appetite.

"Peruvian?"

This brings a smile to my face and a faint growl to my stomach. "That would be perfect."

She slips her arms around me, we kiss, and my disappointment begins to fade.

Maybe the people I saw were Marie and Other Me. Or maybe they're out there somewhen else.

And maybe, just maybe, I'll find them someday.

After all, there's always time.

ACKNOWLEDGMENTS

I am greatly indebted to my editor, Elyse Dinh-McCrillis, for her tireless work; to my friends and two of my favorite authors, Tim Hallinan and Robert Gregory Browne, for their insight and encouragement; and to Dawn Rej, Jill Fulkerson Marnell, Corri Gutzman, Steve Manke, Paulette Feeney, and the "street team" for being early readers and helping to make this novel even better.

I'm glad the story didn't make any of your heads explode.

ABOUT THE AUTHOR

Brett Battles is the Barry Award–winning author of more than twenty novels, including the Jonathan Quinn series, the Project Eden series, and the Alexandra Poe series, the latter of which he wrote with Robert Gregory Browne. He lives in Los Angeles. Learn more about him at brettbattles.com.

Made in the USA
Las Vegas, NV
27 March 2021

20295801R00163